Yellow Bird

A Romance Novel

by Kathryn Kavicky

Table of Contents

PROLOGUE

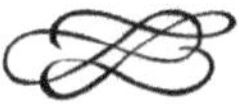

Desiree drifted into a twilight sleep only to look down and see herself curled up in the chair by her father's hospital bed. He rested peacefully, knowing his daughter was by his side. Through the window, she could see the beginning of the sunrise, and a small flock of birds began forming their inflight V-shape, swooping in one direction, then another coming closer to the window. Suddenly, their muted color turned bright yellow as they broke formation, lined up in a straight line, and started a serpentine dance through the sky, soaring high then diving lower and high again, until one little bird landed on the windowsill, pecking at the bell fastened there – faster and faster and faster until the sound was one long steady reverberating chime.

* * *

Desiree jerked awake. "Poppy?" she choked on the words. "Poppy? Oh, Poppy! Noooo!" The heart monitor wasn't beeping. It was a steady line, the chilling monotone hum echoing throughout the room. "No, No, No! Oh, Poppy, No!" Desiree collapsed in tears.

* * *

A sea of faces was all she saw, fighting back tears, grasping the sides of the podium to give her father's eulogy. He shouldn't have died…not yet. He was so vibrant, so full of life, plans, and expectations. Desiree felt robbed – a death sentence - pancreatic cancer…so deadly…so swift to steal everything in its path. Poppy's friends were shocked to hear the news. But Poppy had been matter of fact. The crazy Irishman took his fate in stride, like everything he did, and then planned his own party.

"If yer gonna stand round and cry at me funeral," he told them all, then I'm not comin'! You canna jus' throw me in the river and be done with it. And that goes for you too, Lassie!" he threatened Desiree.

So, they all took the pledge and promised there would be no tears, no maudlin Irish songs, and no depressing poetry. But Bagpipes! Yes, there had to be bagpipes – Irish Bagpipes -- he made them promise. And so, they promised to celebrate his life. Poppy chose the music he wanted to hear.

He picked the photos he wanted everyone to see and remember. He asked his brother Max to tell stories of their raucous childhood, growing up in Brooklyn, and to share Poppy's own personal story about the love of his life – Francine Dubois – the lovely ballet dancer he convinced to become his wife.

It was all Desiree could do to keep his faith and promise him she would be brave and completely respect his wishes. And it all went down just as he wanted. More than a hundred visitors paid their respects at the wake. More than that faced her now, filling up the old Brooklyn church.

"Who are these people?" she mused. "Do I even know them? How do they all know Pat O'Conner? Have I been that absent? Why don't I know them? Have I been so removed I don't know anyone anymore?"

She focused on Janette - her best friend, on her Uncle Max, then blinked back the tears to bring Lil and the other loyal employees into view, and finally on Elliott – dear sweet patient Elliott-- and then it all blurred again, and as the bagpipes started their melancholy hum, Desiree kept her promise, fought back the tears, and remained poised and strong, a replica of her mother. She was an orphan. No parents.

Desiree graciously greeted friends, guests, employees, and business acquaintances, one by one, as dozens and dozens of people filed out the door of the church, paying their last respects. Even the postman came.

"Des, your words were beautiful," comforted Janette. "You totally captured Poppy's whole personality. God, I'll miss him so much – he made me laugh, always!" Janette wrapped Desiree in her arms for one of her amazing mom-like hugs.

"Hmm, thank you." Desiree barely heard her friend but welcomed the hug and the sentiment.

"Thank you. Hardest thing I've ever done, I think."

"I'm sure, love, but listen. I know now really isn't the time, but you know me…what are you going to do? Where are you going now, tonight?"

"Oh, I don't know…I assume to Elliott's or back to my place in Connecticut. Where is he, anyway? I haven't seen him since just before the service."

Janette ignored the last comment. She had her own opinions of Elliott. "Look, you shouldn't be alone tonight. And you're exhausted. I'm only a few blocks from here…come stay with me. We'll order some takeout, I'll give you jammies and a few glasses of wine, and put you to bed."

Desiree smiled. Bless her heart – Janette.

* * *

They bonded in college almost 17 years ago and shared a tiny apartment in New York City when they were just starting out. They were each other's alter ego. Physically, emotionally, and pragmatically different in every way. Janette was brilliant, a whiz with numbers, algorithms, charts, and statistics. Desiree was the creative one – a talented writer but more an artist – quick with the brush and pen able to capture the light, form, and very essence of a face, flower, or landscape. Janette went on to become a marketing genius in real estate, and Desiree pursued a career as a graphic designer, first working a corporate job, then as an independent contractor doing project work for a series of fascinating companies. But her passion was painting, and she was an aspiring illustrator.

Right after graduation, when Desiree wanted to move to New York, Janette's mom invited Desiree to come and stay as long as she needed while she found a job and a place to live. That summer in Brooklyn was a hoot. Janette's family was from the islands of the West Indies – a totally eclectic group of people oozing with personality, cultural diversity, and hearts of gold. Janette's brother, Henry, was the consummate older sibling, placating his mother, who was hoping for a doctor or lawyer and a daughter-in-law, while he quietly pursued a career in architecture, challenging & teasing Janette, flirting with Desiree, and being just the perfect, wonderful host and dance partner. Yes, frequent dance parties were de rigor!

* * *

"That sounds perfect, actually. There's Elliott…give me a moment, OK?"

Desiree touched Elliott's shoulder. "Elliott, I'm going to stay with Janette tonight. I need some 'sister time.'"

"Oh." He sounded disappointed. "Alright. You definitely shouldn't be alone. Are you sure? I thought you'd come back to my place." "I'm sure," she smiled weakly. "I'm just exhausted."

* * *

"Oh my God, this is so good, just what I needed, thank you." Desiree dipped her grilled cheese into the rich and creamy tomato soup.

"It is, right? The ultimate comfy food. It's my signature dish, you know!" Janette wiped the corner of her mouth where the cheese had dribbled from the sandwich. Desiree choked back a laugh, curling her legs up under the cozy crocheted throw, and took another sip of the soup. Janette was no cook. But she definitely knew how to create the most welcoming, warm, and loving environment. They had opted out of take-out food as soon as they changed into flannel PJs. Janette switched on the gas fireplace, opened a bottle of wine, and took a moment to reminisce about all those cold winter nights when they were poor and just starting their careers.

She quickly announced the change, "It's a grilled cheese and tomato soup night!"

"Perfect…the staples of life!"

"So…" Janette turned to face Desiree. "What goes here? I know you've been through a lot these last months with Poppy, but Des, you look terrible!"

"Well…thanks!" she said apologetically. "But yeh… I'm fi……." Desiree started to say she was fine but stopped mid-syllable. This was Janette, who saw through drivel every time, who approached everything in black and white, always cutting to the chase, seeking the truth through the path of least resistance. Damn, she was annoying.

Desiree took a sip of wine. "Elliot asked me to marry him."

Right on cue, Desiree's cell phone vibrated on the table. She ignored it. "Well, that's what you've been wanting, right? Waiting for?" Janette really didn't care much for Elliott. She thought he was weak and needy. Handsome, rich, very nice, very successful, but emotionally inadequate.

"Yes. He asked me a couple of weeks ago- just before Poppy took that turn for worse."

"Are you kidding? Where? Oh, it doesn't matter. What a crappy thing to do. Just another example of his lack of awareness of your feelings. It just seems, Des, it's always about what's best for Elliott. It's all about pretense and timing…his lack of it! For a lawyer, this just amazes me."

Bless her heart. Janette always cut to the chase. "Janette, please don't. He's really not like that. He really does plan everything and weighs every response and outcome. But to be fair, I've been telling him for 3 years it would be great if he could just be more spontaneous. So, he did."

"Umph! Ok, sorry. But his timing really sucked."

Desiree shrugged her shoulders and smiled grimly. "Ya think?

They were both quiet for a moment, staring at the flames in the fireplace. "I have a plan!" Janette perked up immediately.

"Oh boy," thought Desiree. Janette's plans were always bold, confident, and truthful – amazing how she did that. "I'm calling Henry."

"Henry? What for?"

"To book you a room, you ninny! You need to get away, to mourn, to recharge your batteries, to think, and to refocus your energies so you can move forward. What better place than on a beautiful island in the Caribbean, with people you know and love." Janette grabbed her cell phone from the table.

"Janette...wait…"

But Janette had already punched her speed dial and, in seconds, was connected. "Henry…mon frere! Bon soir!"

* * *

Ten years ago, Janette's brother Henry eloped with Raoul, packed up everything, and moved to the island of Saint Martin. It kind of made sense. Janette's mother owned a home there for decades, had dozens of relatives and extended family, and was actually quite the local activist, constantly lobbying for better municipal management on any number of issues. They affectionately called her the unofficial "Mayor" of Philipsburg, the capital of the Dutch side of the island. But she got things done! However, Henry and Raoul preferred the more laid-back vibe of the French side. They bought an old plantation, and with Henry's architectural skills and Raoul's interior design expertise, they renovated and created one of the most beautiful hotels in the Caribbean. They preserved the intense beauty of the main house, hired the best chef for its now 5-star restaurant, and built a complex of 18 luxury villas over the last ten years.

* * *

"Here," Janette passed the phone to Desiree. "Say hello."

"Des! I'm so so sorry about your Poppy! You know I would have come to the funeral, but I really couldn't get away." Henry's lyrical voice resonated deeply over the phone.

"Oh, Henry, please don't worry. I know how you felt about him. But thank you."

"I agree with Janette…you need to come here. Let us take care of you and help you get your spirit back. You know you still owe me a dance!"

Desiree blushed and laughed affectionately. "Henry, you gave me up years ago! But to this day, you are the best dancing partner I've ever had!"

"Good. Then it's settled. I'm reserving one of our villas for you – you can stay as long as you want. It will be fabulous to catch up with you. And we'll have a party in your honor! Just send me your arrival information. I'll send a car."

"Henry…I'm not…" but he had hung up. Desiree shot an annoyed look at her friend. Then shook her head and laughed. "All of you…. You. Your mother, your brother, you're all alike! Incorrigible!"

CHAPTER 1

Happy Hour was just starting, and the myriad of guests were beginning to wander into the lobby in search of the Palm Court, their proverbial oasis. Like all intimate island resorts, the common rooms were open-air, allowing the gentle breezes to do the air-conditioning.

The Lobby of the Las Palmas Hotel was wide and inviting. Imported tiles and ceramics, reminiscent of the Spanish haciendas, created a quiet, cooling image. Wide verandas furnished with overstuffed wicker and rattan furniture surrounded the great room on all sides, looking down to the ocean on the west and to the beautiful hills and cliffs on the east. Giant palms towered over this central meeting place and graced the paths and walkways that led to the individual villas, which served as suites and hotel rooms. Further away, nestled among the dunes and into the hills, were private villas, the owners of which were seldom seen.

In the deepening light, the brilliant red and orange of the fabrics made everything and everybody appeared pink and flushed from the heat of the day. Whitewashed walls absorbed the intensity and provided a rosy halo effect as a backdrop for the Steelband quartet, who would soon begin their calypso serenade.

Strolling through the lobby to the more intimate Cypress Grill, named for the beautiful and hearty wood that paneled the walls and the floor-to-ceiling shutters, Jay Bennett took a seat on the side of the mirrored semi-circular bar, angling his stool so he could watch it all. He loved this time of day, when everyone was mellow from the day's activities, freshly showered, moisturized, and bejeweled, eager for the island's nightlife to begin, when the sun was low in the sky before it dropped from sight when the offshore breezes whispered through the great palms.

"Hello, Georgia, my sweet island princess." Jay grinned at the pretty girl who worked the bar.

"Why, 'ello, Mr. Jay. I thought you were 'all goin' back home today?"

"Couldn't bear it, Georgia. I needed one more magnificent Yellow Bird before I could face the natives!"

Georgia grinned, showing her beautiful bone structure; her sweet, soft voice was like a song. "Well, Mr. Jay, it's you who are the lucky ones. I just happen to 'ave a Yellow Bird waiting right here for you."

With that, she quickly began concocting one of her own recipes, which had made the hotel famous for its exotic drinks. With great fanfare, she set the golden Yellow Bird before him.

"An absolute work of art. Cheers, Princess." Georgia liked this man. He always took a few extra moments to be pleasant and to have a real conversation. As Georgia turned away to take care of another guest, Jay gazed back into his mirror, thinking about returning to the States. He really hated leaving Villa Blanca, but he had been away long enough.

He reviewed the recent details in his head, now oblivious to his surroundings. Six weeks before, Jay had completed a rather unique business deal, a deal that tickled his appreciation for brilliance and creativity. Unfortunately, before the final paperwork was complete, the poor man died. It would have been insolent to have approached the family at such a time to conclude the details when everything was on paper anyway. The actual acquisition could take place anytime. So, Jay had taken some needed time off, stopping in Houston to check on various other investments, finally arriving at "his island." At least, that's the way it felt to him. Someday, he would call this his home and commute to New York. But three weeks was enough time away, he needed to get back to business.

Then he saw her. He had seen her at the pool yesterday for the first time and had marveled at her sophisticated beauty. Today, she looked different. Her hair was loose and rather wild in a totally natural way instead of the tight chignon she had worn tucked up under the large straw hat, but it was definitely her. She reminded him of someone; he never forgot a face. But the who, where, and when eluded him.

She was exquisite, totally at ease in her surroundings, and completely at peace with herself. As she moved from the shadows into the late afternoon sun, her mane of hair glistened with a hundred shades of gold. He was sure he heard the giant palms whispering about the beauty that walked beneath them, but maybe it was only his heart.

Feeling his blood rise, he stared into the mirror, afraid to turn around for fear the vision would vanish. He watched her stroll across the shadowed patio, her long legs stretching graciously, unselfconsciously towards him.

She came straight to the bar, stopping only briefly to greet another guest. Within seconds, she was beside him, leaning against the bar to greet Georgia as if she were an old friend. Jay finally trusted himself to break his mirrored gaze and dared to look at the goddess beside him.

He noticed her tan. It was darker than yesterday, the low-cut jumpsuit showing just a hint of a fainter-tanned breast. He could picture her sunning on a secluded stretch of beach, her hair fanned out over the sand.

"Hello, Georgia," she said brightly. "Any Yellow Birds tonight?"

Jay quickly came back to the present. Close to her like this, he felt breathless. She was truly beautiful. Her skin was as smooth as silk, her exotic eyes were like the darkest Persian blue. The contrast with her magnificent hair was dramatic. She was tall; taller in fact, than he had thought. And her voice, the voice of an angel. "Yes, ma'am," Georgia grinned again. "My, my, these birds are busy tonight."

Georgia hummed the tune of the old calypso song as she quickly whipped up another Yellow Bird.

As she reached for her drink, lifting the glass in cheers to Georgia, Desiree sensed Jay close to her left shoulder.

"I've been admiring your tan," he quipped rather dramatically. Jay grinned and breathed a sigh of relief. He didn't like feeling so vulnerable. At last, he had spoken, and he felt in control again.

Back in New York, such a blatantly flirtatious comment would have made Desiree cringe. But she had mellowed in the island sun and felt gracious and unselfconscious. Absently stirring her drink, she turned towards Jay and, in only a few seconds, dissected him from head to toe.

He was, in fact, adorable. His twinkly blue eyes were mischievous eyes, but honest. His smile was almost cherubic, and he had the cutest dimple on the right side of his cheek. His clothes were classy but simple and basic; the white linen shirt was pressed, sleeves rolled up to just below the elbow, showing strong, tanned, muscular arms and large, perfectly formed hands. He wore no jewelry except a simple diamond stud in his left ear. Desiree watched and listened as he ordered another drink from Georgia and could tell he treated people with respect. He was a nice guy and definitely not a jerk.

Trusting her gut reaction, Desiree laid her big velvet eyes into his and purred, "Why, thank you! I've been working very hard to perfect it."

"God", thought Jay. I'm in love! I love her voice, her laugh, the way she wraps her fingers around her glass, and the way she looks through her lashes as she sips her drink, lookin' me right in the eye!

"Well, how long have you been at this?" He stared right back, letting his eyes sink deeply into hers.

Suddenly, Desiree felt heady and a little dizzy, but it passed just as quickly. Too much sun, she thought, still looking into Jay's eyes. "Every chance I get," she answered. "This is my idea of R&R. Give me a pool, a lounge chair, and a few juicy books, and I'm a very happy woman!"

"Not to mention a beautiful one." Jay lifted his glass in a toast.

There it was again. Desiree felt herself grow flushed. A butterfly flitted through her stomach. This is ridiculous, she thought. I definitely have had too much sun. She broke his gaze and fought to regain her composure. "Thank you, sir! And does such a complimentary gentleman have a name?"

Offering his hand, Jay introduced himself. "My apologies …. Jay Bennett, ma'am, at your service."

"Desiree Dubois." Her smile lit up her entire face.

"Desiree Dubois?" repeated Jay. "That's quite lovely."

"Well, actually, it's my mother's maiden name – I adopted it for business, a pseudonym. It works better on my drawings. I'm actually the product of a cantankerous old Irishman and a French ballet dancer."

Jay laughed, "Well, that must be quite a union! I take it you look like your mother?"

"Except for my hair and my temper!" Desiree's eyes sparkled as she spoke of these two obviously special people. Jay lifted his glass, delighted with the woman who sat by his side. "Well, here's to France and Ireland and …"

"Yellow Birds," finished Desiree as they toasted each other.

CHAPTER 2

Desiree stared into the powder room mirror, approving of what she saw. The little lines that had been around her eyes only two weeks ago were gone. The drawn, pale skin was bronzed and glowing. Her hair, her pride and joy, was silken and streaked from the sun.

The physical breakdown that had hit her after her father's funeral had really taken its toll. In retrospect, she finally realized that this was the first death she had ever faced as an adult. Her mother died when Desiree was only twelve. It was the worst thing a little girl could ever experience. But somehow, she got through the pain, and despite the emptiness she felt, she eventually became accustomed to the new normal, thanks in part to her Uncle Max and Aunt Maggie, friends, and neighbors, but mostly her beloved Poppy. He was her hero, the center of her universe.

He shouldn't have died, not yet. The last three months were just a blur, a foggy dream, more like a nightmare, watching her father so alive, so positive, so strong and virile, change from a positive, optimistic bear of a man to just a shell of himself. The devastation was more than anyone could bear when the doctor said there was nothing more he could do. The overwhelming sadness and despair came as the final blow when, only 3 days later, Pat O'Conner died.

Desiree blinked back the tears, now tears of sweet memories, not the uncontrollable grief that had racked her body a month ago. She concentrated again on how she looked now, how she felt. She knew she could face the world again; she could laugh and have fun.

In fact, she hadn't had this much fun in ages, even before Poppy died.

Jay Bennett was delightful. But he was also sexy with his rugged tan, wonderfully broad shoulders, and narrow hips. His eyes were as blue as the Caribbean and Desiree felt he was undressing her every time he looked at her. She felt strangely uncomfortable under his gaze but terribly excited at the same time. Little butterflies kept flitting across her stomach when he brushed against her. And he was tall. A glorious 6'2. Desiree actually felt petite near him. Well, almost petite. It wasn't often, with her 5'9 frame, to find a man who could lay his arm over her shoulders. In fact, she couldn't remember ever dating a man taller than 5'10 or 11, including Elliott.

"Elliott! Oh, my God!" Desiree stared at herself in disbelief, eyes wide. How does she keep forgetting Elliott? Dear sweet Elliott, waiting so patiently at home while Desiree got her life back together.

* * *

Elliott had been disappointed, but he understood. Desiree couldn't accept his proposal of marriage right now. His timing sucked. Not like him. He always planned everything and weighed every response and outcome. But Desiree was always telling him he needed to be more spontaneous, and he had waited so long, and he did love her so much. After three years and numerous conversations about their future together, Elliott had been so excited when he found the perfect ring that he couldn't wait to propose. It did not go well.

"Elliott!" scolded Desiree with all of her Irish ire in her voice. "Really? Now?" "This is just not the right time. How could you make this about you and me now?" Immediately, Desiree saw the pain in his face then and softened. "Darling, I'm so sorry. I didn't mean to be so harsh, but your timing is really insensitive. My father is dying. I've held in all my emotions because of his wishes, and I just can't deal with anything else".

Elliott wasn't much more understanding following the funeral when Desiree told him of her plans to go away. "Janette's right," said Desiree. "I need to get away, where they have lounge chairs on the beach and little flags on the chairs that I can hoist when I need a drink! I'll be with friends – Henry and Raoul will take good care of me. I promise we'll talk about our future when I get back, OK? I'm really sorry."

* * *

"Don't be ridiculous," she said out loud as she took one last look in the mirror. "There's nothing to feel guilty about. You're simply having a pleasant evening with a new friend. So, why does he give you butterflies? Well, you aren't dead. He's a very handsome man. Desiree put her hand over her thumping heart. "Now, stop that. You're leaving in a few days, and he said he's leaving tomorrow. So, that's that."

CHAPTER 3

When Jay suggested she join him for dinner that night, she said yes. After all, she had to eat! And if not romantic, dinner was, at the very least, amorous. The gardens of the old mansion were ablaze with candlelight, casting deep shadows and golden light over the entire patio. Pink and white linens and vases of exotic flowers dressed every table, and thousands of stars formed a canopy in the midnight blue sky. By candlelight, Desiree was even more beautiful than Jay could have imagined. But he was kept sobered by her great wit and her complete love of food.

"This is absolutely wonderful!" Desiree was just finishing her main course. "I've had delicious food down here, Jay, but this is really exceptional," she smiled contentedly as she delicately pushed the last morsel onto her fork with her knife. "You're a pleasure to watch, Des. I really hate women who pick at their food. What's that all about? Are they watching their diet? Or are they just self-conscious? I like a woman who eats and enjoys it. And I do like getting my money's worth!"

Desiree looked up quickly, just in time to see Jay bite his lower lip to keep from laughing.

"Sorry, I guess I do act a bit ravenous. It must be the island air!"

"You're beautiful when you're ravenous. In fact, I'd bet you're beautiful all the time."

Jay knew she would be. She just had that natural quality combined with her own sense of self. There was no heavy makeup or dramatic eye shadow. Her deep-set eyes were wide, and her lashes were elegantly long, curling ever so softly on her cheeks when she lowered her eyes. She was blessed with high cheekbones, and her lips were full and soft, begging to be kissed. Instead, Jay reached across the table to refill her wine glass, brushing her fingers as he poured.

"Oh, no," Desiree protested, attempting to keep the tone light. "Far from beautiful all the time." Desiree's heart was beating wildly. His touch sent a fire searing through her from her fingers down to the tips of her toes. "You should see me in the morning."

"I'd love to." Jay held her spellbound with his eyes.

"I mean…" Desiree blushed, "I mean, you know, after I, oh damn, Jay, you're getting me all flustered."

"You have no idea what you do to me," Jay sighed. "You're dangerous, woman. You can set hearts on fire."

"Why…. *mon cher monsieur, vos compliments sont trop pour moi!*" Desiree teased in her perfect French.

It was all Desiree could do to break the spell of the moment. Jay laughed, took her fingers gently from the glass, and released them with a quick kiss, but his eyes were full of fire. His whole body ached with the thought of making love to her. But he laughed again and took a long drink of his wine. He would wait. He wanted her to come to him freely.

All evening, Jay sensed some hidden turmoil. Desiree would respond so naturally, exuding an innate sexual desire, and then suddenly reign it in, tempering the passion and flirting. Jay was sure it wasn't coy coquetry. She was as attracted to him as he was to her. He was certain of it. But she wouldn't …or couldn't…let go. Time, Jay thought to himself. She just needs time.

They finished dinner, laughing and enjoying each other's company like an old married couple. People around them thought they were a charming and striking twosome, both so tall and healthy looking yet unique, with Desiree's exotic beauty and Jay's rugged good looks.

"So, my beauty," Jay finally said in a lighter tone than he felt. "Coffee? A nightcap? Some soft music?" He motioned towards the piano bar next to the dining room.

"Well… OK…just one." Desiree took a deep breath and steadied herself. She really was having such a wonderful time; she didn't want it to end. But she knew she would have to keep her emotions under better control.

Over espressos, they shared war stories of college days and careers. And over a nightcap, they discovered they both loved old black-and-white movie classics. Jay's talent for imitating accents and his recall of infamous one-liners were a delight to watch and listen to. And when he asked her to dance, she felt as light as air. She was a good dancer, but Jay made her look even better. His style was relaxed and smooth. And then, he asked her to spend the following day with him. Again, Elliot's face flashed clearly before her, and she felt terribly guilty. The entire evening raced through her head. Dinner with Jay was one thing, but a whole day's outing?

Jay's voice interrupted her thought. "Earth to Desiree…?"

"But I thought you were heading back to the States?" Desiree finally spoke, buying herself some time.

"Well, I was planning on it, but it can wait a few more days. Say, yes, Des. We'll go sailing. We'll sail out to a little island I know about four miles offshore. Only the locals down here really know about it. It's truly beautiful. We can swim and snorkel and have a picnic. What do you say?"

Desiree's common sense took hold. "It sounds divine, Jay, but I really can't. I'm sorry. I actually have plans. Friends of mine from home are here, and I promised to visit. I've been terribly amiss and have kept putting it off."

It actually wasn't a lie. Henry and Raoul had been badgering her all week. She had to go to the party they were planning. Come early, they begged, so we could catch up before everyone else arrived.

Jay looked seriously disappointed. "Oh, too bad." He stared into Des's eyes for just that brief moment, again sending waves of flurries through her belly. "Tell you what," Jay held his cell phone towards her, "please … give me your number? Des, I really had a great time tonight. …and I'd really, really like to see you again when we're back in New York."

Desiree hesitated. It would be rude after such a lovely evening to say no to the phone number. And, yes, she also had a great time, but…. "Tell *you* what," she said, "give me *your* number, and I'll text you when I'm back in New York." She opened her address book and handed the phone to Jay.

"Deal," Jay quickly punched in his number, saved it, and handed the phone back to Desiree, but not before quickly hitting the text button and sending himself her number. "I'll hold you to that!"

"Deal." Desiree nodded and found her eyes locking into Jay's again. She couldn't get past these sporadic, intense feelings. "Thank you. Thank you. I really had a great evening," she said and started to giggle. "I haven't laughed so much in a long, long time!"

Jay took her hand and raised it to his lips. "Good night, Desiree Dubois. Enjoy the rest of your stay and have fun with your friends."

"Travel safe." Desiree turned and headed back to her villa, feeling Jay's eyes watching her go.

As she unlocked the door to her villa, her phone began to vibrate and rang its distinctive chime. Elliott! Desiree kicked the door closed with her toe as she answered the call.

"Hi there," Desiree smiled as she said hello.

"Where have you been?" Elliott questioned before Desiree could speak again. "Didn't you get my messages? I called you three times."

"Oh, Elliott, I'm so sorry. I was out to dinner and didn't hear my phone." "Desiree, it's after midnight. You're just getting back from dinner now? Where did you have dinner?"

"Right here, of course. At the hotel. I'm really sorry, Elliott." Desiree felt guilty she had missed his calls, but his tone annoyed her.

"By yourself?" his voice was accusatory.

"Excuse me?" Why the second degree? "Oh, Elliott," she deflected in her sexiest voice. "Are you jealous?" Desiree loved teasing him when he got like this. But she quickly realized he was in no mood. He seemed angry and very upset. Desiree knew she needed to reassure him. There was no need to further worry him. And she also knew she had been very self-indulgent all evening in her flirtations with Jay Bennett. This is not good, she realized. What happened tonight was a huge mistake. What was I thinking…and why? She needed to make things right.

"Oh Elliott, darling, again, I'm so sorry. We got carried away." But she couldn't tell him the whole truth. She couldn't tell him she had dinner alone with a man she had just met…and again, why? Why would she do that? She was supposed to be engaged – or at least planning on saying yes at last. She tried changing the subject.

"How did your case go today?"

"We?" Elliott homed in on the word "we" and was not happy. "Who is we?" "The people I was with." Desiree hated telling a fib but had to spare his feelings. She couldn't tell Elliott the complete truth. "We met here at the hotel a few days ago (*that part was the truth – she did meet other people a few days ago)*, ran into each other in the bar tonight – you know the Cypress Grill I mentioned to you - and we decided to have dinner together. It was lovely and fun – the Grill had a fabulous calypso band and…."

"It's alright, Desiree. I'm sorry. Forget it. I overreacted. I just get worried. I miss you so much. And thank you, the case went well – we won – a very nice settlement if I do say so." he said proudly.

Desiree's heart broke a little as she heard Elliott's voice soften. Her guilt was overwhelming, and rightly so. "It's OK. Look, I'm very, very tired. It's late. Can I call you tomorrow?"

"Of course. Sleep well, darling. Good night." Elliott disconnected before she could say, "I love you." Damn it, why did he always do that?

* * *

Desiree saw herself running. She could see her house, but it wasn't her house in the distance. A yellow bird came swooping down from a tree, flying along beside her as she ran. Out of breath, she ran into her house and slammed the door behind her, breaking the wings of the little bird. She didn't know what she had been running from. She felt very afraid. Where was Elliott? She ran from room to room and then started up the stairs, but she couldn't get to the top. The stairs kept going, never-ending. Elliott! She kept calling his name. Suddenly, she was at the top of the staircase, in her room, and there was the yellow bird.

* * *

Desiree bolted straight upright in bed! She was breathing hard. "Oh my god!" she sighed in relief. "What a weird dream." She jumped out of bed, made her way to the bathroom, and flipped on the light. Splashing cold water on her face and taking slow, deep breaths, she finally calmed down. There was something in her mind she couldn't see, couldn't remember. A fleeting image, a streak of yellow. It was almost dawn. "Too many yellow birds last night," she mused. "Gotta get back to sleep. Must call Elliott first thing in the morning."

Desiree crawled back under the covers and curled up around her pillow. She tried to think of Elliott, but only Jay's face came to her. She drifted off again with a smile curling her lips.

CHAPTER 4

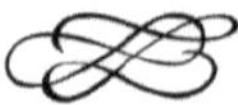

Desiree slept late and woke amazingly refreshed. She didn't remember her dream at all but did have an urgency to call Elliott, as promised. Just as she picked up her phone, a face-time call came in – Janette! "Good morning, sleepy head!" Janette's face appeared.

"Janette! Hey, girl!...and to what do I owe this call? Are you checking up on me?"

"Of course! Haven't heard from you in over a week…what's going on? Have you seen Henry and Raoul? Wow...you look amazing!" Janette stopped, having just focused in on Desiree's face. Desiree laughed, running her fingers through her hair while pulling it up into a scrunchie off her face.

"Well, I slept late this morning. Gotta get my beauty sleep."

"Nooo. That's not what I mean. Your eyes are sparkling. Your skin is glowing! And this is just a cell phone image! Give it up, girlfriend…what's going on?" "Well……" Desiree paused a few seconds. "I had dinner last night with a guy I met here at the hotel…"

Before Desiree could even continue, Janette was all over it. "And????" "Down, girl…it's all innocent…."

Janette interrupted again. "Ah…somehow, I don't think it is. Come on…. I'm all ears…just got a fresh cup of coffee…. come on…. dish!"

Moving to the outside lanai facing the ocean, Desiree took her friend into her confidence, spilling out all the details of the previous night. As she talked, Janette was perfectly silent, listening to every word, captivated by every detail. Desiree left nothing out…. from the pure joy of feeling attractive, pretty, sexy, funny, and witty…to being silly and impulsive, and finally to feeling guilty and sensible.

"Janette, I haven't had this much fun in years! He's handsome and adorable, wicked smart, a great conversationalist, honest, ethical, really comfortable in his own skin… you know what I mean? ….. Oh, Janette…I am sooooo confused! How can I feel this way about a man I just met? This just doesn't make sense to me at all."

"Well, well, well." Janette was grinning from ear to ear. "This is huge, Des. I think, my love, you are at a major crossroads here. You have some serious soul-searching to do. But…. you already knew that, deep down inside. This Jay Bennett has very interestingly become the catalyst that you needed….and….by the way… could very well be the solution as well. Just sayin'."

"Janette, stop. Please. Thank you for listening, as always. But I'm very confused right now. I need to think. Oh…. crap…. I also need to call Elliott! I love you, my friend…. gotta go…" And Desiree disconnected the call.

Several minutes later, Desiree punched the speed dial for Elliott's number, waiting impatiently for the connection. Only the voicemail answered. "I really hate this," she sighed.

* * *

"Hello, you've reached Elliott Grayson. Please leave your name, a detailed message, and the time you are calling. I will return your call as soon as possible."

* * *

Oh, damn, thought Desiree. I hate voicemail. At least be more creative. But then Elliott wasn't creative. Desiree decided to text him instead.

"Hi, darling…. tried calling but missed you. Just a reminder that I'm going to Henry's party tonight, so not sure what time I'll get back. I'll try calling you again later. Need to confirm my flight home… Can't wait to get my hands on you to do, you know what…. Love you so much. D."

Desiree chuckled. She knew those last words would annoy Elliott. But he was so easy…. he was so reserved. It really wasn't nice to tease him so, but she kept trying to loosen him up. It would be great if he was in court when he read the message…they'd wonder why he blushed so much.

For good measure, Desiree called Elliott's office. Eva answered, reminding Desiree that Elliott had another court date that morning. "Of course, I do remember," said Desiree. "Just covering all the bases. Eva, please do tell him I called and remind him to check his text messages. Not to worry. Thank you! As always. Bye."

* * *

Desiree had known Elliott for over three years. His father's law firm handled her father's company, and Elliott had been given the account when he became an associate. When he met Desiree, and they became an "item," Elliott had kept P.O.C. Outfitters, Inc. as a client, even when he became a partner. Elliott adored this woman, would do anything for her, and kept pressuring her to accept his proposal of marriage. But for some reason, she kept avoiding the discussion.

"Elliott, darling," she would say, "Call it my stubborn Irish pride. I just have to get my own business up and running." After working for numerous creative teams as an artist, Desiree launched her own business, illustrating children's books, and was determined to make a go of it on her own steam.

"I can support you, Desiree. You can illustrate to your heart's content," offered Elliott.

"I'm so close now," she said to him just before her father died. "Give me a couple of months to be sure I've made the right decision. Please?"

Elliott was a good man of impeccable background and, in fact, quite well off. He was solid and mature and always in control. He was wonderfully old-fashioned, though perhaps a bit strait-laced and uptight when it came to lovemaking. In their three years of being a "couple," Desiree could only remember once when Elliott really released his inhibitions.

They had spent the weekend at Uncle Max's cabin, and after hiking – Desiree's idea – and rowing on the lake – Elliott's request – Desiree pushed him into the lake and jumped in after him. Of course, the entire event meant stripping off their clothes the minute they got back to the cabin and warming up with a little brandy. Whether it was the heat of the moment or maybe too much brandy, Elliott made wild, passionate love to her right on the floor in front of a roaring fire.

* * *

Desiree smiled at the memory. Sweet Elliott. He still hates talking about that weekend. It makes him blush. But just the memory of that night kept Desiree hoping that she could break down his inhibitions. Maybe after we're married?

"Oh well," Desiree sighed and went to the French doors, opening them wide to let in the sweet, Caribbean morning air. She sent a quick "thanks for the call" to Janette and hit a few emojis. *"Will call you after Henry's party."*

Desiree ordered room service and jumped into the shower. Memories of last night kept creeping into other thoughts of Elliott. She shivered when she remembered the way Jay held her while they danced, and as the hot water pulsated on her back, she suddenly had goosebumps running up and down her spine with the image of him nibbling her finger. Unconsciously, she caught herself reliving his kiss, innocent though it was, and again felt his intentions pressing against her in no uncertain way while they danced.

For a moment, Desiree felt a stab of guilt at the lie she had told Elliott…. some friends she had said. Desiree was suddenly afraid. Why did she feel this way? Why did she feel guilty about deceiving Elliott and then rationalize it away? It was definitely time to go home. Thank goodness Jay Bennett was out of the picture now, heading back to New York today. He was too much of a temptation. But why? Why did she feel herself slipping under his spell? Why, in this moment of truth, was she so attracted to this man she had just met?

CHAPTER 5

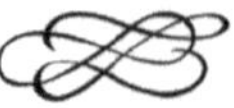

Desiree made a quick turn in front of the mirror, pleased with the results for Henry and Raoul's party. The deep turquoise dress with its crisscross bodice and flirty twirl of a skirt was the color of the sea, setting off the gold in her hair, now pulled to one side in a long ponytail. A stunning gold and turquoise necklace – passed to Desiree from her mother – laid across her collar bones, complimenting thick gold earrings that looked like flattened pebbles. Strappy gold sandals completed the look. Raoul, the fashionista of the couple, would approve.

At 4:00 sharp, what had to be a Rolls Royce of golf carts pulled up to the hotel entrance. It was the next model up from the one used on her arrival. The young driver, dressed in a short, crisp khaki skirt and a tropical shirt, waved and jumped out to escort Desiree to her ride.

"Welcome, Miss. My name's Alyssa. Mr. Henry sent me here to take you to Mande Villa. Watch your step, please."

Desiree stepped up and onto the padded seat of the little blue cart that looked like a fancy convertible. "Just like Henry! Only the best!"

As they traveled the winding roads and paths serpentining through the resort up to Henry and Raoul's home, Alyssa proved to be a wonderful tour guide, identifying additional points of interest, unique foliage, and the more private areas of the resort restricted to owners only. As they rode, Desiree mused at the memory of her arrival ten days ago.

* * *

The handsome, tanned, impeccably groomed, and seriously-in-shape man that greeted Desiree at the front of the hotel was a far cry from the lanky and wiry Henry of ten years ago. "Desiree! Ma Cherie! You're as gorgeous as ever! Maybe a tad tired around the eyes, but darling, we'll take care of that! Leave it to Raoul and me and our beautiful island."

"Oh, Henry – so wonderful to see you too! And YOU look amazing. Island life definitely agrees with you! I can't believe how long it's been. And this estate! The hotel! Janette told me all about it, but words don't do it justice."

"Come, I'll give you the Grand tour!" Henry loaded her luggage into the little blue golf cart, and off they went to tour the magnificent plantation and hotel compound, ending at her own rooms – La Villa Jaune – the yellow villa.

"How beautiful. Are all the villas different colors?"

"Ah…you noticed. But not just random colors. This is my mother's work. You know her – you remember how superstitious she was?" Desiree smiled in agreement. Henry continued, *"She believed that the spirit realm loves to communicate with colors and that every color is able to deliver a spiritual message. So, of course, she insisted color had to play a part here. And you know how that goes…"*

"She always got her way," Desiree chuckled.

"Certainement! So, it was easier to go with her than against her. Though we both admit now – Raoul and I – she was right. We agreed to name every villa a different color – but with great purpose. Every color must symbolize and create a special and meaningful experience for our guests. So, you, my dear, will stay in this one - La Villa Jaune- and if Ma Mere was correct – you will receive a spiritual message filled with joy, optimism and gain the strength to take on the next steps of your journey."

"Henry, that's really beautiful…and weird! But I love it! Thank you." Desiree reached out and hugged her friend. Her "villa"- La Villa Jaune- was the carriage house of the original estate – strategically positioned away from the old, sprawling anti-bellum mansion (now the main hotel) with its many salons and public areas. Painted a soft and creamy yellow with off-white trim, framed with enormous flowering pink and red mandevillas and surrounded by tall palms, the bungalow- style accommodations just oozed security, comfort, and luxury.

"Oh…Henry…this is just beautiful…and huge! My little cottage in Connecticut would fit in one room!"

"This is your home for as long as you want it or need it – a week, a month, a whole year!"

Desiree laughed. "Wow! Henry, I'm not relocating!"

"Well, you know what I mean. You're family. So…. these are your orders…. you will relax and sun and swim and read and do whatever you want to do. And next Friday… Raoul and I are having a party…it's one of our annual house parties, but we're dedicating it to you! "

"ONE of your annual parties?"

"Of course…we have them at least 5 times a year!"

"Oh Henry, maybe you haven't changed so much – just gotten better with age! No one throws a better party than you!"

"Then it's settled…YOU will be our guest of honor….and this one is also for our staff, other special guests, and any owners who are on the island. Cocktails… dinner…. and of course…. dancing! I'll send a ride for you.

* * *

"What can I do to help?" Desiree offered the minute she lifted from the little golf cart. Henry was there to meet her, of course, and Raoul came up behind him. Hugs and compliments all around.

"Raoul! You gorgeous man! Hello! And thank you, too, for your amazing hospitality. You are both too, too good to me!"

"Darling, you are our little sister…. you know that. We're here for you forever." Raoul took her hand and twirled her around…. "Stunning, my dear," he said. "A bit too thin…you need some meat on those gorgeous bones, but beautiful as ever!

Desiree felt incredibly humbled. "Take it all in," she told herself. "Embrace it. Treasure it. They ARE your family."

Calypso and Merengue Music echoed throughout the lush property, enveloping and permeating every corner of the magnificent grounds of Mandevilla – from the wide open gates flanked by tall lighter palms to the stone and tiled patio surrounding an Olympic-sized lighted pool. Dozens of tables covered in vibrant, colorful cloths and luminaria candles provided discreet seating for anyone needing some moments of privacy. There was an open bar on one side of the pool and a huge buffet table on the other – each laden with food and drinks and served by a rotating & smiling staff – so all could take part in the festivities.

Desiree took it all in…. "This…" mused Desiree…. "is the way it should be. So casually simple yet perfectly executed. When I get married…I want it to be like this."

"Ready, my dear? You look stunning tonight, by the way! Let's show them how it's done!" Henry grabbed Desiree's hand and waist, twirling her onto the center of the dance floor. They started with the fun and lively calypso, then eased into a seductive salsa followed by merengue. Everything Henry had ever taught her about island dancing came back two-fold…the music crescendoed, the other guests stepped far back to allow the two to show their stuff – it was *Dancing with the Stars* in person – they were stunning, sweeping the dance floor from one end to the other, gathering applause along the way.

"Oh my god…. I'm so out of shape, Henry!" gasped Desiree at last, laughing as she grabbed his face between her hands and gave him a brotherly kiss. "Thank you! I needed that!"

Desiree moved towards one of the tables to get a drink. Sipping the tart island concoction, she chatted with a young couple on their honeymoon while watching other guests mingling, dancing, eating, and having a wonderful time.

Henry and Raoul certainly knew how to throw a great party. They were the consummate hosts, and their friends and staff adored them.

Lost in thought, she heard behind her now, just a whisper in her ear, "Now, *that* was impressive!"

Desiree caught her breath!!! She whipped around… "Jay???" "Hey, Princess! Hello…. Yes…it's me!! Surprised?"

"How…. what….?" Desiree was speechless. "I thought you were leaving today?"

"Well, I was until Henry called me and reminded me about his party! What are YOU doing here?" Jay locked his eyes into hers.

"Henry and Raoul are the friends I mentioned. I've known them for over 15 years! Henry's sister and I are friends from college – they're my second family."

At that moment, Henry joined them, enveloping the two of them between his arms. "You two have met? You know each other?"

Desiree started to blush. Jay took it on and shared the story of their "date" from the previous night.

"It wasn't a date," insisted Desiree. Jay just continued on, leaving out no detail while throwing in a few innuendos.

"Well, well, well," Henry mused, grinning all the while. "Don't think I could have planned that one any better."

The rest of the evening passed in a blur. Henry and Raoul introduced Desiree to everyone – from the staff to several other owners and some specially invited guests of the hotel. They loved sharing how they all knew each other, Henry's and Desiree's humorous and conflicting stories of those early days in Brooklyn, gossiping about the escapades of Janette and Desiree, the dance parties, and hot summer nights in Manhattan. Several staff members made sure they said hello. Georgia, the lovely mixologist and creator of the signature Yellowbirds, grinned a knowing smile and waved when she spotted them from across the patio. Jay stayed at Desiree's side, listening to every word, taking in every detail, and dancing nearly every dance. Together, they made a stunning and charming couple, chatting easily with each other and with other guests.

At last, with plates in hand, Jay led Desiree to one of the little tables. They ate in silence for a few minutes, taking in the sparkling lights reflecting from the pool, the gaiety of the party guests, and the sweet refrain of a familiar calypso song by Harry Belafonte.

"So, Ms. Desiree Dubois," Jay cleared his voice and smiled. "Hmmm," Desiree was lost in thought.

"Now that we know each other better, and it seems we have Henry's stamp of approval, *now* will you go sailing with me? Tomorrow?"

"Well, I don't need Henry's approval." "Oh, you don't, do you."

"No, I don't…and OK, I'd love to." As the words came out of her mouth, Desiree caught her breath, slapping her hand across her mouth, eyes wide. "Uhhh!" "Oh damn," she said to herself. "What am I thinking? Why did I say yes?" She felt butterflies in her stomach again, or was it fear?

Jay choked on his drink, laughing at the same time.

"My dear Desiree, you look like you saw a ghost! Whatever are you afraid of?" "Nothing. I'm fine. Excuse me for a moment, please? I need to find the ladies' room." And as she walked away, she called back over her shoulder, "And yes, I'd love to go sailing!"

Desiree ran into Henry on the way. "There you are…. Hello, Darling! Having a good time?" Henry put an affectionate arm around her.

"Perfectly lovely! Thank you so much!" Desiree bit her lip. "Henry….do you have a minute?"

"Of course. What's up?" Henry steered her to the side of the patio, giving a casual wave to guests and, of course, to Raoul.

"Jay Bennett. How well do you know him?"

"Hmmm…oh, quite well, actually." Henry smiled to himself. "Almost since Raoul and I moved here. I guess about 8 years or so. He was one of our first owners. His family had roots here. In fact, he was one of our initial investors. Why?" Henry cocked his head quizzically. "You two seem to be hitting it off rather nicely."

"Well, he's certainly nice and funny, and he's coming on to me, big time!" "Darling, have you looked in the mirror?"

"That's not what I mean."

"Des, you are one of the loveliest and most wonderful women I know. You're wicked smart…kind… funny…. generous…a good and loyal friend…. and yes, beautiful – inside and out. You know…. if things had been different, I would have married you myself!"

"Oh Henry…I love you. Thank you." Desiree took a deep sigh. "I have a problem. I know Janette has told you about Elliott and me. We've been together over three years now. He's an amazing man. He's asked me to marry him – several times."

"And??? Isn't that wonderful? Isn't that what you always hoped for?" "Well…I thought it was until now. Until I met this Jay Bennett, that is. He's gotten under my skin. He makes me laugh, Henry. And with just a look, he gives me butterflies. I'm all discombobulated…I'm feeling things I never felt with Elliott, even in the beginning. I keep imagining how life would be with him… with Jay…. I'm having weird dreams…literally!"

"And what's wrong with that? The feelings, that is. And my mother would say other stuff about the dreams."

"I don't know. I feel…I feel…torn…. like I'm betraying Elliott. I'm here having an amazing time while he's in New York. I like how I feel here…with Jay…with his attention. I feel more alive than I've felt in a long, long time."

"Oh, Des…my adorable little sister…" Henry pulled Desiree towards him, enveloping her in his long arms, gently kissing the top of her head. "You've been through a life-altering experience. You've lost your sweet Poppy…your father… your rock. You're about to launch the newest phase of your career, to realize your future after years of just dreaming about it. And you've inherited your father's business and have a company and its employees to worry about. That's a lot, Des. You deserve a little fun and excitement!"

"I told Jay I'd go sailing with him tomorrow."

"Hmmm…so you did, did you? And what's wrong with that? He's a good guy, Des. He's honest, ethical, a good businessman, one with strong convictions, and a gentleman – at least as far as I've ever seen. I'd say he's pretty comfortable in his own skin…pretty easy on the eyes, too, if I do say so myself!"

"Henry!! Stop that." But Desiree laughed at Henry's playful comment, slapping his arm affectionately.

"That's my girl. Des…look…embrace the life you have now, today. You've been through a lot. There's nothing written in stone, and nothing so committed that can't be changed if need be. Trust yourself to do the right thing. Not only for you but for Elliott and the other people who have come to depend on you." Desiree was silent for some time. A million thoughts raced through her head.

Finally, "I love you, Henry. Always the big brother! Thank you."

Joining Desiree in the little golf cart, they were silent on the ride back to the villas. "Madame?" Jay offered his hand and escorted her to the door of her Villa Jeune. "I'm really happy you said yes, Des."

"Do I need to bring anything?"

"Nothing. I'll take care of everything. Oh, I guess you should bring your bathing suit unless you're into nude swimming," he grinned. "And sneakers… you do have sneakers, don't you?" looking down at her perfectly manicured feet. "Yes. I have sneakers," she answered a bit defensively. "And I'll bring a suit, thank you!"

Jay grinned as he reached over, placing an arm over each of her shoulders, looking her straight in the eye, and gently pulling her to him. He wanted so much to kiss her hard on her lips, to wrap his arms around her, but he opted instead for a warm and soft kiss that brushed her lips, lingering for only a moment. Desiree responded easily. Then she tensed. His lips spoke of friendship, but his body was taut with desire. Desiree fought with herself to stay calm, and Jay sensed it immediately. He released his hold on her and, instead, cradled her face in his hands.

He looked her squarely in the eyes. "Hmmmm," he sighed. "I'm leaving you now, Des, but I really don't want to." Then he kissed her again, quickly this time, on the tip of her nose, then turned and strode off in the moonlight, calling back over his shoulder, "I'll see you at 10!"

23

CHAPTER 6

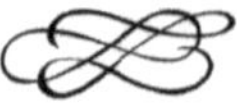

J ay pulled his red jeep into a free spot at the Marina. He nodded towards the harbor.

"There she is."

Desiree squinted against the glare and looked out to where he pointed. There were four sailboats moored in the same area. "Which one?"

"The little one," Jay grinned.

"The little one?" She echoed amazed. "They're all huge!" "No, mine's the smallest. She only sleeps eight."

"Jay! That's huge! Are you kidding? Come on, which one, really."

Jay put his arm around Desiree and gently directed her gaze a bit more to the left. "There," he whispered against her hair. "The one with the yellow and blue spinnaker and the dark wood hull."

"Oh, Jay, she's beautiful! She looks kind of old fashioned, you know, like the sailboat in *High Society*, with Grace Kelly, the True Love, remember?"

"Ah, yes, she was 'yar'." They laughed together, remembering their conversation about old movies.

"But this one's all mine. I bought her 'bout five years ago. It took three years just to bring back her beauty. It was my greatest dream to have a boat like her. And when I found her, no one else was going to touch her."

"You really did the work all yourself?" Desiree was mesmerized by the boat's sleek lines. She really didn't know much about boats in general, but one couldn't help being impressed with this little beauty. "What did you name her?" Desiree asked, still staring out into the harbor.

"Sure, you won't laugh?"

Desiree looked up at Jay only to find his eyes twinkling with delight.

"No, of course not!" "MY DESIRE."

"Pardon?"

"MY DESIRE. That's her name." "No!" Desiree felt her cheeks get hot. "Yes! Cross my heart and…"

"Well, isn't that a coincidence!"

Jay was outwardly laughing now. "Isn't it, though? I always believed in fate." "Umph!" Desiree sucked in her breath and regained her composure. "Well, are we going aboard?"

"Absolutely! Let's get the dingy."

* * *

On board, the little boat was more beautiful than she was from the shore. Jay had restored her to her 1950s splendor, and Desiree felt she *was* Grace Kelly stepping back in time.

Below deck, the small galley was completely equipped with every convenience. Two small bunk rooms had been opened up to make an intimate master suite complete with a full-size captain's bed. All of the wood, decks, tables, and cabinets were deep, rich mahogany, sanded and buffed to a satiny smooth finish. The cushions and bed linens were a royal blue and white stripe, everything crisp and efficient.

Following Jay's expert guidance, Desiree helped him set the sails, and as they tacked out of the harbor, she felt like a bird, totally relaxed and at ease, happier than she could ever remember.

"Me thinks you've done this before, my beauty!" Jay teased her in his best pirate voice.

Desiree couldn't help herself. She was grinning from ear to ear, thrilled with the anticipation of the perfect sailing day. Elliot had taught her quite a bit over the years, sailing in Long Island Sound along the Eastern shore with his parents.

But this was different. This was free. Unencumbered. As she watched, waiting for her next set of instructions, she studied Jay with her artistic eye, comparing him to a Rodin sculpture. His hair blew away from his face, leaving a broad and slightly furrowed brow showing off his 2-day beard, his eyes squinting in concentration as he watched every movement the sails made. She marveled at his agility despite his large, muscular body. With the strength of Thor throwing a thunderbolt, he heaved the main sail, hauling

25

the ropes and steering the little boat, always in control, always anticipating the wind's next move.

Desiree studied the firm muscles and tendons in his long-tanned legs and, with a practiced eye, traced every sinewy line from his broad shoulders down to his waist. She was acutely aware of his every movement, and as his body tensed and relaxed with each gesture he made, Desiree felt her own knees weaken.

Jay Bennett was a powerful presence. He couldn't be ignored. As she stared at him, she could feel herself falling under his spell, losing her own self-control. She found herself fantasizing about the kind of lover he would be. Passionate? Demanding? Tender?

"Hey! Desiree! Let out the rope; watch your head! Let's go!"

"Oh my God! Sorry!"Desiree crashed back into reality and quickly jumped to attention. The boat righted herself, and Desiree blinked against the brilliant sky.

"Where were you? What were you thinking? We almost capsized!"

"Sorry! So sorry! It's been a while." Desiree hoped he didn't see her flushed cheeks.

"Well, come on, Girl! We've got places to go!"

For the next hour, they sailed majestically through the wind, cutting waves and leaning precariously, first to the starboard and then to the port. It was totally exhilarating and exciting and strangely erotic. Desiree felt the electricity in the air, and the way Jay kept looking at her, she was sure he felt it, too.

CHAPTER 7

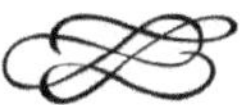

At last, on the horizon, they spied the islands that Jay had boasted about. They were everything he had claimed. Dead ahead, only about three hundred yards wide and a mile long, was one of four of the *Pequenas Islas* clustered together, forming a large half circle, sparkling in the ocean. Like soft granulated sugar, the wide sandy beach glistened and twinkled in the midday sun. Low shrubs and the twining branches of the mangroves stretching down the center of the island formed a wall of private dens, natural "beach huts," and passages providing shade from the intense heat and leading to the other side.

A dozen other boats were anchored at various spots along the island, all of them very protective of their little paradise. Desiree recognized several couples from last night's party. One group had built a small beach fire to fry and serve up the tiny local fish just caught to anyone interested. Jay anchored his boat close to a group of his friends – sailboats and cruisers alike – where they spent a few hours swimming and snorkeling and then hitching a lift to shore with one couple; they joined the beachcombers munching on sandwiches, fruit, and the freshly fried fish. They laughed and told Desiree stories of the times when Jay had first come to the islands as a "gringo".

Of course, he denied most of it…laughing it off and at himself but occasionally nearly blushing with embarrassment. His friends obviously adored him but gave him no slack!

"Come on, let's go for a walk," Jay whispered to Desiree sometime later. "I want to show you my little island." Turning to the others, Jay grinned, "Enough of this destructive rhetoric! I have a reputation to protect! We'll see you guys in a bit."

"If you get lost, meet us at the Caves tonight!" Jedd called after them. "New band playing…. hey… don't do anything we wouldn't do!"

"Yea…yea…yea," Jay laughed and grabbed Desiree's hand with one hand while waving backwards with the other towards his friends.

They strode off down towards the opposite end of the island, their bare feet sinking deeply into the soft granular sand, and then, taking her elbow, Jay steered her into one of the tree-lined passages – the unique mangrove trees that thrive on saltwater...

"Where are we going?"

"Sssssh!" He put his finger on her lips and smiled down at her. "You'll see. Come on."

A few yards later, they emerged into a little clearing, completely surrounded on three sides by the same shrubs. But in front lay only a stretch of sand and the ocean. Desiree felt stranded, adrift on the sea. Jay's presence beside her was overwhelming and comforting. She could barely speak.

"Oh, Jay, this is eerie." Desiree shivered in the hot sun.

"It is strange, isn't it. When I first found it, I sat here for hours, completely mesmerized by the view."

"But it feels so lonely here, so isolated. I mean, if we hadn't just left all your friends five minutes ago, I would swear we were the only people left on Earth!" Jay put his arms around her, resting his chin on her head, facing the water.

Together, they looked out past the horizon. "I'd love to be the only person left on earth with you."

Desiree tilted her head to look up at him, but this time, Jay wasn't grinning. His eyes were full of fire. He turned her around to face him. "You feel the same, don't you?" It was more of a statement than a question.

Desiree broke the gaze. "I… I… don't know," she stammered. "You frighten me, Jay."

"Frighten you? My God, why? Look at me." He waited till he could look her straight in the eye. "Desiree, please don't be frightened."

His look softened. "You are the most exciting woman I have ever met. You're like a wild exotic animal that has been confined too long. You're restless, you're pacing, you're searching for something. I want to help you find it and share it with you. Let me help you. I know you want me to. I can see it in your eyes! I can feel it when I touch you."

Jay could contain himself no longer. He pulled Desiree to him, almost roughly. Pressing her against himself, he kissed her hard on the lips, wrapping his arms around her and caressing her bare back. Her skin was smooth and silky, glistening in the sun. Desiree lost her breath and her control all at the same time. She was no match for Jay's hot kisses. Her arms moved up around his neck, and her lips parted.

Jay's tongue searched for hers as his hands moved down to caress her buttocks. He could feel her muscles contracting under the thin fabric of her suit. Her breasts pressed against his bare chest. She felt every muscle, every nerve in Jay's body responding to their kisses. She smoothed her own hands down his long spine and around his tight derriere, feeling him thrust towards her. She arched her back gently and relaxed even more completely into his arms as they kissed and danced under the sun.

Half-consciously, in what seemed like hours, but only minutes later, Desiree became aware of the hot sun beating on her back. She was acutely aware of her scanty attire, sensing the soft cotton barely covering her bikini like a sheath between them. Slowly, she fought to refocus on reality. She pulled Jay's arms down from her neck, gently easing herself from his embrace.

"Jay, please, let's stop. This is going much too fast. We can't do this. "I'm supposed to be in love with someone else." At least I think I am, she said I'm not ready for this. I'm supposed to be in love with someone else." At least I think I am, she said in her own mind.

"Woah, really? That doesn't make sense. Are you talking about this guy, Elliott? The one who is handling your father's estate? Just good friends, I thought you said."

"Yes. Elliott. And we *are* good friends for a little more than three years. And I thought I was in love. Then he proposed to me just before I came here, right after the funeral. His timing was lousy." Desiree sighed deeply. "Part of me getting away was to think, to try and figure out how I really feel about him."

"Des, you kissed me as passionately as I kissed you. How can you be in love with Elliott and kiss me like that? You're deceiving yourself. Let yourself go. Listen to your heart."

"I don't know." Desiree turned away with tears in her eyes. "I'm very confused. This is more than I can think about right now."

Jay's heart went out to her. She was a strong woman, but at this moment, there on this little patch of sand surrounded by trees and water, she was as vulnerable as a child.

And there it was. The flash of an image. A face was torn by pain but still elusive.

"I'm sorry, my dear sweet Desiree. I'm sorry, but damn it, woman, you make it very hard on a man..."

Desiree smiled weakly. His reference wasn't lost on her. And she couldn't ignore her own involvement in this intense and ardent demonstration of affection.

"I promise..." Jay whispered but with determination, "I will never push you. BUT I will tell you this…and be forewarned… I think I'm falling in love with you. Do you understand? And I'll wait for you to feel the same about me."

"Come on, let's head back to the boat. It's getting late."

CHAPTER 8

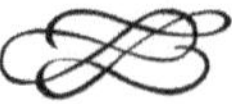

Despite her confusion, Desiree felt strangely comforted walking beside Jay. They didn't touch now, and even though Desiree was lost in thought, Jay's presence was comforting yet unmistakable. Desiree felt physically at ease, but her emotions were in turmoil. When her thoughts were on Elliott, Jay's face came into view; when she tried to concentrate on Jay, Elliott's face appeared.

She realized she was being very unfair to Elliott. He trusted her, and she was deceiving that trust. And she wasn't really being honest with Jay either. She would leave for New York tomorrow morning, and as soon as she saw Elliott, she would…. she would what? Accept a proposal? Set a wedding date? That wasn't honest, either.

Desiree could not deny her incredibly mounting feelings for Jay Bennett. What happened to the nice girl who wanted to settle down and have babies? "Who am I?" she said over and over to herself.

"Well, who in the hell are you? What do you want? Who do you want?" she chided herself, "why haven't you married Elliott?" Desiree was getting more confused than ever. "Something's rotten in Denmark," she thought. "I cannot allow Jay to get any closer, and I cannot keep lying to Elliott. And I thought I was getting my life in order! All I've done is screw it up!"

As they neared the spot where they had moored the boat, they noticed the beach was deserted. The last launch was just disappearing from view. MY DESIRE rocked gently on her anchor as the sun dropped dramatically lower into the horizon.

"I didn't realize we were gone so long!" commented Desiree, amazed. "God, what a beautiful sunset."

"Neither did I." Jay stood with his hands on his hips, staring out to sea. "Des, we have a problem."

"What?"

"We can't sail back."

"What!"

"I'm really sorry. I swear I didn't plan this. The wind died down too much, the tide is out, and not to mention it's getting too dark."

"What? What do you mean? You mean this yacht of yours doesn't have a motor? Can't we call for help? How about the Coast Guard? Do you have a radio…is there cell service?" Desiree reached into her bag to grab her cell phone, only to find it missing.

"Oh my god! "she said out loud."I left my cell in the hotel? Seriously? Really? What was I thinking?"

"Calm down. First, there is no cell service out here anyway. And yes… the boat has a motor… but it needs a new starter… which is on order… but…"

Desiree wasn't interested in explanations! "No motor? Seriously? So… you mean we're stuck? We're stuck on this island in the middle of the ocean all night?" Desiree felt the bile in her stomach for the second time in as many days. But her voice was angry. "On this island all night?" Desiree was getting more panicked by the second, but her voice was angry.

"I'm afraid so." Jay nodded, smothering a smile.

"You mean, you and I on this little boat, together, all night? What are we going to eat?"

Now he burst out laughing. "Eat? Are you kidding? You're stranded…. on a deserted island…alone…. with me….and you're worried about what you're going to eat?"

Desiree folded her arms across her chest, thumping her foot in the sand. Her eyes became little slits, and her voice grew louder.

"Yes, damn it! I'm hungry! Those friggin' little fish and sandwiches didn't exactly do it for me. And when I get hungry, I get angry, and when I'm angry, I'm not a very nice person. In fact….and don't you dare stand there laughing at me, Jay Bennett, I'm pissed! You have some nerve stranding me out here with you…That is some low-down, rotten trick. If you want me so badly, why don't you just throw me to the sand and take me? Or are you going to seduce me while the waves gently rock us to sleep? How romantic! You know all the right moves, don't you? How dare you do this to me!"

"WHOA! Desiree! Do you hear yourself?" Jay moved closer. "Don't touch me!"

"Desiree, calm down. Please." Jay was truly apologetic. He reached out and took Desiree in his arms. "I promise I didn't plan this. And I also promise I will not seduce you. Though I admit, it's not going to be easy." He saw the serious panic in her eyes. "I'm serious. Trust me. Ok?"

Desiree stared into his eyes, and she knew he meant what he said; she was ashamed of herself for reacting so childishly. "I'm sorry. I guess I overreacted. It was stupid."

"It wasn't stupid. It was real. But I must say you do have quite a temper.

From the Irish side, I take it?"

Desiree blushed. "My biggest fault. I have absolutely no control over it. My mother used to shake her head in dismay. *'Ah…ma cheri…zer is no hope… il n'y a pas d'espoir. Vous ne deviendrez jamais une dame…you will never become a lady…. You are just like your papa… 'tu es comme ton papa…mon dieu!'"*

"Sweet…now that's better." Jay tweaked her nose. "Now cheer up. We'll make the best of this. Pretend we're camping. But first, let's get back to the boat." "But we'll have to swim!"

"And that would be another yes."

"I have no dry clothes, only those shorts and this silly coverup I wore this morning. I'll freeze when I get out."

"Complain, complain, complain. I thought you were the outdoor type?"

"I have my limits…and you are definitely pushing them. Hmph! Stranded on an island." He cocked an eye at her. "Just sayin'," she finished contritely.

"Fear not, *damn pranzel.* Trust me. Come on. Give me your shoes and your bag. Let's go."

They waded into the water, which was calm and warm from the hot sun. They swam a few yards to the boat. Jay threw the bag over the side, then hoisted himself up first and pulled Desiree in. Millions of little goosebumps appeared on her the moment she hit the cool evening air. Her teeth began to chatter. Jay threw a big towel over her and started to rub her down.

"Thanks, I can manage." Desiree pulled away. She trusted Jay, but she wasn't sure she trusted herself. Their kiss on the beach still burned in her memory, and she needed all the self-control she could muster.

"Now," Jay said, ignoring her defensiveness, "go down into the cabin. In the bottom drawer under the bed are some sweaters, and there's some draw-string sweats on the top. Help yourself. I think you'll be warmer…and safer," he winked, "in those, instead of those skimpy shorts and top you wore this morning."

"Great." Thank God! She thought. "Be back in a few minutes. What about food?" She called over her shoulder.

"Don't worry. I've got it covered."

Desiree went below and found the clothes. Finding her hairbrush on the bottom of her tote, a small tube of moisturizer, lipstick, and a clean pair of undies (her mother always told her to never travel without an extra pair – just in case), she pulled together a less than glamourous but relaxed and comfortable image of herself. She brushed her hair and toweled it dry, pulling the now wildly curly hair into a make-do ponytail. She felt immediately warmer…and safer (she smiled) as she tightened the string on the white sweat.

"Great fit," she yelled sarcastically. She pulled on a big navy blue and white sweater that fell to her thighs and was able to roll the sleeves up three times. "Grace Kelly, eat your heart out," she said to herself.

By the time she finished, a good half hour had passed. She had heard Jay rummaging around in the galley, but nothing could have prepared her for what met her on deck.

"What's all this?' Desiree looked in amazement at the nothing-less-than-lavish arrangement that now occupied the entire hatch area of the deck. A white linen cloth covered the hatch, forming an intimate table for two. The old oil lantern, now lit, cast amber shadows across the deck. Blue and white spattered dishes, real silver, and champagne glasses finished the vignette. But the real eye-stopper was the tiny hibachi heating up its coals.

"I thought this wasn't planned?" Desiree felt her blood begin to boil.

"This wasn't. Lunch was. Remember? But between meeting Jess and Mark and the others and taking our little constitutional, we never got around to it. So, voila, ma petite! We have dinner for two!"

"Oh. Well, this certainly beats a can of beans." Desiree stopped. "What's wrong?"

Jay was staring at her, arms across his chest. He nodded to her appearance. "How in the world can you look so damn beautiful with no makeup and baggy clothes? Actually, you'd probably look great in a potato sack!"

"Maintenant! But of course! Monsieur Bennett." Desiree resurrected her French accent. She did a runway turn as she asked in her own voice, "So, do you think Women's Wear Daily would like to feature the latest in sailing attire?"

"Like I said, you would sell in a sack." Jay felt his blood surge yet again for the umpteenth time that day. God, this woman had an incredible pull on his manhood…. not to mention his emotions.

"So, what's for dinner?' Desiree quickly changed the subject as Jay recouped his composure...

"Well, you come on over, watch the chef at work. Caribbean style. Le Chien Chaud!'" Jay held up two skewers of huge hot dogs speared lengthwise -- laid them on the open charcoal grill, and opened the champagne.

"Madame?" "Hot dogs?"

"But of course! And…since you asked…. a can of beans!" He held up the now-open can of sweetened Caribbean beans, emptying them into a small pot. "Did you forget I was a Boy Scout? Always prepared! I earned over 50 badges! And truth be known, hot dogs are my favorite meal!"

"And they go with Champagne?" Desiree was holding back her laughter. Jay was delightful!

"Of course! Everything goes with Champagne! And champagne should never go to waste!!"

Desiree laughed outright at his antics – tossing the grill utensils like a Hibachi chef, accenting his grilling procedure and expertise.

"Finally, madame?"

"Oui, si'l vous plait." Desiree settled back on the cushions Jay had provided and took a sip of the delightfully dry champagne. He was so sexy and a joy to watch as he fussed with his creations. And even more amazing was the fact that he was as relaxed making dinner as he was hoisting the sails.

Desiree still didn't know much about his private life, only that he had never been married, though once engaged. Both parents were alive and well and living in Arizona. He had a married sister out in Seattle with four wild and woolly nieces. He wanted children of his own and was the president and co-partner of Bennett and Bagstrom Engineers, a small engineering firm. But he also had considerable investments (obviously) in real estate and various other related firms around the country. Judging by his lifestyle, he wasn't exactly poor.

But then, neither was Desiree. Her mother's inheritance had enabled her to buy a little two-bedroom farmhouse- cottage in southern Connecticut. In addition, her father had given her part of the profits when they sold the house she had grown up in. This helped her start her own business. Now, her father's estate, which was to be settled upon her return, would undoubtedly make her quite comfortable. Her own business as a free-lance illustrator had its ups and downs, and she had been through some pretty lean periods, but a more promising future was on the horizon.

For a moment, Desiree found herself thinking about what life with Jay Bennett would be like. Living in her little cottage, vacationing on MY DESIRE, relaxed and at ease with life and her conscience.

Then Elliott invaded her thoughts. She tried to picture life with Elliott. Funny, but it was something she had never been able to imagine. Is that why she could never fully commit to an engagement? There was always a grey area… like tall buildings in the city. Life with Elliott was rushed and efficient. A series of cocktail parties and dinners, theater, and the opera, and weekends in the Hamptons. Not that Desiree didn't love the arts; she was passionate about them, especially ballet. After all, her mother was a dancer. But in Elliott's world, being involved in that scene was a commitment, not a passion. That always annoyed her.

"Des?Hello?Earth to Desiree?"

"What? Oh, Jay, I'm sorry. I was just mellowing out. This is so good! I feel so relaxed. How're the Hot Dogs!"

"Done. And perfect, if I do say so myself. I'm ready to serve. Are you ready?" "Famished."

CHAPTER 9

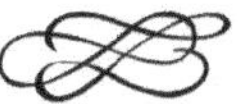

With great fanfare, Jay laid the halved hot dogs (now stuffed with melted cheese) on a platter (with toasted buns and warmed baked beans on the side) in the middle of their table, poured another round of champagne, and dropped down on the cushions across from Desiree.

They lifted their glasses. "Bon Appetit!" they said in unison. "Dig in!"

It was the best meal Desiree had ever tasted. The romantic surroundings, the water, the night breeze, the gentle sway of the boat, and certainly the bubbles in the champagne all contributed to a total mood. Desiree sopped every little morsel of meat, dressings, and condiments off her plate and then licked each finger individually before going back for more.

"I do have napkins." Jay leaned on his elbows, watching her.

"Oh, no… not necessary. This is too good to waste one tiny taste on a napkin…" "Desiree, I have never seen a woman eat like you do."

"That's what Elliott always says. I'm afraid I embarrass him; he hates to eat with his fingers. That's why he won't eat lobster or crabs or greasy hamburgers!" She licked her fingers again and took another sip of champagne. "I love greasy hamburgers, don't you?"

"You are so delightful," Jay laughed and let the reference to Elliott go. He already knew that that relationship was potentially on the cutting room floor. Not because of him…but because of Desiree's inability to commit. They had already shared a lot of information and philosophies about life in the short time they had known each other. However, she had never referred to Elliott in criticizing terms. She was usually so defensive of him and their relationship. What does she really feel…deep down inside? Again…Jay let it go.

Finally, Desiree had sated her appetite and leaned back against the side of the boat. Holding her glass, she stared up at the sky that had filled dramatically with stars.

"How can you possibly wish on a star tonight? There's so many. It's awesome."

Jay came around and sat down beside her. "It is magnificent, isn't it? There is nothing quite so peaceful."

"Oh, I don't know. Sometimes, I lay in my own backyard in the summer and stare up into the Connecticut sky. It's pretty impressive."

"You love that little house, don't you?"

"It's mine. No one or nothing can take it away. It's bought and paid for."

"You sound bitter, not proud."

"Do I? Sorry. Sometimes, I still get angry about my father dying on me."

"You never did say how it happened."

"Cancer. He'd had it for months but refused to tell anyone till nearly the end. He couldn't hide it anymore. He always lived life to its fullest, always busy. If he wasn't working, he was fishing or trying out a new invention. He and my Uncle Max went to their cabin up in the mountains every weekend. Sometimes I went too. They taught me how to bait a hook when I was only six. Ma Mere despised fishing, but she went along when I was small. She did it for Poppy, and he went to the ballet with her. He usually fell asleep, but she never complained. They were special. They were always so in tune with each other, so relaxed and accepting.

Desiree sighed and settled back into the cushions as she rambled on about her family, intertwining stories about the cabin and the country, life in New York City, her mother's passion, her father's obsessions and inventions, and the effect it all had on them both. She spoke softly, as if to herself, but Jay hung on to every word. Something she had said … his inventions?

"You said your dad had inventions?"

Desiree laughed. "Oh yes. Hundreds of them. Some died on the drawing board. Some blew up in the garage. A few are still buried in the patent office, I'm sure."

"Did any make it?"

"One. But Poppy will never get to see it."

"What happened?" Jay's curiosity was triggered, his innate senses were alerted, and he had a sick feeling in his stomach.

"Well, actually, it was a revision of one he had invented with my grandfather when Poppy was only 10 years old."

"Ten years old? Are you kidding me?"

"Nope…cross my heart," Desiree made the X on her left breast. "I'm not kidding." She took another sip of the champagne.

"The family business, dating back nearly 50 years, was a small mail-order camping supply company, kind of like L.L. Bean or Orvis, but a LOT smaller. It was meat and potatoes for our family. But my grandfather, like Poppy, loved to invent things. During the war – that would be Korean – Grandpa had come up with a line of specialized survival equipment. You know, the kind used in the deepest, darkest Africa or Asia? At about the same time, my dad was experimenting with charcoal and water. Well, together, they devised a line of equipment that included a mini water purification system, which could make any water drinkable, in small quantities, of course. Over time, to make a long story short, while small groups, little towns, etc., were benefiting from the system, the US Army learned of it, contracted for its use, and ended up supporting our military and our own family for years by using the product."

"You mean the army gave your grandfather contracts to supply this equipment and the water system."

"Exactly. It lasted through the Korean and, later, the Vietnam War, and even in the Middle East. But eventually, Grandpa's inside contact person retired, and like many government projects, ours fell through the cracks.

"But obviously, that's not the end of this story."

"Not when you're dealing with manic inventors!" Desiree laughed. "They never stopped tweaking, and along the way, Grandpa and Poppy adapted the mini water system for the camper crowd, and it became standard issue in our catalog."

"I know…I have one!" interrupted Jay.

"You're kidding? Really?"

"I do…and it's GREAT! It really works."

"Well, of course, it works," Desiree said smugly, but deep down, she was impressed and delighted. She continued, "And then, always trying to build that better mouse trap, Poppy took the system even further and modified it to work on a grander scale."

Jay sat perfectly still, his arm still around her, his mind racing. His thoughts were wild. All were wild. All the pieces were falling into place. Jay knew the story only too well.

* * *

Jay loved the little tack shop in Cranford Lake. It was a capsule in time from the 1930s, a 70-year-old wooden structure as sturdy today as it was then. The floor-to-ceiling racks, glass-faced cabinets, and large flat drawers filled with beautiful lures of all kinds and colors, and probably a hundred or more photos of proud anglers – men, women, and kids – taken through the decades showing off their catch, revealed the undisputed history of the Lake and its tiny town. Jay headed to the back of the store where the best fly-fishing lures were hiding. Here is where he went to uncover another gem to add to his collection. Jay first saw Pat O'Conner as the Irishman was "arguing" with a larger version of himself over the benefits of live bait over lures for trout. Jay hid his grin as he couldn't help but eavesdrop on the two men sparring back and forth, badgering each other for ten minutes.

"Max, ye're a stubborn mule, ye know! Those flashy things just dunna' work in this lake!"

"Say all ye want, Paddy, but I disagree! Lures are like parsley on the p'taters…. they'll taste the same, but they look a hell of a lot better! Just like a woman in a beautiful dress! Tell me your eye doesn't take a turn when she's sportin' something bright and pretty! Tell me YOU prefer a woman in a brown sack!"

"What in god's name does a woman's dress 'ave to do with the type of fishin' lures?" Trying to swallow his laugh, the man named Paddy shook his head, feigning disbelief at what he just heard.

Feeling guilty at eavesdropping, Jay discreetly reversed his steps and headed out the door, chuckling at the obvious enjoyment the two men took, baiting each other. That evening, Jay stopped at the main lodge for a nightcap, and there at the bar was the one called Paddy.

"Eh, Laddie," he said, turning to Jay and raising the drink in his hand.

"Sláinte! … Cheers! Nice night. You from here? Don't think I've seen ye before."

"Oh, I've only been here a few times – I like the fishing," said Jay. "How about you? Didn't I see you in the tack shop today?"

"Did ye now? Aye, I was. Come up nearly every weekend. Did we talk? Don't rightly remember. Don't have much space left up here," he laughed as he tapped a finger to his head.

Jay smiled. "Uhm…no, we didn't. I saw you and your friend "discussing" bait, lures and women's dresses this afternoon."

"Ah ha! Aye! That was me brother, Max. Stubborn old fool! But I love him! Thinks he knows about fishin'. He doesn't…but he does know how to make money! He's a wall street wiz from the old days. And he loves the ladies!" Paddy took a drink from his glass and stuck out his strong hand."

"Name's Patrick…Patrick O'Conner."

"Jay Bennett…it's a pleasure, Sir!"

And the conversation started… and continued for several hours into the late evening. Jay shared his passions and talked about his life and his business. He learned about Patrick's camping supply company, about his deceased wife, about his daughter, and about his obsession with inventing things. The end of the evening was the beginning of a sincere friendship, an immediate bonding most often seen between father and son, and though they didn't know it at the time, it was the seed that kick-started a chain of events no one could have seen coming!

* * *

"What do you mean?" Jay forced himself to ask Desriee, knowingly anticipating how the rest of the story would unfold.

"Cranford, the little town where we have a family cabin?" Jay nodded… waiting…feeling sick to his stomach.

Desiree continued the story, oblivious of Jay's growing discomfort. "Cranford discovered the beginnings of pollution in its drinking water. It came from chemicals that were being used on the farms around the area. Poppy donated his system, after more modifications, to help clean up the water. It worked better than anyone ever imagined. The preliminary results, which came out about 6 months ago, were really impressive. The final results will be out this summer. But Poppy will never see it."

Sitting here with Desiree, listening to her recounting of her father's eccentricities, discoveries, and revelations, Jay remembered the day Pat O'Conner presented him with the offer of a deal, a deal that tickled his appreciation for Pat's brilliance and creativity. The man certainly had more than enough room in his head for his vision and a definitive plan for a solution to his problem. They were casting for trout, a pastime they had enjoyed together many times as their friendship evolved.

* * *

"I 'ave a proposition for ye, laddie," said Pat. "I've done some research on ye. Asked around. You're a good man. You're smart. You're honest… ethical. So, hear me out." Pat now shared the whole story of his dilemma, along with the shocking news of his diagnosis. The man had pancreatic cancer – a death sentence. He asked Jay to be his emissary, so to speak, to carry out his plans on his behalf. "I know it won't be easy. And I wager ye'll have to be clever. And know this: that if you accept my terms, I trust you to carry out my instructions to the end. 'Cause if ye don't, cross my heart, I'll come back to haunt ye for the rest of your days!"

* * *

Jay squirmed in his place at the memory and re-adjusted his position.

"I'm sorry, Jay." Desiree leaned forward, turning slightly. "I've bored you to death."

"No. No. Not at all. Don't move." Jay reassured her and softly stroked her hair. He didn't want her to see his face. The fates were definitely working overtime. The illusive image that had been haunting him since meeting Desiree became clear. Without a doubt, Desiree's father was the same Patrick O'Conner, the crazy, eccentric inventor who sold his business and his purification system to Jay's parent company only three months ago. And Desiree was Pat O'Conner's daughter! And they had bonded…Jay and the old man. And yes, now with Desiree. But her name? Dubois? The name she used to introduce herself to him that night at the bar over Yellowbirds– Desiree Dubois, her mother's maiden name -- muddied the waters. But then there was her face. Clear as day now, he remembered her from the back of the church the day of Pat-O'Conner's funeral. Hair pulled starkly back, the drawn and sad face of a lovely woman about to give a eulogy. He didn't stay. He had paid his respects. He had seen the man before he died. He left before she spoke.

* * *

How on earth was he going to proceed? She was special. But he had made a pledge to her father. And now the man was dead. *"This is private, between you and me."* O'Conner had said. *"No one is to know about this until*

42

after the final papers are signed and the whole deal is done. Not my daughter, not my brother, not the employees. No one! Agreed?" Jay had agreed. He had even agreed when O'Conner insisted Jay's lawyers, rather than his own, draw up the papers. Jay had thought the whole thing a little strange and melodramatic, but the man was clearly an eccentric and undoubtedly had his reasons.

* * *

In just a few short months, everything was different. Would his promise to Pat O'Conner be important now? Who was to know that he, Jay, would meet and fall in love with the man's daughter? It was bizarre. He wanted to tell Desiree everything. There was karma here; he knew it on both sides. Crazy as it seemed, he truly believed they were meant to be. But it would have to wait.

Desiree sighed again, this time a little sadly. Almost abruptly, Jay interrupted her thoughts, struggling to keep his voice light.

"Come on, Sailor. Time for bed."

Desiree glanced towards the hold. "Both of us? Down there?"

"No." Jay said quietly and comfortingly, "You sleep down there. I'll stand watch up here." Jay kissed her like a brother, patted her behind, and sent her down the galley stairs.

Desiree went like a good little girl. As she lay in the captain's bed, she felt the boat sway under her, rocking her like a baby. Soon, she drifted off to sleep, her last thought of Jay and the way he stroked her hair as they sat under the stars.

* * *

Later that night, she dreamt of the bird again. This time, the bird was soaring high in the sky, out of reach, in and out of the clouds, appearing and then disappearing again behind a brilliant sun. She saw herself standing on a sandy beach, reaching up towards the bird. Suddenly, she was flying with the yellow bird, holding its delicate wing but feeling nothing. She flew high up into the sky and back towards the sea, elated and glorious, laughing and crying at the same time. She wasn't afraid. The yellow bird kept her calm. Suddenly, the bird was gone. She panicked and glanced down, realizing how high she had flown. Down, down, down she fell, diving, gliding, free falling out of control. She was going to crash. She braced herself for disaster. She screamed and felt the bed beneath her!

CHAPTER 10

MY DESIRE sailed into the harbor at 11:00 the next morning. Her crew was calm and passive, each locked into his own thoughts and feelings. Jay was preoccupied with working out a game plan on how to complete the business arrangement for Pat O'Conner without involving Desiree. It did not look promising.

Desiree, equally caught up in her own thoughts, barely noticed Jay's aloofness. Her mood swung up and down, reveling in the sense of peace she had felt last night, then building in tension as she thought about Elliott and her return to New York, and lastly, feeling a marked uneasiness as she relived her strange, haunting dream.

They didn't talk much either as they drove back to the hotel. Conversation at this time seemed trite and unnecessary. Desiree had insisted that Jay not drive her to the plane. She hated goodbyes, especially at airports.

"Can I come in for a moment?" asked Jay as they reached her door. She nodded with a smile as she opened the door wide, silently inviting him in, throwing her tote bag on the front table in the beautiful suite. She started towards the lanai as Jay grabbed her arm and turned her towards him. He took her in his arms, staring her down with intense eyes. It was the first time he had touched her since his brotherly kiss last night. "I refuse to let you go without a proper kiss."

"Jay, please."

"Hush!" Jay put his finger to her lips and pulled her closer into his arms. Desiree's breath caught in her throat as the memories of their time on the beach and the boat washed over her like a giant wave. She heard the surf in her ears again. She felt Jay grow hard against her, and as she looked deep into his eyes, she wanted nothing more than to let him kiss her – deeply, passionately.

In seconds, their tongues were stretching deep inside each other's mouths, begging, teasing, caressing.

Without even thinking, Desiree wrapped her arms tightly around Jay's neck and pulled herself closer. Her passion was mounting. It was becoming unbearable. Arching her back, she gently, unselfconsciously rocked herself against his thigh. In one swift movement, Jay turned their locked bodies sideways and eased down onto a king-size bed, curling his body around Desiree, feeling the gentle breeze washing over their bodies. There, with her eyes closed, she was lost in ecstasy.

Slowly, he unbuttoned her shirt, caressing her breasts as he traced her tan lines with his finger. His tongue darted in and out of her mouth, searching for her own, and then, carefully, smoothly, seductively, he sucked her tongue into his mouth. Jay reached down into Desiree's very soul, and without hesitation, she reached up to grab his. He released her tongue and began kissing her eyes, her lips, her throat, and now her round pounding breasts. He could feel her quiver beneath him, alive and passionate. Desiree let out a gasp. He moved downwards across her belly, kissing and licking every inch of warm, salty skin.

Desiree's passion was mounting. It was becoming unbearable. She wanted more; she wanted to feel those powerful legs wrapped around her thighs and to entwine her body with his, to feel his full power inside of her. Any second, she would beg Jay to love her; all of her reserve of the last two days would be for naught. She wanted him. God, with all of her heart, she wanted him.

But suddenly, from the deep recesses of her conscience, her logical mind took over. She was engaged to Elliott, and she could not, she would not make love to another man while that state existed.

"STOP! Jay, stop!" Desiree's voice broke in panic. "I can't do this, not now." "What! Are you crazy? Now you say stop?" Jay had played Mr. Nice Guy as far as he could. He pulled back and looked at her with a heated glare. "I'm sorry, Jay. I know it's not fair."

Suddenly, her cell phone was ringing on the front table where she had left it. It was Elliott's ringtone. "Elliott!" she gasped. "I have to answer that!" She wasn't free. She was in turmoil, emotionally entangled, bound by unresolved promises to another man, to Elliott, who loved her.

"I'm so sorry! I …have to…. answer that." Desiree's voice broke in panic. "I can't do this, not now."

Jay's eyes turned steely and hard. "What?" "I'm sorry, Jay. I know it's not fair."

"Fair? It's inhuman. You flirt, you entice me for two days; you tell me you're confused; I tell you I'll wait, and then today, when we kiss, you start rocking up against me like a dog in heat! You let me lay you down and unbutton your shirt. Lady, you were begging me to make love to you! Pardon my French, but you practically came in your pants!"

"Jay!" Desiree sat up and buttoned her shirt. "I said I was sorry. Ok?" she repeated the apology defensively. "I did want you to make love to me. I wanted it. And I want to love you as well. More than you know. But I'm engaged, and until I fix things with Elliott, I…"

"Elliott, Elliott, Elliott! Damn it, Des, I'm sick and tired of hearing about Elliott." Jay was annoyed, and his ego was hurt. "And according to you, you're NOT engaged!"

As the phone stopped ringing, he stalked through the French doors to the veranda. For a long time, he stood there with his hands shoved deep into his pockets, staring at the sea. Desire watched him, feeling guilty. Finally, Jay turned and came back inside. His eyes had softened, but his voice was determined.

"I know we haven't known each other very long, 72 hours to be exact. But we have something here, I'm sure of it. I've never felt this way so quickly about a woman. I want to see you in New York… often. But I cannot compete with Elliott if you keep allowing him to interfere. You have to work this out yourself, Des. Decide how you feel about Elliott and about me."

"You mean make a choice?"

"Yes, make a choice. You're not being fair to him, either. If you love Elliott and you want to marry him…then do it. I won't like it, but I'll leave you alone and wish you well. But you're responding very amorously to me, my dear. Is that the voice of a woman happily in love and wanting to be engaged?"

"No, but…"

"There are no buts. Obviously, you're not the type to have a serious relationship with two men at the same time, right? So, Des, make a decision. Either marry Elliott or break up with him. Let me love you or don't. I'll accept any decision you make. But I will not see you again unless you're rid of Elliott. Because, Desiree, I've fallen in love with you. I love you."

With that, Jay turned and strode to the door and opened it to leave. "Think it over. I'll accept whatever you decide. Au Revoir, ma petite."

Desiree stood frozen, staring at the door, not believing what she had just heard.

"Oh, my God!" she heard herself say. Her cell phone rang again. Elliott. She let it go to voice mail.

CHAPTER 11

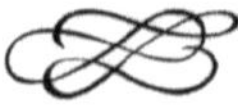

Desiree sat numb, staring out the window of the 727. She still couldn't believe that Jay had said he loved her. After only three days? How can he be so sure? It had taken Elliott almost two years before he told her he was in love with her. But then Elliott deliberated over which pair of socks to wear. There was no room in Elliott's life for impulse.

Desiree remembered the day she brought home fruit, cheese, and wine and suggested they eat in bed instead of going out. Elliott was annoyed and refused to cancel the reservations he had made two days before. "I'm a good customer, Desiree," he had said. "I refuse to cancel at the last minute for bread and cheese." "Would it make a difference if it was caviar and champagne?" chastised Desiree.

"No."

"Hmmm…just as I thought. You know, Elliott, you're getting to be an old fart! Loosen up!"

"Desiree, really, do you have to be so crass?"

And the fight was on. Eventually, of course, Elliott apologized, and they made up, but the wine and cheese was put away, and Desiree traded her black teddy for a dinner suit.

I wonder what Jay would have done under the circumstances, thought Desiree. She smiled. She knew what he would have done. Jay was an action person. He thought, he felt, and then he did. There was no question in Desiree's mind that Jay Bennett said what he meant and did what he said. In the brief hours that they had known each other, he had made that fact perfectly clear.

Desiree liked that quality and considered it just that, a quality. A lot of people would find it offensive. She herself tried to live by the same standards. Her father had taught her well.

* * *

"Be smart enough to listen to your heart, lassie," he had crooned to her over and over again. *"And brave enough to fight for it with all your soul."*

* * *

But lately, Desiree realized she was compromising more and more where Elliott was concerned. Not that compromise wasn't vital to a loving and healthy relationship. But it shouldn't all be one-sided.

She closed her eyes and wistfully envisioned Elliott waiting at the airport. Elegant and aloof, tanned from the weekend - maybe some Spring skiing in Vermont. His hair would be tousled, much to his dismay. Desiree loved the way it curled up at the nap of his neck and took great pleasure in running her nails through it whenever she could.

She could see him comb the top locks of his hair with his fingers, intently watching the gate. Would he grab her excitedly and swing her around? Or give her a bear of a hug, possessively wrapping his strong arms around her?

His kiss would be powerful and full on the lips, not too long to attract attention, but long enough to let her know he missed her. The kind of kiss that held promises of more. Then he'd hold her at arm's length and look deep into her eyes. "Oh, Desiree," he'd croon her name. "I love you so much. I've missed you. I've got a wonderful surprise for you," he would say seductively.

* * *

"Ladies and Gentlemen, we are now approaching JFK International Airport. Please be sure your seat belts are fastened, put all tray tables in their full upright position, and turn off all electronics until we are on the ground...."

* * *

Desiree woke immediately and shook her head to clear her thoughts. She took out her compact and applied fresh lipstick and blush, brushed her hair, then smoothed it with her fingers, letting the natural waves fall again softly around her face. She adjusted the pashmina around her neck and straightened her shirt. Her tan was a beautiful honey color and was complimented by simple gold jewelry and the diamond studs that Elliott had given her for her birthday. She looked rested, bright-eyed, and quietly elegant. Elliott would approve.

As she left Customs, Desiree saw Elliott before he saw her. True to her daydream, he was tan and distinguished-looking. He wore his blue blazer casually over his favorite white polo shirt. And his hair was curling up at the base of his neck.

When he saw her, Elliott's face broke into a huge grin, and his eyes actually had tears of joy. Desiree never remembered seeing him so animated. He waved rather frantically, catching himself just before he was ready to shout her name.

"Desir…" Elliott stopped and waited until she was closer. "Darling!" He wrapped his arms around her and held her close. Only then did he whisper, "Desiree, I've missed you so much."

* * *

Desiree had called him soon after Jay had left. He was frantic and angry. "Where on earth have you been? I've left you messages. I called the hotel. I've called everywhere! I even called Henry. No one knew where you were…you could have been kidnapped! I've been frantic!"

"Oh, Elliott, I'm really fine. And so, so sorry…really. I went sailing yesterday with some friends (there was that lie again), and I had forgotten to take my phone with me (which was true). We went to a little club when we got back to where this amazing jazz group was playing. And it was very late when I got in. I'll tell you all about it when I get home." With that, she was able to calm Elliott down and assure him that all really was fine.

* * *

Desiree felt her heart go out to him and beat a few extra beats. Dear sweet Elliott. How much he must care to allow himself even this much public emotion. She put her arms around his neck and pulled him close.

"Oh, Elliott, I've missed you too. It's been too long. I should have come back a week ago," Desiree thought quickly to herself.

They stood together, arms entwined. Releasing themselves a little, Desiree pressed her lips against Elliott's, only to feel him pull away.

"Not here, Darling. Later." Elliott kissed her on her forehead and gently pulled her arms down from around his neck. "Let me look at you. You look wonderful, absolutely beautiful."

Elliott's voice was warm and loving, and his eyes spoke of his love for her, even if his words could not. But Desiree was disappointed. All she wanted right now was to be kissed and to be told she was loved.

"Thank you, Darling," said Desiree with more enthusiasm than she felt. Elliott was already taking care of the luggage. Once they were in the car, he started talking and filled Desiree in on all the news.

"So…the Hortons are planning a little dinner party in our honor this weekend. You know all the regulars, Kim and Alex. Jonathan and Megan, Tad and Susan, the Randalls, and the Greeleys. And we're invited to dinner tomorrow night at Mom's. Just the four of us. In fact, I figured we could look at a few houses since we'll be up there. I've already spoken to Joan Spencer, you know, Mom's friendly real estate contact, and she said she has a couple of beauties that aren't even on the market yet."

But Desiree wasn't listening. She was back on MY DESIRE, watching Jay trim the sails and grill his hot dogs! Suddenly, she realized they were driving towards the city instead of Connecticut.

"Elliott, where are we going?" Her voice was tense.

"To my place, of course. I've planned a little romantic dinner for two." "What do you mean, of course," then her voice softened. "Oh, Elliott, I'm sorry. That really sounds wonderful, but can't we do that another night? I was counting on being in my own house tonight. We can stop on the way and get some romantic food near my place, can't we?" Desiree smiled provocatively but was afraid Elliott might be insistent.

Elliott looked at her and couldn't resist her smile. God, she was beautiful. He was a lucky man. He wanted to make love to her right now! To throw all protocol aside and take her there on the road, in the night. He imagined her lying under him, her hair spread out around her as he caressed every inch of her body, and finally, feeling her soft, warm skin quiver at his touch. If only he could allow himself the satisfaction of his fantasies. Elliott looked back to the road and took a deep breath.

"Of course, darling. I should have realized. There's nothing at the apartment that can't wait for another night. You do want my company, don't you?" Elliott grinned at Desiree, pleased with his own joke.

"Don't be silly. Who else?" Desiree almost choked over her own words. She must stop putting double meanings into everything.

They chatted comfortably now, Desiree filling Elliott in on all she had done, the party at Henry's, his beautiful hotel. She told him of Georgia, the lovely staff, of Jedd and Monica, and the various people she had met… well, almost all.

"And so," Elliott continued, "what about the sailing trip? Same people?" "Yes." Desiree lied without hesitation. "Beautiful boat, perfect day, and really fun." She told him about the beachside fishing and grilling and described the island and the other dozen people she had met that day. She made no mention of Jay in particular. Of course, no mention of the intimacy she had experienced sailing mano a mano with him alone on his boat, and certainly no mention of being stranded overnight on the island, drinking champagne, and dreaming on the stars.

Desiree was feeling terribly uncomfortable. Jay was right. She had to come to terms with her feelings. This emotional roller coaster wasn't fair to Jay or to Elliott, and it certainly wasn't healthy for Desiree. ''A Femme Fatale, I'm not," she said under her breath.

"What was that, darling?" Elliott looked at her and smiled.

"What? Oh, I said I'm famished. Let's stop at Nicki's." Nicki was Desiree's favorite little Italian restaurant less than a mile from her house. They served deep-dish pizza, homemade pasta, obscenely delicious garlic bread, and sauces made to order. In fact, bring in your own pot, and they'll fill it to the brim for takeout!

"I thought you wanted to get home?" Elliott sounded disappointed.

"I did…I do…but you can only eat fresh seafood and island fare so many days in a row! It's good for my soul…. OK? Do you mind terribly?"

"I never mind anything about you." At least I didn't used to, she thought.

He controlled his impulse to comment on Desiree's recent attitude. She was interestingly and unquestionably different. He couldn't put his finger on it. She had certainly had enough problems lately and had been under a tremendous strain.

But it was more than that. Desiree's entire personality seemed to be changing. She had always been so agreeable. But more and more often, she would get defensive over little things and support a cause with a passion that made Elliott uncomfortable.

And then her behavior while she was away , was confusing. She wouldn't call for days and then leave sexy, suggestive messages. She had even started dressing differently. Elliott had been instrumental in graduating her from the jeans and sweatshirts of college to a more refined style. Gone was the aspiring free-spirited artist Elliott had met over three years ago, and vanished was the young ingenue with whom he had fallen in love. Sitting beside him now was an elegant, sophisticated, and incredibly talented woman. Elliott realized Desiree had grown up.

CHAPTER 12

Desiree had never been so glad to see her home. Here, she felt safe and secure. As the front door swung wide, she was immediately enveloped with a sense of being in a cocoon. She had taken great care to fill the little house with comfort and memories, and as she walked through it now, turning on each well-placed lamp, the rooms came alive and filled Desiree with peace.

It was an old farmhouse, part barn and part added-on construction, with tall beamed ceilings, old roll-out casement windows, and highly glossed wide-panel oak floors and ceilings. The barn siding walls were painted a soft white long past, absorbing but not swallowing the light from the wraparound windows. Sheer curtains, framed by a rich, floral tapestry and gold silk drape, softened every view onto the intimate garden lawn filled with wild knock-out roses that would bloom rampantly from spring through summer. In front of the huge fireplace, like two giant pandas, were the overstuffed tapestry fabric chairs that had belonged to Desiree's mother. Above the fireplace, on the wide recycled wood mantel, rested a beautiful and tranquil painting of water lilies by Desiree's grandmother. Ivory and gold hand-tufted area rugs, a sleek yet comfy sofa, and dozens of glass pillars and slender candle sticks awaited their lighting to complete the mood.

The rest of the house was equally as personal. The kitchen was the second largest room in the house, a true farmhouse kitchen, with lower ceilings and old, glass-paned wooden cabinets filled with blue willow China from France and a random assortment of Irish, French, and even German glass and crystal, all of which had been in Desiree's family for generations. Sometimes, Desiree felt she was living in the past, but she loved and treasured all of it. The future was outside. This was her heritage.

Upstairs, the two bedrooms were identical in size. Framed with nearly life- size ballet prints by Dega, Desiree's bedroomheld only a solid mahogany English armoire, a thread-bare Oriental rug of questionable value, and a customized four-poster bed handmade by her great uncle, a little rickety, held together with spit and glue (as her dad used to say), and in need of refinishing, it had been handed down for so long that no one except Desiree was willing to take it on for refurbishing. She just didn't care. It was worth it, and it will be done!

Desiree's studio, by stark contrast, was all but bare. There was an old wooden hutch for supplies and the drawing board that her father had made for her when she was fifteen. Every inch of the walls was covered with Desiree's illustrations and sketches. The built-in bookshelves that formed a wide window seat were the home of her doll collection and the books that her drawings were in. She called it…this special space… The Children's Room.

Elliott didn't like her house. He was never at ease here. His style was less cluttered, modern, and streamlined. Desiree's place was stifling, in his opinion, even claustrophobic. Elliott always preferred to think about tomorrow; the past (and all that encumbered it) made him feel smothered. He had always avoided spending too much time in Desiree's house, preferring his own designer-decorated penthouse with its panoramic views of the East River. But he did marvel at Desiree's incredible decorative talent, her ability to read a person's needs and create a mood or a lifestyle. It was the artist in her. She had her own sense of belonging and had an amazing ability to help others find theirs. He was rather envious of it. It was a feeling he had never been able to experience, and so a trait he could never share.

After checking through the house and making sure everything was as she had left it, Desiree quickly sorted through her mail. She was delighted to find the confirming letter that she had been retained to illustrate T.M. Poppins' newest book. They had worked together twice before, and it had always been mutually enjoyable. Poppins wrote wonderful stories about children's fantasies and the illustrations were always a tremendous challenge. So, first thing Monday, it was off to Manhattan for an organizational meeting.

Elliott had just come out of the kitchen with two glasses. Wine for Desiree and a Cognac for himself. "A little nightcap, darling?"

"Oh, yes. Thank you. Perfect." Desiree plopped down in one of the big chairs and stretched her toes towards the fire that was now burning gently, taking the early March chill off the room. "I'm so glad to be home."

She smiled at Elliott, who was resting in the opposite chair. "Thank you for not protesting about coming back here tonight and for being so agreeable about stopping at Nicki's for dinner. I know you would have preferred your own place." "I love you, and I want you to be happy." Elliott took a sip of his brandy and leaned forward. Reaching for her hand, "Are you happy, Desiree?"

"Very." Desiree avoided the hand, leaned her head back, and closed her eyes. The fire was wonderful, spreading its warmth up and down her body. She remembered feeling this warm only yesterday, standing on the little beach so close to Jay's arms. Her eyes flew open, only to see Elliott close to her, bending down to kiss her.

Moving even closer, his lips pressed against hers, warm and persuasive. She kissed him lightly, quickly, not allowing him to press deeper, yet not wanting to pull away abruptly. Her heart was beating wildly, not from desire but from panic. She hadn't seen Elliott in over three weeks; she had wanted his kisses at the airport, and now she was pulling away.

Luckily, Elliott did not sense her turmoil; he hugged her and kissed her again lightly on her nose. "I love you. You're beautiful." He sat back in his chair and cleared his throat. "Desiree, we have to talk.

"You mean about your proposal? I know…" Elliott cut her off. "No, dear, about your father's estate."

"Oh, Elliott, not now. "That was just like Elliott. Always the lawyer. "Can't it wait till tomorrow?"

"It's very important, Darling. There's a lot going on that you aren't aware of." "What do you mean?"

''I mean, everything is not the way you thought."

"Am I poor?" Desiree really wasn't in the mood for this discussion, and her voice showed it.

"Don't be crass."

"Well, am I? Was Poppy broke? Is that what you're trying to tell me?" "No, not exactly. But there are serious complications."

"Elliott, I really don't want to discuss this now. We have all day tomorrow.

Can't it wait?"

"Yes, of course. I'm sorry. I shouldn't have even brought it up."

"Thank you. Now, what I really want to do is take a hot bath and go to bed.

Are you coming?"

"Yes. You go on up. I'll lock up for you."

CHAPTER 13

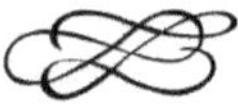

Desiree eased herself into the almost scalding water. The old claw-footed tub was filled to the brim with bubbles. Resting her head on the back rim, Desiree felt the anxiety of the last hours melt away. She was glad to be home; she was glad to start work again on Monday. Tomorrow, she would have to face whatever bad news Elliott had about her father's estate. And she would have to deal with looking at houses and dining with Elliott's family. Somehow, she had to get out of that house-hunting venture. She knew Elliott was going to pressure her to set a wedding date. Desiree didn't blame him, but she also knew she was even less certain about her feelings for him than when she left New York three weeks ago. Jay had seen to that.

After her bath, Desiree smoothed moisturizer all over her body, pulled on a delicate peach silk chemise, brushed her hair, and went towards the bedroom. Elliott was already in bed reading. She looked at him from the bathroom door and admired his wide shoulders and perfect physique. His hair was disheveled, the way she liked it, and his reading glasses were perched on the tip of his nose, giving him a professorial look. He was really very sexy.

Desiree crawled in beside him and snuggled up. The faint scent of his aftershave wafted from his skin. He was warm; the hair on his arms and legs was soft. He took off his glasses, threw the paper to the floor, and turned out the light. Elliott hated making love in the light. A few times, Desiree managed to use candlelight. Tonight, though, there was at least a full moon. Elliott rolled over towards Desiree and began caressing her arms, her shoulders, running the back of his fingers gently down her cheek. His touch was tender but hurried. He was terribly aroused by his earlier revelations about Desiree. He was as excited and eager as a new lover. Desiree sensed the change. Three weeks ago, it would have delighted her. Tonight, it only added to her confusion.

Minutes later, Elliott eased himself onto Desiree, whispering that he loved her and needed her. In the moonlight, he could see the silhouette of her face with her hair spread out against the pillow. He felt the passions of his fantasies take over, and he wanted her now. Desiree wrapped her arms around him and hugged him lovingly, like the true friend he had become, but not the lover she desired. She realized she could not make love with him. Not tonight, and maybe not ever again.

Jay's presence was haunting her; his words resounded in her ears. *"Decide how you feel about Elliott and about me. Make a choice. If you love Elliott, marry him. But know that I love you, I love you."* Those were the words that haunted her now. "Elliott…. Elliott…" Desiree pushed gently against his shoulder. "I'm so sorry.

I can't make love right now. I thought the bath would relax me, but I'm just too exhausted and too uptight."

"What's wrong?" Elliott was truly concerned.

"I don't know," lied Desiree. "What you said about Poppy's estate…. that's really bothering me. And I guess I'm just tired from the trip; it's been a long day." Elliott suspected she wasn't telling the truth. And he also sensed there was something else seriously bothering her. For the third time that night, he put Desiree's wishes before his own. It wasn't easy, especially now. Her timing was rotten. But he accepted her words. He hugged her and kissed her gently. "We'll talk in the morning."

Desiree kissed him on the cheek and tried to cuddle beside him. But even that was uncomfortable. As soon as she was sure Elliott had fallen asleep, Desiree eased away and rolled over to her side of the bed. Hours later, she fell into a restless sleep.

Desiree and Elliott both slept late the next morning. After breakfast, Desiree called her best friend, Janette, and then called her Uncle Max. Janette was eager to hear the very latest on the Desiree and Jay story! Uncle Max was just delighted to hear from her, and Desiree made plans to see them each the following week.

Desiree knew that Elliott was expecting an explanation of her actions last night. In fact, he deserved one. But she just couldn't bring herself to discuss everything just yet. She hoped her visit with Janette would help her put things in perspective. Janette was her best friend since college and had always been her alter ego. Somehow, Janette's point of view, though usually opposite of Desiree's, always helped Desiree see things more clearly. If only she could keep Elliott at bay until then. She decided the lesser of two evils right now was to hear what he had to say about her father's estate. She had a feeling that this talk was going to upset her, but better now than later.

About noon, Desiree offered Elliott some fresh coffee and told him she was ready to hear what he had to say about her father.

"Of course, darling. I'll be as brief as possible." That meant that Elliott had bad news, for sure.

"Elliott, I don't like the sound of this. It seems very ominous," Desiree was sitting at the big oak table, staring into her cup. When she looked up, Elliott had a very stern look on his face; he was in lawyer mode, and Desiree knew that meant business.

"It's not ominous, but I'm afraid it will be rather a shock to you."

"I said I'm ready. For heaven's sake, Elliott, save the dramatics for a jury." Once Desiree made up her mind about something, she wanted to get it over with. But actually, she didn't feel as confident as she sounded.

"Sorry." Elliott smiled apologetically, as he pulled up the chair beside her. He took a deep breath.

"Here it is in a nutshell. P.O.C. Outfitters, for all practical purposes, is bankrupt."

"What!" Desiree choked on her coffee. "That's impossible!"

"It's fact." Elliott looked her squarely in the eyes. "Your father has been borrowing money from the company for years to subsidize his "inventions" as you all call them. Specifically, that water purification system that he gave to Cranford."

"He wouldn't do that," defended Desiree. "He would never jeopardize the company and all our people, they're family! There must be some mistake."

"There's no mistake." Desiree heard the disapproval, almost contempt, in Elliott's voice. He had never believed in Pat O'Conner's inventions. He considered them the playthings of an eccentric old man. Now, this made it worse.

''He would have paid it all back," Desiree stated matter of factly.

"I'm sure he intended to." conceded Elliott. "But unfortunately, he's dead, and you are the heir to a bankrupt company. In fact, Desiree, I really recommend that you file CHAPTER 11 immediately and lay it all to rest."

"Well, why don't we just announce it to the whole world while we're at it." She stared at Elliott. "I will not file for bankruptcy. What about our people, Lil and the rest of them? They need that company. It's their entire life. No, there must be another way." Desiree sat lost in thought, thinking about where she could raise enough money to pay off the creditors.

"The water system!" Desiree's voice brightened. "The reports over five months ago were dramatic. Even then, Poppy was talking about how valuable it would be to towns like Cranford. We can sell the invention. In fact, I can't believe he never tried to sell it himself!"

"Maybe." Elliott was cautious. Actually, he had already thought of it himself. Despite his personal feelings about O'Conner's inventions, he couldn't dispute the findings of EPA officials.

"I've already put out some feelers to some engineering firms and to a big sanitation company. But Desiree, you have to remember that the experiment in Cranford won't be finished until August, and the final results won't even be tabulated until October, at least. You can't afford to wait that long. There are creditors standing in line."

"I'll pay them." Desiree looked defiantly at Elliott.

"Desiree, we're talking about two hundred thousand dollars!"

"I don't care. If it takes me the rest of my life, I'll pay them back."

"Now you're being melodramatic. Think for a minute what we're talking about."

"I know what we're talking about… my father's reputation."

"Obviously, Desiree, your father got so involved with his damn inventions that he lost sight of reality. He robbed the company of its future, its employees of their pensions, and you of your inheritance. *That's* his reputation!"

Desiree jumped up from the table. She threw her shoulders back, and the fire came into her eyes. "That's enough, Elliott! You don't have to be so cruel. My father wasn't like that. He must have had a plan. He loved that company and those people. They were his family. And he loved you too, Mr. Grayson, so watch what you say. Don't you dare slur his name! Now, I think you'd better go. Please give my regrets to your mother. I won't be joining them for dinner." Desiree turned and stormed out of the room, choking back her tears.

A few minutes later, she heard the door slam and the sound of Elliott's car speeding away. She lay on her bed, devastated. Elliott thought her father was a fool; the company her grandfather had started would die; her father's inventions, his entire life's dreams would be traded for a bad debt. Something had to be done; Pat O'Conner deserved a better epitaph.

CHAPTER 14

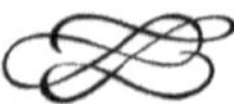

Monday morning dawned bright and clear. It was a beautiful spring day, and Desiree felt rested and in control again. She was convinced that she would find a way to salvage her father's reputation and, hopefully, the company.

She really didn't know how, but her motto was always to think positively.

She had a ten o'clock appointment in New York with T.M. Poppins to begin work on the illustrations for his new book. After that, she was meeting Uncle Max for lunch. She dressed carefully, choosing a navy-blue double-breasted blazer, pencil skirt, a soft white silk shirt, tiny pearls, and the "family crest," a stunning pin of pearls, garnets and sapphires in the shape of a miniature crown. It had been a gift from Uncle Max.

Desiree pulled her hair back into a loose chignon and topped her look off with pearl and gold earrings. A little blush and deep coral lipstick, she was the epitome of good health and sophistication. As she took one last glance in the mirror, she caught herself wondering how Jay would think she looked.

Jay! With all the trauma of family wills and inheritances, Desiree had completely forgotten about her love life. Now, it all came rushing back.

"This is just too much," said Desiree to herself. "I don't need this. Why can't my life be simple? Oh, for the sands of that beach and a yellow bird."

Desiree blushed just thinking of that beautiful oasis. "It already seemed like a year ago. Enough!" She chastised herself. "You have work to do."

The meeting with Poppins was wonderful. Desiree liked the man and respected him more than any other author she had ever worked with. He was very creative and had a vivid imagination. This book was about a pair of ducks who took up residence in a little pond, forming a special friendship with the little girl who lived there. They worked for over three hours, at the end of which Desiree had the outlines for the first three illustrations. There would be twenty in all. They had agreed on watercolors, Desiree's favorite medium. She said her goodbyes and hurried off to grab a taxi as she texted her uncle. She was already half an hour late.

Maxwell O'Conner had never been interested in the camping supply company except to use its equipment when he went fishing. Instead, he had headed for the wilds of Wall Street when he was only nineteen. He fought and scratched his way to the top, making a good living and retiring with more than a comfortable pension. Fishing with his brother and others had become a convenient and casual pastime.

Max took one look at his niece and knew something was different. It wasn't her looks, though he was certain she was more beautiful than the last time he had seen her. And, of course, she had been distraught at his brother's funeral. No, this was something more important. Something to do with the heart. He was sure of it.

"Uncle Max!" Desiree grabbed him around the neck and squeezed him hard. She looked up into his eyes, grinning from ear to ear. They were the only family they each had now, but there had always been a special bond between them.

Uncle Max was five years older than his brother and had been both brother and father to Pat O'Conner and uncle and grandfather to Desiree. He was a bear of a man, taller than Desiree and at least twenty pounds overweight. But his eyes twinkled almost all the time, and when he laughed, they all but disappeared into the creases that were his eyelids. His laugh was boisterous and mellow, his skin was wrinkled from years in the sun. His heart most certainly was made of gold, for no request was ever refused. Desiree was convinced that he was Santa Claus incarnate.

"Desi, me darlin'," he hugged her equally as hard. "Let me look at you, Lassie. Now, don't ye look so fine. That vacation you took was good for ye. Maybe it was more than just a vacation?"

"Uncle Max, whatever *are* you talking about?"

"You look awfully pretty, Desi, and there's something around your eyes.

They're the eyes of a young girl in love."

"Well, of course, Uncle Max. I'm engaged to Elliott. Or are you getting senile in your old age?" teased Desiree.

"My mind's as sharp as a tack. Elliott's a wimp, and you're not engaged.

Someone else. I think there's someone else."

"Uncle Max!" Desiree grew scarlet. She was used to his blatant dislike of Elliott, but she never could get used to his incredible sixth sense. How did he know about Jay? He must be a wizard. She also could never lie to him.

"Well, yes, I did meet a rather interesting man last week." "Ah ha!" Max slapped his knee in delight. "I knew it!" "What do you mean, you knew it?"

"I can tell, darlin'. I know ye like I know myself. Those big blue eyes of yours always tell me about your heart. And I've never seen them shine like they are now with that dishrag you call a fiancée. So, what's his name? Are you going to tell me about him?"

"You're as gossipy as an old woman." Desiree laughed as she shook a finger at him. But tell him she did.

"His name is Jay Bennett. We met at the hotel. He's from New York, and I gather he's quite rich. At least he acts that way. And his boat…"

"His boat?"

"Yes, we went sailing." "Ah ha!"

"Will you please quit ah-ahing! It was perfectly innocent," She lied. "Did you kiss him?"

"Uncle Max! I really don't see what business it is of yours!"

"Ok, ok. I'll back off. But keep me posted on this young man, promise?"

"If there's anything to post, you'll be the first to know. I promise."

Max then changed the subject. "I take it Elliott told you the news about Paddy's company."

"Yes. How long have you known?"

"I'm afraid I knew about his takin' the money for a while now. But I canna' believe that it's that bad… but then, those inventions of his always did mean everything to him."

"But Uncle Max, surely Poppy must have had some sort of plan. He wouldn't let everything go down the drain like that."

"I think so too, darlin'. But I also think the poor man died before he could see it through."

"Didn't he tell you anything?"

"Not a thing. He was a very stubborn, private man, ye know." "What're we going to do?"

"I don't rightly know, but I do think that Paddy's invention is the key."

Together, they laid out a game plan that included contacting engineering firms, sanitation companies, and other companies that might be interested in buying the filtration system. Maybe they could sell it based on the preliminary results. If they could get enough money to pay off the company's debts, they could at least close the doors quietly and preserve everyone's good name. Obviously, there would be no inheritance for Desiree, nor severance and pensions for the loyal employees. But you could only do what you could do.

Lunch was otherwise delightful. Uncle Max had a new female friend and invited Desiree to join them for dinner later that week. Max's love life tickled Desiree. He would date a woman for three or four months, then be celibate for four months and start again. He was kind and very considerate, and each woman considered him a real friend even after the affair was over. Desiree kept hoping that one day, he would settle down with one of them. But Max always said no one would ever take the place of his Maggie. And that had been over ten years ago.

CHAPTER 15

Late that night, Desiree dreamt of the yellow bird again. *It sat at the foot of her bed, perched on the footboard. In its sweet sing-song voice, it spoke to her of loves lost and loves found. "But, beware," sang the little bird, "all is not what it seems to be." The little yellow bird took flight and soared about the room.*

* * *

Then, (still dreaming) Desiree was standing on the banks of a wide river. She saw the bird high in the air flying away from her. She called to it. "Come back, come back, little bird… please come back!" The bird turned and laughed and flew down to the far shore, where it lit upon the sand and fell asleep. Uncle Max was there, as were Elliott and her father. Her father picked up the yellow bird and put it in his pocket. Then he disappeared.

* * *

This time, when Desiree woke up, she wrote it all down. These haunting dreams were beginning to affect her life. She decided she had to find out what they all meant. Most people never even thought about their dreams, let alone tried to analyze them. And though her own logic told her it was nonsense, the romantic in her yearned for an explanation.

Desiree only knew two people who understood dreams. Her mother had been one, her innate abilities making a believer even out of Pat O'Conner. Lil McInnis was the other.

* * *

Lil McInnis had been P.O.C Outfitters' right arm for thirty years. Pat O'Conner couldn't run the company without her. She knew everything and everybody. Lil was the first person in every morning and the last one to leave at night; she made the coffee and kept the inventory. She was on a first-name basis with practically every customer and vendor and always made a point of asking about their respective families.

If you wanted to know the local gossip, ask Lil. But if you wanted to share a secret, the FBI couldn't get it out of her. A widow for well over twenty years, she put her daughter through medical school and kept a stern and loving eye on Desiree. When she thought "Mr. O" (as she called him) was too lenient with his daughter, Lil added her own two cents, but she was equally as defensive when Pat O'Conner came down too hard on Desiree; at those times, Lil intervened as only a mother can.

Lil grieved deeply when Pat' O'Conner died. She had lost a great friend and perhaps even a part of herself. For as well as she knew him, he probably knew her even better.

Desiree was like her second daughter, and over the years, they, too, had developed a special bond. Lil looked around her apartment and checked the table once more in anticipation. Everything was ready for dinner. Desiree would arrive in about ten minutes. It was probably the first home-cooked meal she had in months, thought Lil. She had made Desiree's favorite, roast beef with Yorkshire pudding, oven-baked potatoes, fresh carrots, and green beans, and, of course, Lil's famous sherry trifle for dessert.

When the bell rang, Lil patted her short, greyish-blonde hair and straightened her skirt. Her wide Irish face, scrubbed and shiny, showed off her porcelain complexion and formed the perfect frame for her deep blue eyes. Bubbling over with anticipation, she flung open the door.

"Desiree! Honey! Come in, come in. Lord, you are a vision." Lil could not believe her eyes. Desiree had truly blossomed during the last few weeks. She was the most striking combination of her father and mother that Lil could ever have imagined.

"Lil!" Desiree threw her arms around the older woman and hugged her tightly. "I've missed you oh so much!" Desiree paused, sniffing the air. "Something smells like roast and pudding."

"Of course. What else would I make for you when you haven't eaten in months."

"Hardly." laughed Desiree, patting her stomach. "In fact, I'd say I've been eating extremely well."

"So? Do I detect some interesting news?"

Desiree stepped back and held out the bouquet of lilies she held in her arms. "Here you go, your favorite." She had coyly changed the subject. Why did everyone think she had some incredible revelation to discuss? Did they all know something she didn't?

"Oh, Desiree, you shouldn't have. They're gorgeous. Thank you, dear. Now, come in, and let's hear all about this vacation of yours."

They sat in the living room with a glass of sherry and a plate of brie and crackers. Desiree filled Lil in on her trip, all except Jay. She planned on telling her friend, but later.

During dinner, they caught up on the local news and traded fond memories about Desiree's father. They really hadn't had a chance to do this since the funeral. Desiree avoided any mention of the company's present state of affairs. She didn't know what Lil knew and didn't, and certainly didn't have the heart to break the news to Lil now. But then Desiree was sure it would all work out. Many laughs and a few tears later, the conversation finally turned again to Desiree's personal life.

Lil came right to the point. "So, what else is it that you want to talk to me about?"

Desiree squirmed in her seat. "You always do seem to read my mind, Lil." Desiree looked at her friend and smiled. "I've been having some strange dreams lately.

Lil's eyebrows shot up. "Oh?" Lil knew that Desiree had always been skeptical about these special talents that she had shared with her mother. But unlike Francine Dubois-O'Conner, Lil McInnis learned the process from her own mother and grandmother. They all had sworn it was an inherited gift, one that should be nurtured and not be taken lightly.

Desiree found it all fascinating and curiously entertaining. And now, despite all logical reasoning, she found herself pouring out her dreams to Lil.

"I keep dreaming about a yellow bird. It seems to be everywhere I go. It turns up in my house, on the beach, in my bedroom. Once, I was even able to fly along with it. Once, I slammed a door on it and broke its wing. And just the other night, I saw Poppy with the bird. He put it in his pocket."

"Oh Desiree, this is exciting. I didn't think you'd ever come to me with your dreams. I thought you didn't believe in dreams?"

"Lil, these dreams are driving me crazy. At first, I thought I had had too much to drink. You see, yellow bird is the name of a drink at the hotel… but now I don't know. I feel very strange when I wake up. Sometimes I'm even scared." "Oh, darling, there is never anything to be frightened about. Your dreams are just that, yours. You just have to understand them, that's all. Let's move to the living room. And just let me run and get my books and a pen and paper." Lil went into the next room and was back in seconds.

"All right. Ready? Now, relax and think back to the first dream, and try to tell each one to me in sequence. Remember as much detail as you can. No matter how silly it seems, tell me everything."

Desiree leaned comfortably back in her chair, resting her head on the little doily, but was able to see Lil clearly. Lil picked up her pen and pad and started to take notes as Desiree recounted each dream. There was a smile on Lil's lips as she wrote, and occasionally, she asked a question to clarify a thought. She kept nodding and writing and smiling. After about half an hour, Desiree announced that that was all she could remember.

"That's fine. Now, just give me some time to go over everything. Why don't you go into the kitchen and make some coffee? And while we have dessert, I'll tell you what I think."

By the time the coffee was ready, Lil had completed her analysis. Desiree carried in the tray loaded with bowls of trifle, Lil's antique coffee pot and two large mugs.

Desiree kicked off her shoes and curled up on the couch. She tasted the trifle.

"Fabulous! Will you part with this recipe yet?" "Never!"

Desiree made a face. Lil cleared her throat.

"Alright then. First off, when a woman dreams about a bird, she is usually dreaming about herself. You must be having some serious thoughts about yourself these days. Yes?"

Desiree nodded.

Lil continued. "And, when the bird is yellow, it usually has more than one meaning, each one being contradictory to the other. It can symbolize stages of good luck or bad luck. It can relate to finances – good and bad. It can also be a sign of betrayal or changes in the heart."

"Great…that's rather vague, don't you think?" Desiree's skepticism was showing.

"Now, now… don't be cheeky. Depending on what the yellow bird does and the vitality of the bird dictates its behavior. Flying yellow birds foretell an interesting event. But it also indicates you have been worried about a particular problem with a relationship in the past."

"Lil! This isn't helpful!" Desiree was frustrated. "This is all over the place!"

"Patience, dear. I think the important thing in these first dreams is the color of the bird. Since it's yellow or golden, it suggests fire or passion. That's a given. Who or what the bird represents is the next thing to consider. It could be a masculine presence, or it could be you." Lil looked up. Desiree was listening intently, if not skeptically.

"Now, I personally think the bird is you. In the first dream, you're searching for something. That's why you are running. Somewhere in your subconscious, you probably know what you're running from or towards, but you don't want to admit it. I think the yellow bird either is or represents that something. Recognize who or what the yellow bird is, and you'll know what you're looking for.

"This is very confusing, Lil. How can the yellow bird be me and someone or something else at the same time?"

"That's what makes dreams so interesting, dear. Our minds can do all sorts of things." Lil looked back at her notes. "For example, when you called out for Elliott, that is only your logical mind talking. I don't think Elliott is the issue here, the yellow bird is. Concentrate on the yellow bird."

Lil glanced at her notes again. "Now, this is important. You say you broke the wings of the bird -- you are holding back about something, showing great restraint. When you slammed the door on the bird, you were ''clipping *your* wings." In a sense, you're trying to ignore the truth. Do you follow, Desiree?" Lil's voice was calm and reassuring.

Desiree felt the hair rise up on her arms. The woman must be a witch. It was almost as if she had been a fly on the wall. Desiree nodded, amazed, and answered Lil's question. "Yes, only too well. But tell me. What about this masculine presence? Is that Elliott?" Desiree asked hopefully.

Lil smiled at her young friend. "So, there is more to this than you are letting me in on, isn't there?"

"Come on, Lil. I promise I'll tell you everything. What about the male presence? Is it Elliott?"

"You tell me." "Lil!"

"Ok, ok. Even though there is only one bird, I think the bird is both you and a man. They seem to be interchanging constantly as your dreams progress. It might be Elliott, but it could be someone else. Is there a man who's causing this soul-searching that you're doing?"

"Probably. Go on." Desiree was getting impatient.

Lil raised an eyebrow at Desiree but went on calmly. "The stairs that you climb and can't get to the top? Well, that is purely sexual, something you can't or won't allow yourself to reach."

Desiree sat with her mouth open. "Who are you, Freud? I don't believe this. Lil."

"What don't you believe?"

"I'll explain later; go on." Desiree was fascinated. Lil was right on target. Desiree already knew that the yellow bird was Jay and herself. His power was overwhelming, and his very presence had forced her to re-evaluate her whole being.

"All right," said Lil. "Now for the second dream. The yellow bird is soaring among the clouds and the 'golden' sun, and you are flying with it. The soaring is again a search for something; the golden sun usually stands for truth and intuition. So, I would say in this dream that the yellow bird, meaning you, is looking for that truth.

Desiree sat speechless and let Lil go on.

"But then you see yourself flying with the bird and finally falling. It could be that the bird is the truth and that your attempts to fly with him are your own attempts to recognize it. When you started to fall, it was because you can't accept the truth."

Lil looked at Desiree. "This is all very revealing, my dear. Would you care to fill me in on the details?"

"Yes, yes, I will. But first, tell me about the third dream. The yellow bird in Poppy's pocket and the taunting message that all is not what it seems."

"Yes, let me see." Lil went back to her notes. "OK, you are standing on a riverbank looking at the other side. Desiree, my dear, you must feel that life is passing you by. That is the only definition for that image. But why? The river itself represents your destiny, your fortune, and since you said the river was very wide, it means your future is great and very positive.

Desiree felt goose bumps up and down her arms. There was no fortune; she was heir to nothing except maybe her father's invention. But dreams could not tell the future, they only revealed what was already present. What great destiny was she avoiding? Jay again?

Lil had continued. "Everything is related to the fate of the yellow bird. When your father puts the bird in his pocket, the bird becomes hidden; the truth is hidden. Perhaps you're not seeing the truth. Darling, you have a very important decision to make. And I'm afraid this yellow bird will keep nagging at you until you do."

Desiree poured two glasses of wine. "Lil, you are truly amazing. I think I have just become a true believer in dreams! Here, have some wine and get ready for a great story."

For the next hour, Desiree told Lil everything about Jay. She left out nothing. Hearing her own words, she realized what she had known almost from the beginning - that she already loved this man. He had awakened in her feelings that she never knew existed. Jay was alive and passionate and exciting and caring. Life with him would be "life," not mere existence.

Her feelings for Elliott were based on friendship. He had been present in her life before she knew who she was. She had allowed Elliott to dictate her feelings and mold her responses. He was a sweet man; he meant well. But she needed someone who could allow her, even encourage her to grow. Elliott had no room in his ordered life for growing pains and the passions they might unleash.

Yes, Jay was the yellow bird; he was truth and passion, inspiration and destiny.

CHAPTER 16

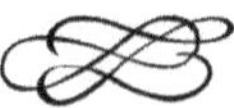

"Elliott? Hi, it's me." Desiree took a deep breath. She had been avoiding Elliott for days now. He had sent beautiful, long-stemmed red roses to apologize for the other night. He had texted and called and left sweet and apologetic messages on her voicemail. Desiree knew he thought she was playing hard to get. But she had been trying to muster up the courage to break off the engagement that never was.

Finally, Desiree realized that Elliott was not the right man for her. Jay had awakened a myriad of feelings in her, and she owed it to herself to come to terms with them all. Maybe Jay wasn't the right man. But she knew she wasn't the right girl for Elliott either. She could never conform to the picture-perfect ideal of a woman and wife he wanted. Elliott was organized, orderly, and methodical. His entire life was one of neatness; it lacked complexities; it lacked character.

God knows Desiree had tried to adapt. But there was always something that just wouldn't harmonize. They didn't like the same music or enjoy reading the same books; he was modern; she was traditional; he was a purist; she was an incurable romantic. Even her own name caused him embarrassment. "Desiree," Elliott had mused when they first met, "how…. passionate."

"Desiree, darling!" Elliott was ecstatic to hear her voice. "I didn't think you'd ever call. Did you get the roses? I'm sorry, darling, I really am. It was very rude of me."

"It's all right, really. Thank you, though. They're beautiful. Elliott, can you meet me for drinks tonight? I have to talk to you."

"Of course. Why don't you come by the office first? I'd like to go over some papers with you about the company."

"Yes, all right." Desiree hated the thought of delaying this talk any longer, but she knew she needed to take care of the company, too. She had put that on the back burner for as long as she could. "I'll be there about four."

"See you then, darling. Bye."

* * *

Desiree took a last glance in the mirror. Now that she had made her decision about Elliott, she felt a hundred percent better. She felt she was in control again, that she was in charge of her own life. She had dressed carefully, wanting to look her very best, for herself, though, not for Elliott. It was a wonderful feeling. She was in a monochromatic mood today; she wore Ralph Lauren's black wool pants with a soft grey cashmere sweater with an asymmetrical cowl-neck collar and a fitted cropped wool jacket. With it, she paired grey and black suede pumps, simple pearls, and silver jewelry. She looked fabulous.

Everyone at Elliott's office welcomed her warmly and commented on how stunning she looked. Elliott noticed it, too. There was an attitude about her that was different. It was more of the new Desiree, and he found it very exciting.

"Darling, come in. You look beautiful. Is that a new outfit?"

"No, I just threw a few things together. But thank you." Desiree sat down in the big leather chair across from Elliott's desk, feeling a little bit smug but definitely good about herself. "Is your father in today?"

"No, he had a litigation today and then went home. Mother and Dad both want you to come up this weekend. But we can talk about that later. First, let's go over these papers."

Elliott showed Desiree all the papers supporting the company's financial standing. It was all very depressing. There, in black and white, was over two hundred thousand dollars borrowed by Pat O'Conner over a five-year period. Each entry was properly documented, obviously done with every good intention of paying it back. But the end result was that P.O.C. Outfitters had been running on credit for over a year and now could not even meet next month's salaries.

Again, he encouraged her to file for bankruptcy. And again, she refused.

"Not yet, Elliott. I have to try to work this out first. What have you found out about the water system?"

"Everything is still very positive in Cranford. Monthly reports from the E.P.A. are steadily improving."

"Good, so I want to try and sell now. What's it worth?"

"Only one company has examined the possibility so far. But they are a very small operation and would rather wait for more conclusive evidence." Desiree looked disappointed.

"Don't panic," Elliott reassured her. "I'm also waiting to hear from Brown and Ferris. They are the leaders in the sanitation and waste treatment business. If anyone can see this thing's potential, they can."

Elliott cleared his throat. "Anyway, it so happens I went to school with a guy whose brother went to work for them. They're sending one of their engineers up to Cranford this week."

"Oh, Elliott! That's wonderful." Desiree was ecstatic.

Elliott held up his hand. "Whoa. Desiree. No promises, now. But I've put them in touch with Ed Kreiger up there. He's expecting them on Friday and will let us know how it goes. Ok?"

"More than OK. Thank you. I know you're not thrilled with this idea."

"It's all right. Anyway, maybe you're right." Elliott was so wonderfully positive and supportive that Desiree couldn't believe he was the same man. A twinge of guilt passed over her as she thought of their impending conversation. It was a beautiful, brisk, and sunny March afternoon, and Elliott had suggested the Café Carlyle at the historic hotel of the same name on the Upper East Side.   It was Elliott's nod to Desiree's love of history and old-world charm. From his office, it was a leisurely stroll from Columbus Circle and across town at 76th Street. They made small talk while they walked, and Desiree wished Elliott wasn't being so romantic. Why couldn't he have demonstrated this effort sooner? And how long would it last? He had tried periodically before, but sooner or later, Elliott's staunch reserve always took over.

They took a table in the corner of the renowned bar. Elliott ordered their regulars. After they were served, Desiree opened the conversation.

"Elliott, I have something very important to tell you."

"I'm all ears." He was smiling contentedly, and suddenly Desiree realized he must think she wanted to set the wedding date.

Oh, God. She said to herself. He's not going to make this easy.

Desiree took a deep breath and plunged in. She never was one to mince words.

"Elliott, I'm breaking off our engagement."

"What?" Elliott almost spit into his drink. "What did you say?"

"I'm breaking off our engagement. Or rather, I'm not accepting your proposal. We're not right for each other. We never have been. You keep trying to change me, and I keep trying to change you. It's not fair to either of us."

There, it was out at last. No icing on this cake! Rather harsh. Oh, you think? Desiree took a huge gulp of her drink and leaned back against the banquet. She could see the pain in Elliott's eyes, but in her heart, she knew she was right. She leaned forward and touched his hand. Elliott flinched.

"Elliott, try to listen to me. I'm sorry I blurted it out this way. I've realized I've been trying to sort out my feelings for over three months. You're part of the reason I went away after Poppy's funeral. You're so kind and very generous. You've always treated me with the utmost respect. You deserve a partner who feels exactly the same way you do and who wants the same things. But something is missing. I love you, but not the way a woman should love a man. I'm not 'in love' with you. I love you more like a wonderful friend."

"Who is he?" "What?"

"I said, who is he? Who is it that you do love like a man!" "Elliott! You're getting the wrong idea."

"Am I?" Elliott looked at her in amazement. He was angry and terribly hurt, and he wanted to hurt back. To him, it was suddenly all very clear. He had noticed her changing, and now he knew why. "How long has this been going on?"

"Nothing is going on. This has nothing to do with anyone but me."

But Desiree knew she wasn't telling the whole truth. Oh, why was this getting out of hand? This was not the way it was supposed to happen.

"Elliott, try to listen. Please?"

"I'm listening." But Elliott was staring straight ahead with a rather comical expression on his face. The noise and clammer of the popular bar became muted and blurred. Finally, he focused on Desiree's words.

"You've been trying to change me since the day you met me. You advised me on what to wear, how to act, how to talk, everything. At first, I was flattered. I was rather naïve, I admit, and I probably needed some guidance. But you never appreciated who I was, and you resent it when I try to be me.

Elliott opened his mouth to speak, but Desiree kept on. Now that she had gathered momentum, she didn't want to weaken. Her emotions had taken over; her words poured out over one another, free-falling like a stream of consciousness. "You hate being kissed in public; you cringe when I call you sexy; you get embarrassed when we make love with the lights on. Even now, you hate to talk about anything intimate. God, Elliott, you don't even like my name. Change it to Diane, you told me one night." Desiree choked back a sob; tears streamed down her cheeks.

"I tried to give you everything a girl could want." Elliott handed her his handkerchief.

"Oh, I know you did." she paused to wipe her nose. "And I know it came from your heart. But Elliott, where is your soul? Your passion?"

Elliott knew Desiree was right. He fought with it himself like the night he wanted to make love to Desiree on the side of the road. And the times he had wanted to throw his arms around her and tell her he loved her. But something always held him back. In every phase of his life, he took the risk-free path. From grade school through college and even in his practice, Elliott made no spontaneous decisions. Every little detail was always ironed out in advance. And now, because of it, he was losing Desiree.

Elliott composed himself and braced himself for the answer to his question. He had to know. "Is there someone else, Desiree? Are you in love with another man?"

Desiree thought carefully. She really did not know if she was in love with Jay Bennett. But she did know that he was the catalyst for this new self-awareness. And she knew that she would see Jay again.

"I'm not in love with anyone else." Desiree looked Elliott right in the eye. "But I cannot lie to you, Elliott. I did meet someone. I met him last week while I was away. I honestly don't know how I feel about him, but he is responsible for how I feel about myself right now. In a few short days, he helped me realize what I've been wrestling with for months. Does that make sense?"

"Did you sleep with him?"

"Elliott! Haven't you heard a word I said?" "Did you?"

"Elliott, I love you, and I certainly believed I was in love with my future husband. I did not sleep with another man." Desiree looked down and lowered her voice, almost whispering, "But because my feelings were so mixed up, I couldn't make love with you the other night either."

Elliott sighed deeply and downed the rest of his drink. "So, I guess there's not much else to say."

"I'm sorry, I'm really so sorry."

"Yeah." Elliott absently stirred his empty glass.

"I hope we can be friends." Even before she had finished her words, Desiree knew how trite they sounded.

"Oh, Desiree, don't." Elliott echoed her feelings. "Let's just let things go peacefully. I'll turn over your father's account to James with my recommendations. He'll do a good job for you."

"No. Elliott, please stay on the account. My father would want you to see it through. And so do I. Please."

He looked at her. God, she was beautiful. "I'll think about it. Thank you for asking. Now, Desiree, I think I'd like to be alone. I'll get you a cab to the train." "Please, don't worry. I'll be all right." Desiree reached into the pocket of her jacket and took out the little blue Tiffany box with the diamond ring Elliott had given her. She laid it on the table by Elliott's hand, softly touching his fingers. Finally, she stood up from the table and kissed Elliott on the cheek, gently brushing her hand across his hair. She wasn't sure, but she thought she felt his tear on her lips.

Elliott watched her glide from the room, a vision, his goddess, gone. He motioned to the waiter, and then he got thoroughly and disgustingly drunk.

CHAPTER 17

After that, the rest of the week totally fell apart. Desiree's best friend Janette was called out of town on business, so their plans were postponed. Uncle Max and his new girlfriend decided to go to the Bahamas and canceled their dinner with Desiree. Great! She said to herself. All this terrific introspection and not a soul to share it with.

None of Desiree's ideas for the illustrations would cooperate with the paper, and she was left staring at a blank drawing board. And to top it all off, now that she knew she wanted to see Jay again, she debated. Should she call him? Maybe I'll just send a text, she thought. She picked up her phone and found his number, beginning a message. No…she erased it. Too corny. She tried again….no, not that either…too sentimental. How 'bout…. oh rats… this is impossible.

Desiree's emotions went up and down. She cried over Elliott, but she felt no guilt. She went from being nervous and afraid to feeling secure and on top of the world. All the typical symptoms of ending an affair. In the end, she knew she was right and in control of her life.

She spent the weekend cleaning closets and deciding what parts of her wardrobe were going to the Salvation Army. Finally, on Sunday, she drove into Brooklyn to her father's apartment. It was time she went through his personal papers.

His office looked as if he had just walked out the day before. His desk was cluttered with papers, and the shelves around the room were lined with books -- scientific, biographical, and espionage. What a character he had been. Thomas Edison and Robert Ludlum rolled into the body of a leprechaun.

There were drawings of future inventions, pictures of Desiree, and, of course, Pat and his ballerina, Francine, Desiree's mother. Desiree loved the picture of their wedding – the elegant, porcelain-skinned French beauty and prima ballerina Francine Dubois, arm in arm with the dashing and dignified Patrick James O'Conner, walking down the aisle of the old church. The story of that day remained pure romance to everyone who had attended – how the bride left her groom speechless when she appeared in a stunning *blue* lace gown – her gift to her husband honoring Irish tradition. And Patrick O'Conner, himself, so grand and proud, dressed in his full County Tartan, complete with its double-breasted jacket and waistcoat.

There were dozens of other photos framed or just thumbtacked to his bulletin board of summer barbeques at POC, fishing with his brother Max, the one where Desiree's mother caught her first fish, the cabin in Cranford, their original home where they lived as a family, and Desiree's favorite…her first dance recital – Ma Mere, Poppy, and Desiree dressed like fairy princess holding a huge bouquet of white tulips and lilacs.

Desiree felt herself tearing up – just another of many episodes since her father died. But she smiled. She missed him. "Oh, Poppy," she said out loud. "What on earth did you have in mind? How did you intend to pay back your debt?" For hours, she sorted through his papers, looking for a clue.

There were dozens of E.P.A reports from Cranford, newspaper clippings reporting the growing problem of contaminated drinking water in small towns all around the country, and stories of whole neighborhoods being shut down due to water infected by pesticides and chemical waste.

There was a congratulatory letter from the regional director of the environmental control board, and still in its envelope, an invitation to speak to the Eastern United States Clean Water Advisory Council on World Water Day – a dignified and celebratory event created in 1993 by the UN General Assembly to educate the world about the importance of water in general, and to raise awareness about the global freshwater crisis. The overall goal, then and now, was to ensure safe water and sanitation through the protection and management of freshwater supplies, not just for small inland lakes *but for all* by the year 2030. Desiree found phone numbers without names and names without numbers.

Somehow, her father had always known who was who and what was what. She thumbed through his appointment book to find nothing but initials (a habit that had driven her mother crazy).

Weekends were marked "F w/ M," which meant fishing with Max, or "D w/ DE," which meant dinner with Desiree and Elliott. It went on: "Dr.T."(doctor's appointment), "POC IV" (inventory for the company), and so on. The very day he went into the hospital, he had marked MJB/SOC. God only knows who or what that meant.

Desiree rummaged through Poppy's desk and found a set of keys for the filing cabinet, a thick file marked personal, more pictures, and a safety deposit key. "Oh, Poppy," said Desiree. "Whatever does this belong to? You were the worst organizer in the world. How could you let your life get so messy."

Desiree took the key, the papers, and the pictures and stuffed them into a large box she found in the kitchen. At the back of the hall closet, she also found his kilt. Gently lifting it from its hanger, she hugged it tightly to her heart and carefully laid it on top of the box of papers and pictures. She would come back later that week and sort through the rest of the place, deciding what to keep and what to give to Good Will.

Actually, there was very little to save. After Desiree had left for college and they sold the house she had grown up in, Poppy had lived a rather spartan existence, choosing to put any extra money into his inventions. His clothes were all at least 20 years old, and the furniture was older than that. Thank goodness for Mrs. Jenkins, who had come in every other day to clean and take care of him. Otherwise, he probably wouldn't have even eaten.

Desiree looked around one last time, turned out the lights, and locked the door. This CHAPTER was closed.

CHAPTER 18

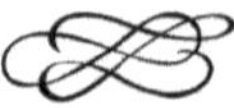

Later that night, Desiree curled up in her bed with a cup of tea and the big file marked personal that she had taken from her father's desk. For over two hours, she poured through the reams of paper, discarding most of it. Poppy had kept every single piece of correspondence he had ever received and considered all of it "personal." Desiree laughed. He was such a character.

But she kept searching. She was sure somewhere she would find some clue to her father's plans to repay the money. Finally, Desiree's determination paid off.... sort of. Mixed in with various letters and notations, she found two pieces of paper stapled together. One was a handwritten, rough draft of a note penned by her father. Many words had been scratched out and rewritten as if he was searching for the proper words. The second was an answer to his note. It was a more formal letter, addressed to Patrick O' Conner, but also written in script. They read as follows:

Dear MB,

Your interest in and support of the Cranford Water Experiment is greatly appreciated. I'm delighted you foresee the same potential as I do. I would indeed be interested in discussing the terms of the sale. Join me for lunch on Monday next.

There was no date on Poppy's scribbled note. Whether it was ever sent remains a mystery. But, according to the second letter, the meeting obviously took place. The letter was addressed to Desiree's father and was dated January 25, only a month before his death! It read:

Dear Mr. O' Conner:

Your offer is intriguing. In fact, it is generous, though you drive a hard bargain. Per our conversation, I herein accept all conditions of the sale and will have my lawyers draw up the appropriate papers per your instructions.

Regards,

?????

Here was the rub. The initials used to sign that letter were totally unreadable. The best Desiree could figure out was that it was three letters scrawled together in a flamboyant flourish.

But it was here. The proof that her father had made plans. He himself had contracted to sell the invention. All she had to do was find this person!

Suddenly, Desiree sobered. What a needle in a haystack. Who on earth was this person, and how would she find him or her or it. Surely, if the deal had been closed, the new owner would have come forward by now. Desiree rubbed her head. More complications. Nothing was easy.

Desiree was lost in thought when she realized her cell was vibrating on the table next to her. She picked it up absent-mindedly.

"Hello." She heard music playing in the background.

"Yellow bird high up in the banana tree." The familiar calypso tune brought an instant laugh to her voice.

"Jay!"

"You recognized my voice?"

"No… the song! Though I don't know any other person alive who sings like you do!"

"Hello, beautiful. I've missed you terribly."

"Oh, Jay. I've… Hey… how did you get this number? "You gave it to me, remember?"

"No, I distinctly remember you gave me yours."

"Ah, it's the old sleight of hand trick. A quick blind text from your phone to mine when I added my number."

"Why you…"

"Sneaky bum…" Jay finished the sentence for her, laughing.

Desiree was delighted. She couldn't be angry. "Guess I'll just have to be a lot more careful handing over my phone to strangers."

"Well, I wouldn't exactly call me a stranger!" Desiree felt herself blush.

"Everything all right? Are you all right?"

"Oh… you have no idea! So much has happened." Desiree's words were falling over each other. "But I'm fine. In fact, I couldn't be better, well, maybe a little better," she added coyly.

"Watch it, my dear. Be careful what you wish for. You might get it." "That's what I mean."

"Are you serious? Have you been thinking?"

"I've done a lot more than think. I've become a positive action player," Desiree waited expectantly. Jay was silent on the other end. Desiree continued. "I've made some changes since I've been back, Jay." Absent-mindedly, she curled and uncurled her hair around her finger and cuddled down into the pillows.

"You have, have you." Desiree could hear the smile in his voice.

"I have. And I want to tell you all about them. But not over the phone. This deserves eye-to-eye contact." She lowered her voice, letting her tone get sexy and suggestive. Desiree was excited.

Jay could hear it in her voice, too. And he was equally as elated. It was all he had been hoping for. They quickly made plans for the following night. Desiree invited him to her place. She felt very strongly about being on home ground, and anyway, she wanted a chance to show off her own entertaining abilities.

"Jay, by the way, I wanted to call you, and I did try to text you, but I just couldn't find the right words."

"You can tell me in person then…tomorrow, Good night, Des."

Desiree put her father's papers aside. Perhaps Jay could help her solve that dilemma. In the meantime, she planned on getting her beauty sleep. She turned out the light and snuggled down under the big eiderdown. But now she was too excited to sleep and nervous. She wanted everything to be perfect tomorrow. She had much to do, much to do.

CHAPTER 19

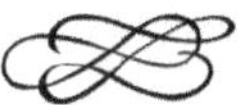

Desiree rose early the next morning and immediately reserved the next four hours for the illustrations. After the mental block she had experienced the last few days, she was far behind. When her brain was fogged, when she needed some clarity, some natural inspiration was usually the remedy, and a visit to the museum and nature center a few miles from her house was always a good choice. A historic icon in the region, the Nature Center was originally a working farm that evolved into a comprehensive nature, cultural, and educational experience.

In truth, Desiree just preferred to walk the grounds, feed the goats, and hang out around the pond to watch the ducks, geese, swans, otters, and all of the waterfowl that found a home there. It was an oasis – as much for them as it was for Desiree.

It was cold on this windy March day, but just what she needed. Sitting on the far side of the huge pond, slightly sheltered by weeping willow trees, Desiree spotted a pair of mallard ducks – the male and female hanging out together, seemingly quite dedicated to each other. Desiree was fascinated and asked the young volunteer about them.

"Oh, they are our most romantic residents! They mate for life, you know, and every Spring, they come back here to the pond, lay their eggs, and raise their ducklings!"

"Seriously?" Desiree was fascinated. "Do you mind if I take a couple of pictures? Would they mind?" Desiree laughed as she took out her cell phone.

"Of course! They love their picture being taken! In fact, we have albums full of them from the last five years!"

"That is amazing," said Desiree. "Seems love is in the air everywhere!"

Desiree's imagination started to percolate – here were the stars of Mr. Poppins' book. She recalled the copy he had shared with her.

* * *

"Harry was a handsome duck with blue-tinged wing feathers and a neck so deeply green, it looked as if he had a silk ascot tied around his throat. His chest was broad and strong and colored a rich, dark, velvety brown, the same shade as an otter's wet skin. In fact, if a duck had buttons on his chest, Harry's would appear to be a handmade vest from the best tailor in town.

When floating in the water, Harry looked as regal as an ocean liner sailing on the Atlantic, and on land, Harry was as grand as any proper gentleman, standing almost 18 inches tall — chest thrown out, neck extended, and head held high. One could almost see a smile on Harry's beak while he surveyed his surroundings like a proud landowner. There was only one thing about his looks that Harry didn't like… and that was his feet! He had the biggest, brightest, reddest-orange, most widely webbed feet anyone had ever seen!"

* * *

The longer she watched, the more enthralled she became. She took a dozen or more pictures and headed back to her house, thanking the sweet volunteer. In her studio, her brushes flew over the paper, and in record time, she had the first set of illustrations based on what she had seen with her own eyes. She knew Mr. Poppins would be pleased. She called him immediately and said she'd express mail them down to him that afternoon. He would have them by tomorrow.

"Excellent, My Dear. Excellent. I'll look forward to seeing them. Perhaps you'll bring the next set in person, and we could have lunch. My garden is just dying to burst open and demanding to be seen."

"Absolutely, Mr. Poppins. I'll plan on it. Have a nice day now. Bye-bye."

Next, Desiree tore through the house, tidying up the clutter she had let accumulate since her return. She pulled her big round oak table in front of the fireplace, between the two chairs, and set it with her grandmother's finest linens and blue willow china. Since her own garden wasn't alive yet, she would stop by the florist and pick up some tulips. Then she brought in more wood, fluffed the pillows, grabbed her coat, and left for the village. The wind had picked up, and   the sun had given way to dark storm clouds, but nothing could ruin her mood. After mailing the drawings, she bought a couple of Cornish hens, fresh asparagus, mushrooms, wild rice, two bottles of wine, French bread, strawberries, and an absolutely sinful, year-on-your-hips chocolate mousse for dessert.

By five thirty, she had everything totally organized and timed to serve dinner at eight. Desiree smiled to herself, pleased with her preparations, and went upstairs. Finally, she was ready to pamper herself. She drew her bath and sunk down into the bubbles with tea bags on her eyes. She forced herself to relax and stayed there for a solid half hour. She absolutely was not going to meet Jay at the door, looking frazzled.

But of course, nothing ever goes the way one plans. Desiree managed to break two nails, realized she forgot to buy the tulips and split the cork inside the wine bottle!

"Damn, damn, double damn! Seriously?" she chided herself.

It was a quarter to seven, and Jay was due in only fifteen minutes! Desiree ran up to the bathroom and slammed the door.

"STOP!" she screamed to herself in the mirror. "Look what you're doing to yourself! Calm down. Count to ten. Take a deep breath."

Desiree looked at her eyes. Her pupils were dilated. "My God, Desiree. You look like a mad woman! Where is the calm, relaxed, in-control woman that sashayed across the patio only two weeks ago? Remember that goddess?"

Desiree laughed at herself. She never had thought she'd be so nervous. She was like a young schoolgirl on her first date. Carefully, she splashed cool water on herface and wrists. Deep breaths. Count. 10-9-8…. Again, a deep breath. There, she felt better. She felt her heart slow down. Her eyes softened. Her muscles relaxed. The doorbell rang.

CHAPTER 20

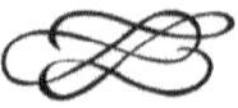

When she opened the door, she was totally unprepared for the waves of feelings that washed over her. In only seconds, she was back on the beach, sailing on MY DESIRE and soaring like the little yellow bird of her dreams. Desiree stared at Jay, unable to speak, swept away into his soul.

Jay, too, was mesmerized. The image he carried in his mind could never do her justice. Desiree was more beautiful, more exquisite than he could ever describe. Her hair was pulled into a low, loose ponytail, allowing curly wisps to frame her face, and the deep blue ankle-length wool sweater dress skimming her body made her eyes glow like Persian jewels. Small gold earrings glistened in her ears, catching the flames of the shimmering firelight. The look was simple, easy, and unaffected. She was framed like a rich oil painting by the soft colors of the room behind her.

Finally, it was Desiree who broke the silence.

"Jay!" she was slightly breathless. "Don't just stand there, come in, come in… Wow…it's gotten so cold!" She pulled him through the door, bringing the frosty night air with him. Touching him made it all real. She looked into his eyes. They were crinkled and laughing.

"Well, I never!" Jay boomed. "I never thought we would both be totally speechless!"

"A Ripley's first, I'm sure," chimed in Desiree. This time, she noticed that Jay's arms were full of packages. "What on earth…"

"I thought you'd never ask. Here, take these." He handed her two bottles of champagne. "And this." a paper bag filled with miniature pears and red grapes. "And these." A huge bouquet of lilacs and white tulips.

"Oh, Jay. This wasn't necessary. Thank you! They're all magnificent!" She turned, heading into the kitchen with the packages.

"Only the best for you, my dear. Only the best." Jay was right behind her. "Now, I really need something from you?"

"What?" Desiree was fussing with the flowers. "Hmmmm, tulips, she said to herself. "lilacs? Amazing." "Des?"

Desiree turned and looked up. Jay was practically nose to nose. She felt her heartbeat quicken and the pit of her stomach fall to her knees. Jay pulled her to him, and in one movement, his arms were around her and hers around him. Their lips met, their tongues entwined, and their passion erupted with an intensity that neither of them could calm. All the unsaid feelings and emotions rushed over them, drowning them in their wake. They looked deeply into each other's eyes, holding the gaze for what seemed an eternity, relishing and reveling in a newly found freedom.

Finally, the tensions of those lost moments passed, and together, they relaxed and looked at one another with a new understanding. Desiree spoke first.

"I have so much to tell you, Jay."

"You just told me all I need to know, Des."

"Yes, I know. But there is really so much more. But first, I believe you came to this establishment for dinner."

"I was wondering how long it would take you to remember that fact. I'm starving, woman. All this emotional stuff builds up an appetite!"

Their old rapport was back. Once again, they were completely at ease in each other's company. The conversation was lively and animated. They laughed and joked and told stories. Jay adored her little house and everything in it.

"It's really you, Des. I can see you and your whole ancestry right here under one roof. It's a bit flowery for my taste, mind you. But a few stripes and solids here and there, maybe an old worn leather chair, and it could be quite a comfy little love nest."

"Aren't we jumping ahead a little fast?" Desiree looked sternly at Jay but, deep down inside, was delighted by his comments. She really didn't know where all this was going to lead, but she was heading in, full speed ahead.

Over dinner, she told him about Elliott. After much coaxing, she confessed her crazy dreams and Lil's interpretation of them. Jay pooh-poohed the whole thing but didn't doubt the integrity of Desiree's conclusions concerning her own feelings.

"And how do you feel about Elliott now?" His concern was genuine, though he admitted to himself he was still a little jealous and wary.

"Elliott and I have known each other a lot of years," explained Desiree. "I suppose we can never be friends now. Those ideals never seem to work. But I really do have some very special feelings for him. I always will." Jay tightened his jaw.

Desiree continued quickly. "But I've realized that I was trying too hard to make things work between us. He's not right for me. And I don't think I could ever have made Elliott truly happy either."

"From what I've heard, Elliott doesn't know how to be happy," Jay said sarcastically.

"Don't Jay. Sarcasm doesn't become you. And it's totally unnecessary!" Desiree said defensively.

"Sorry. You're right. That was my male ego talking."

"I'm sorry I hurt Elliott. But I know I'm on the right track for myself. And…" Desiree lifted the bottle of wine to refill his glass, "I'm pretty sure you're in the race too."

Jay lifted his glass in a toast and winked, "Here's lookin' at you, kid."

Together, they cleared the table and tidied the kitchen. They worked easily together, bumping elbows and touching hands, chatting like old friends.

While they worked, Desiree filled Jay in on the problems with her father's company. She also told him about the two letters and how she knew those letters were the key to her father's plans.

"If I can't find a way to pay back those debts, I'll have to declare bankruptcy, and everything Poppy worked so hard to achieve will just disappear. Not to mention all the people… especially Lil. What would she do? She was planning on retiring next year. She wouldn't have a penny."

Jay's mind was going a mile a minute, trying to focus on Desiree's words. He, of course, knew the entire story. He also knew that the protection of the company and its employees was the heart of the deal he had struck with Pat O' Conner. No one, except O' Conner and himself, would ever have known the details of this rather clandestine plan. Now, because of O'Conner's untimely death, Desiree was left with a mess. And he – Jay – was holding the key to it all. The fates could be cruel. Who would have guessed they would introduce him to Desiree before the dye was cast. Who could have predicted he would fall madly in love with her? And he was under oath to protect the old man's wishes. These were precarious waters. It was a triple conflict that challenged a man's integrity. Jay knew what he had to do and would honor that. And he hoped that, in the end, Desiree's own sense of honor would help her understand his actions. So, what to say? He had to suggest or offer something. He had to extend his help without jeopardizing his promise. "Well…you know…." he finally said, "I know a few engineering firms myself. I'll be glad to make a few calls for you." "Oh, Jay, that would be great. I'd really appreciate it."

"But first, my dear," Jay's eyes twinkled, "…Alexa! Play "Washin' Dishes" by Jack Johnson." The infamous 'voice' immediately responded and stopped the current music track to announce *'Washin' Dishes by Jack Johnson on Amazon Music.* As the soft rock, swing tempo song started to play, Jay grabbed Desiree's hand, twirled her away from the sink, under his arm, and danced her around the kitchen.

Caught by surprise but never missing a beat, Desiree slipped easily into the rhythm, grinning while Jay crooned the words *'in the morning when the world came awake before you knew me, I knew your name…. when you saw me washing dishes….one day I could take you away…'*

Laughing now, Desiree was delighted. "You amaze me! You sing, you dance, you have the most eclectic collection of songs….is there anything you can't do?" One last twirl as the song ended, Jay pulled her close and kissed her quick.

The dance was the perfect distraction to get Desiree's mind off her father's business. Until he saw her eyes well up with tears. "Des, what's wrong?" Jay lifted her chin gently.

"I remember…. I remember…my mother and Poppy danced in the kitchen," she said wistfully. "I haven't thought of that in years. I was like nine or ten….and I would hide behind the kitchen door and peak around it… ma mere taught him to waltz, and he taught her how to do the Irish step-dance…oh, he wasn't very good…, but what he lacked in talent, he gained in enthusiasm! She would pretend to not know how to do the dance. Of course, she did. And they would laugh, and always end with a slow dance…. hmmmph…. well…. enough of that…."

Desiree sent Jay out to check on the fire while she finished the last of the chores. Shaking off her melancholy, she loaded a big silver tray with the champagne, strawberries, pears, grapes, and that wonderfully sinful chocolate mousse. Back in the living room, they took their respective places and dug in. This was Desiree's favorite part of any dinner.

"What is this? A Viennese coffee hour?" Jay dropped a strawberry into each bubbling glass. "Maybe you should rethink your career. You know, bar mitzvahs, weddings, affairs?"

Desiree giggled. "Well, I only brought the berries and the mousse. You, may I remind you, are responsible for the rest!"

"Guilty, as charged. And they are delectable, I must say. Here, taste." Jay sliced a piece of the pear and leaned across the table. Desiree parted her lips and let him slide the soft, cool fruit into her mouth. Her eyes never left his. She returned the favor with a perfectly round, crisp grape.

They sipped the champagne and continued in this manner until Desiree, choosing her moment carefully, waited until Jay's eyes were slightly closed and then popped a huge piece of mousse into his mouth. His eyes flew open, and his head jerked enough that he managed to smear chocolate across one cheek. Desiree laughed gleefully, leaning back in her chair.

"Cute." Jay grinned at her, wiping his mouth with his finger. "So, the lady wants to play." Desiree's laughter turned to a shriek when Jay jumped up from the chair and closed in on her with an even bigger piece of cake.

"Don't you dare get chocolate on my furniture!" screamed Desiree.

"You should have thought of that before, my dear!" He leered in his best Simon LeGree voice as he twirled an imaginary mustache.

Desiree scrambled out of her chair from the opposite side, slid between the table and the fireplace, and around the back of Jay's chair. He countered her move, then stood still, waiting for her next one, the mousse dangling precariously on his open palm.

All the while, Desiree was laughing giddily, and Jay was slinging bad-guy one- liners in a dozen different accents.

"What's that!" Desiree suddenly screamed and pointed over Jay's shoulder. "What?" Jay turned his head for a second, and Desiree jumped in front of him and ran to the kitchen, shrieking in delight.

Jay followed in hot pursuit, feigning a scene from an old silent movie, "You'll pay for this, Pauline! He sneered again, twirling his invisible mustache, "I'll tie you to the table leg and make you eat the entire mousse! Only I will ever love you then, you'll have to be with me forever!"

"No! No! A thousand times, no! I will never eat the mousse!"

The champagne had done its job. Tears of laughter were streaming down Desiree's face. She had positioned herself between the sink and the kitchen table and now realized in mock horror that she was trapped.

Jay leered at her from the kitchen door, still holding the mousse! Seconds later, he was leaning over her. He had grabbed one of her wrists with one hand and was ready to shove the chocolate into her face with the other when it finally splattered to the floor.

Without missing a beat, Jay darted into the living room, grabbed the poker from the fireplace, brandishing it like a sword, and leaped into the kitchen, roaring in his best pirate voice, swishing at the mouse, "ARR! Damn You Villain! You mouse, you! ….. Fear not, Woman! You're mine!" And while Desiree was laughing hysterically, Jay leaned over her, smothering her laughter with kisses.

Desiree was already weak in the knees. Jay's attempted kiss finished the job. They both collapsed on the floor, totally out of control. Many minutes passed before they both sobered. Jay looked her squarely in the eyes.

"I love you, you crazy, sensitive, beautiful, food-loving woman. You're everything I have ever been looking for. I want to protect you from all of the villains and pirates of this world."

And then he kissed her, hard and passionately, yet with great tenderness. There was no doubt in Desiree's mind that he meant every word that he said. Desiree responded without any guilt. She kissed him as passionately as he did her. She opened her soul and invited him in.

Suddenly, a huge crack of thunder followed by lightning that lit up the entire room rocked the very foundation of the little house! And all went dark!

"Oh my God!" Desiree felt herself shaking. "What on earth was that?" She ran to the front windows, then the door, but all was black outside. Thank goodness for the dozens of luminaria candles she had placed around the rooms. "I think a tree went over!" she opened the door to peer out. It was snowing!

"Are you kidding me? It's March, for heaven's sake! This is bizarre!"

Jay came up behind her… "So, this happens often?"

"Well, yes, I lose power a lot…we're in the country, you know." "And do you have a generator?"

"Ah…that would be a no."

"Hmmm. I see. So, you are here, alone in the dark, frequently when the lights go out?"

"That would be a yes." Desiree was still giggling from the champagne. "Well, obviously, I can't leave you to fend for yourself tonight." "Well, of course, you can't, Dudley. You're a Boy Scout, after all!"

"Yes, I am. And I'm always prepared…. except tonight… I have no idea how to fix this problem, Jay said sheepishly. "And I can't possibly leave you alone." "Well, then. You'll just have to stay the night to be sure I stay safe." Desiree was feeling extremely cheeky.

Jay ventured outside and brought in more wood for the fire while Desiree gathered up some extra blankets. The house was quickly getting chilly now that the power and heat were off.

"Help me with this table, please," she asked as she started pulling the table back from the fireplace. Piling up pillows in front of the fireplace, using the big chairs to lean against, Desiree and Jay snuggled down into the comfort of the make-shift campsite.

CHAPTER 21

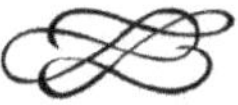

"Well….it seems the fates are working again," observed Jay as they got comfy in front of the fire with their glasses in hand. "Hmmm... perhaps…"

"Really? Not a believer in fate?"

"Yes…I am …But…I do confess… if the lights hadn't gone out… I'd have asked you to stay…"

"Really?"

"Yes…I would have…"

"Hmmm...so sorry the outage messed that up." "What's messed up? I'm here…" she said provocatively.

"Ummm...yes, so you are …. Des, are you sure you're OK with this? With us like this…right now?" he leaned closer. She could feel his breath on her face…

"Yes…I'm OK," she said as he stroked her arms and her shoulders, til finally, he said, "Can you get out of this dress?'

Dess burst out laughing – the intensity of the moment broken – "Yes… give me a minute…ok?'

Desiree shook off the moment, pulled herself up from the comforters, grabbed a candle, and headed toward the stairs…. "God, it's cold out here!" she yelled back as she climbed to the second floor. Her mood was somewhat tempered by the cold air. But at the top, in her bedroom, in one swell swoop, she stripped off the dress, grabbed a chemise, and headed back down the stairs, barefoot and semi-naked! Fueled by the wine, the conversation, and the incredibly unexpected romantic circumstances of a blackout, her mood was intoxicated. She felt sexy, and gripping the banister to avoid falling, she made her way back downstairs… step by step. When she turned the corner towards the living room and the temporary campsite, she lost her breath, nearly hiccupping with emotion….

He stood there now, bare-chested, with two glasses in his hand. The light from the fireplace radiated off the muscles on his body. His muscles glistened as if oiled, and yet, his stance was easy and comfortable and relaxed – a man who was comfortable in his own skin, not at all conscientious of how absolutely gorgeous he appeared to others! His own breath caught in his throat when he looked at her in the soft yellow chemise, just barely skimming her body. "Damn, girl," he said just loud enough for her to hear.

"Now," said Jay softly to Desiree as he moved closer and looked at every inch of her, placing his arms around her and pulling her close. "Where were we?" The low burning fire and luminarias throughout the room sent beautiful light and shadows dancing against the walls, giving everything an amber glow. Desiree felt her cheeks blush, her entire body trembling, knowing what she wanted most.

"You look beautiful. Are you OK?" he asked. He took her face in his hands. "You're shaking. Are you cold?" Desiree shook her head, staring at him, speechless.

"What's wrong. Did I grow two heads or something?" She giggled. "No, I just feel like I'm on a set, and the director is about to yell action."

"Sssh. Don't say a word. You don't have to." Jay pulled her to him, embracing her, holding her, making her feel warm and wanted.

He kissed her on her lips. They were sweet and moist, tasting like wine and chocolate. He felt them tremble slightly. "Relax." He said. "Trust me. Close your eyes." He softly kissed each one. "Don't think about anything." He kissed her ear and then her neck. "Let your thoughts soar like a bird, like a yellow bird, high up in the sky, without a care in the world."

As he spoke, they slowly sank into the pillows, comforters, and linens Desiree had piled onto the floor in front of the fireplace. And as she sunk deeper and deeper into the pillows, relaxing at every word, she felt as if in a trance. She slid her arms around Jay's neck and arched her back as he lowered his face onto her breast. With his tongue, he pushed the silk aside to find her nipple stiff and erect. "You smell delicious," he mumbled and kissed each bud, moving from one to the other, back to her shoulders and her long, sinewy throat.

Desiree returned the caresses, kissing his shoulders and neck while sliding her own hands down his lean and muscular back to his buttocks. She traced the top of his trousers with her hands, circling back towards herself, pushing to release the entanglement of fabric between them.

Jay lifted his hips, allowing Desiree to ease off his remaining clothes. She caught them with her foot and flung them aside. She gasped. At last, she could feel every inch of him against her. His skin was hot through the thin silk of her chemise, and the memory of their kiss on the beach was vivid.

But this was now. Jay lifted the pale silk over her head and stopped to gaze down at the vision beneath him. "You are magnificent. I love you more than you know."

Then began his descent towards her belly, caressing and kissing every inch along the way. For a long time, Desiree lay oblivious to everything except Jay. He took her from one plateau to another, each time the intensity becoming more and more unbearable, yet exultant. Finally, when she thought she could bear no more, he was inside her. She arched her back and held him tightly, slowly moving in a wave together until they burst within each other.

Afterward, they lay holding each other, not talking. Jay went into the kitchen and made them tea, and they curled back under the covers, eating cookies and fruit. Later that night, they made love again, and still, for a third time. Jay was a sensitive lover, but he was also playful and creative. Together, they experimented, laughing at their awkwardness and reveling in their pure enjoyment.

Finally, hours later, they fell into a deep sleep, wrapped in each other's arms. Desiree dreamt of the yellow bird again, and when she awoke, there was no mistaking the message of this dream.

* * *

Two yellow birds flew through the clouds, darting in and out of the shadows cast by the sun. Playfully, they chased each other across the skies, at last joining their wings together to become one.

* * *

Morning dawned sweet and comfortable without any awkwardness or regrets. The lights were on, and Desiree was singing in the kitchen when Jay joined her.

"Hello, sleepyhead." She handed him a cup of coffee.

"You're certainly up bright and early," Jay scowled. So, he was grumpy in the morning. Well, you couldn't have everything.

"Aren't we pleasant?"

Jay grinned. "Only until my first cup of coffee."

"Ok, but," teased Desiree, "it's not exactly early. It's already 10 o'clock." "Perfect. A very respectable hour for a young couple to rise." He had come close to her and wrapped his arms about her, nuzzling her neck from behind. "What's that about rising?" Desiree could distinctly feel his mounting urges through her skirt.

"Didn't you wear yourself out last night, m'lord?" "Never, where you're concerned."

"Power's back on," Desiree diverted Jay's physical reaction to her words. "But the yard's a mess. My landscaper called, and he'll be here later today. What an amazing storm last night…"

"Wasn't it, though?" Jay's play on words made Desire blush.

She turned around, spatula in hand, and purred, "Then you should have waited, and I would've brought you breakfast "in bed," referring to the pile of blankets still on the living room floor.

"Madame! I'm shocked. Absolutely shocked. What kind of place is this, anyway?"

Desiree kissed him then, feeling wonderfully warm and cozy. "So, what will it be? French toast? Waffles? Bacon and eggs?"

"Nothing, darling. Really. All kidding aside, I must be off. Are you sure you're OK? I have some very important business to attend to, but I could rearrange my schedule."

"No… I'm good. Years of living here have awakened the pioneering spirit in me. This is nothing!"

"OK, but I'll call you later. How would you like to come with me upstate this weekend?"

"Oh, I don't think I can. I planned to spend the weekend with Janette. I told you about her. I haven't seen her since after my father's funeral."

"You mean you'd rather spend the weekend with her than me?" He sounded really hurt.

"No. It's not that. It's just…" Desiree searched for the right words. Then she saw Jay grin.

"You're so fun to tease!" Jay hugged her. Desiree breathed a sigh of relief. "Thank God. I thought you were one of those jealous types."

"Oh, I am. Just be careful who you're standing me up for! Seriously, I understand. And I'm glad you have such a good friend. I'd like to meet her."

"Well, that can certainly be arranged. How about lunch on Friday? I'll be in town anyway. My treat."

"Oh, no. If I'm having lunch with two beautiful women, I'm buying. I have a reputation to protect."

"Ok. Ok. You win."

"Good. Now, is it Ok I shower? I've got to get out of here."

CHAPTER 22

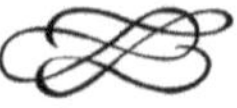

The rest of the week passed by at record speed. Desiree's new schedule included not only her work on the illustrations but two days a week at P.O.C. Outfitters. There were still orders to fill and creditors to handle. Lil had finally been told of the bleak situation. She was visibly upset, but she stuck out her chin with all of her Irish moxi and convinced herself it would all work out. She trusted Desiree like she had trusted Pat O'Conner. And Desiree's determination was no easy thing to fight.

Aside from these pressures, Desiree was on cloud nine. Lil saw the change in her immediately and jumped right in with her usual blunt observations.

"You look like the cat that ate the yellow bird," she stated that first morning over coffee.

Desiree blushed. "Thanks to you." "Well?"

"Well, what?"

"Desiree O' Conner, you know damn well what I mean. I take it you've told Mr. Jay Bennett of your intentions."

"You could say that." Desiree chuckled. "And I assume you've told Elliott."

"Of course. "Desiree looked seriously at Lil. "You know me better than that, Lil. It wasn't very pleasant, and I doubt if Elliott will ever speak to me again. I'm afraid I hurt him terribly."

"He'll get over it. Most men do. And Elliott especially. If one's emotions aren't taxed to the limit, it doesn't hurt so much."

"Lil, that's not very sensitive of you."

"But it's the truth where Elliott is concerned. You just never saw it. Everyone else did."

"So I keep hearing." Desiree was getting bored with this conversation. "Nice of everyone to tell me now."

"You wouldn't have listened before, dear. But I'm sorry. You're right. Anyway, you've done the right thing. Now, when do I get to meet this hunk!"

"Soon, Lil, very soon."

Meanwhile, sitting at her father's desk, Desiree was calling everyone on his old Rolodex to try and track down the source of the two letters. She had even brought in her father's hand-scribbled notes and called the numbers that had no names. Two of them seemed terribly familiar, and she burst out laughing when, after dialing the first of them, Uncle Max answered the phone!

"Uncle Max! Is that you?"

"Ai, of course it is, lassie. Who'd ye think it was at the other end of this number?"

Desiree quickly explained to Uncle Max. He was fascinated by the letters but had no clue as to their meaning.

"This is the answer to our problems, Uncle Max. I just know it. I've got to find the man who made this deal."

"Have you talked to Elliott about it?" Uncle Max asked. "Maybe he knows something. He is the company's lawyer."

Desiree hesitated. "Umm, Elliott probably doesn't want to speak to me."

"What happened, darlin'? Did the two of ye have a fight?" Max tried to be sympathetic despite his dislike of Elliott.

"I broke up with him. I called off the wedding."

"Ah ha!" Max's face broke into a grin from ear to ear that Desiree could sense over the phone.

"Now, stop that!" Desiree couldn't help but smile herself. She could never be angry at Uncle Max, and any thought of Jay, even such a backhanded one, brought a twinkle to her own eye. And Uncle Max could sense that through the phone, too.

"So, you finally threw out that dishrag. Good for you. I take it you had some additional motive behind it?"

"Well, let's say that I have been doing a lot of soul-searching lately, and I've started to make some changes in my life."

"All right, dearie. I'll wait for the details. But I want to meet this new beau of yours and soon. Invite him for supper as soon as I get back. I'm leaving for my fishing trip with Lydia tomorrow morning. Now, I must go, lassie. Love you. Bye."

''Bye, bye Uncle Max. I love you too." Desiree hung up laughing.

Uncle Max made her day. But back to business. There was one more number in Poppy's scribble, but as familiar as it seemed, Desiree couldn't place it, and there was no answer when she called it. That left only one more source. She would have to call Elliott.

"Elliott? This is Desiree."

''I do still recognize your voice." Elliott was hurting, and being curt was his only way to protect himself.

"Elliott, please. Don't be rude. How are you?" Desiree persisted. "All right, I guess. You?"

"Fine. The reason why I called is about P.O.C. I told you I still want you to handle our legal matters. I want you to stay on as our lawyer. Please. As a friend. For Poppy."

"You know I will, Desiree." Elliott's voice had softened. "What do you need." "Thank you." Desiree smiled. She felt she had made some progress. "First, I want to know what happened last week in Cranford?"

"As a matter of fact, I was going to call you about this. I have good news and bad news. The good news is that I think we have a buyer!"

"Oh, Elliott, really? What did they say?"

"They say that that crazy father of yours is a genius! His water purification system can save little towns like Cranford thousands and thousands of taxpayer dollars. They also feel that with a few more modifications, they can incorporate it into their own building codes and market it to a whole new client. It's the answer to small towns who don't need a huge sewer system."

"Oh, Elliott, that's fabulous. How much?"

"That's the bad news. There's still a risk without all of the EPA reports being in. And as you know, that won't be for seven more months in October."

"Yes, yes, Elliott. I know. But how much?"

"They'll buy it now for $100,000, and they'll assume all responsibility for the project."

"But Elliott, $100,000 won't save P.O.C. It might pay the outstanding bills and the creditors, but I can't operate the company and pay salaries, too!"

"I know, Desiree. But you can close the doors without any debts."

Desiree's mind worked quickly. Elliott was trying to talk her into the easy way out. She wanted it all. She was not going to see P.O.C. die.

She said to Elliott, "They want to steal it from me, Elliott. There's very little risk involved in buying that system now, or they wouldn't be willing to take on the responsibility. They're going to reap the profits and the publicity if they buy it now. What's it worth seven months from now? Did they tell you that?"

"They wouldn't commit. They said maybe triple that or even more."

"And I wonder how much they can profit from it? Millions?" Desiree's Irish temper was flaring. Her father knew its potential. He had already made a deal. She had to find whoever it was. She told Elliott about the letters.

"Why didn't you say so before? I wouldn't have gone through this whole charade."

"I only came across them two nights ago, Elliott. Don't be so testy. Listen." She read him the two notes. "What do you think?"

"I think you're right. But unless this guy comes forward, they might as well not even exist."

"Think, Elliott. Ask your father. Someone must know something."

"Your father was a very private man, Desiree. If he wanted something to be kept a secret, he did. That's what made him such a difficult client. He never told his lawyers anything."

"I know, Elliott. I know. Please, do what you can."

"I will. But Desiree, there's a failsafe point. If we can't find your missing deal maker, then I strongly advise you to take the $100,000. Otherwise, you're looking at total bankruptcy."

"I'll think about it. Bye."

CHAPTER 23

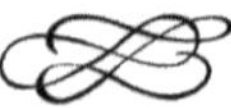

By Thursday night, Desiree was exhausted. The pressures of dealing with a faltering company, trying to keep morals high, and maintaining her own creative energies while she worked on the illustrations were too much. A weekend doing nothing but gossiping, antiquing, and doing "girl stuff" was just what she needed.

Of course, the daily calls from Jay had a very positive effect on her mood. He was always witty and entertaining and outrageously sexy over the phone. He could make her blush with only a word or a phrase. And his gift for the romantic was not to be outdone.

On Wednesday afternoon in the office, Lil had knocked on the door to deliver a handwritten note that had arrived for Desiree. Of course, Lil stayed around to hear its contents. Blushing, Desiree read it out loud:

Come dine with me at six o'clock
I'll meet you at the big tic toc
That stands outside your office door
The one that always says it's four.

My carriage is the color black
I'll be the one who's in the back
With roses and a heart on fire.
For you, my dear, my Sweet Desire.

"You'd better grab this one, Desiree," Lil shook her finger at her young friend. "They threw away the mold when they made him. And they say chivalry is dead!" Lil turned and left the office, clucking like an old mother hen.

Desiree was flattered, elated, excited, and had at least a dozen other feelings all at the same time. No one had ever treated her so grandly, so special, except for Poppy and Uncle Max. But one can't classify fathers and uncles in the affairs of the heart.

Sure enough, at six o'clock, right outside P.O.C.'s doors, under the clock that had stopped at four o'clock 20 years ago, was a black hansom cab complete with one very handsome man and a dozen white roses in the passenger's seat.

Jay looked dashing, sitting back in the elegant old carriage. If time could be turned back, Desiree was sure he would have been a landbaron or a plantation owner. She laughed as she envisioned a portlier Jay in a white suit, holding a silver-tipped cane between his knees.

"What's so funny?"

"Just a daydream…oh, Jay! This is terribly romantic. If I'd known, I could have worn a white lawn dress or something!" Desiree grabbed his outstretched hand and climbed in beside him, feeling instantly transported to a simpler time. They toured the old streets of Brooklyn, through the Heights, and down the promenade, watching a magnificent sun setting over the city. When they finally stopped to eat, Mama Lou, the robust proprietor of the tiny Italian Restaurant, welcomed Jay with a big bear hug and then pinched Desiree's cheek, telling Jay to feed her better.

"Don't let this skinny frame fool you, Lou," Jay teased. "This woman can out eat me!"

"Good, good." grinned Mama Lou. "I like a girls that a canna eat! Now, sit! I bring you the besta pasta in all a Brooklyn. Maybe all a New York."

It was a wonderful, spontaneous, romantic evening, and Desiree was sure she was falling in love. Jay, too, shared more of his innermost feelings than he had in their past conversations. His parents were both living but had moved to the West Coast to be closer to their grandchildren. Jay's sister and brother-in-law lived in Seattle with two fiery little girls and an Irish setter. Desiree had known Jay had been engaged about four years ago, but he had never volunteered any details about why the relationship ended. Finally, that night, over dinner, he talked about how his fiancée had been killed in a car accident a month before the wedding.

To ease his pain and allow time to mend the wound, he had thrown himself into his work, consequently building up a miniature empire of small businesses and investments. His prime interest was real estate – like Henry had mentioned, he was an investor at Las Palmas and the Villas, but he had his degree in engineering. The combination, along with the managerial expertise of his partner, made them a formidable team. Together, they bought and/or merged ten different companies and industrial sites in four and a half years.

"Want to buy a bankrupt camping supply company?" Desiree asked longingly.

Jay had been waiting for this to come up, which is part of the reason he had been so evasive about his business deals. He stalled for time.

"Desire! My God. Sometimes I can't see the forest for the trees. I've been so involved in falling in love with you that aside from reaching out to a few contacts, I never even thought about a business proposition. Maybe I should speak to Elliott? I can't make any promises, you know. You have to realize, Des, that sometimes it's just too late. Sometimes, you do just have to let go."

"Oh, Jay, I know. I'm trying to prepare myself for that possibility. But I won't go down without a fight. Talk to him. But you have to promise not to let him know that you and I are… you know."

"Are you kidding? I'll tell him the whole story!" "Don't you dare!!"

"Ah! Caught ya!" Jay laughed and leaned over to kiss her. "You're much too gullible, Des. Better watch yourself. Someone may take extreme advantage of you someday."

"I thought you were going to protect me from all those Pirates?"

"But who's going to protect you from me?" he sneered teasingly while twirling that invisible mustache again.

After dinner, they took a cab to Manhattan. Desiree was nestled comfortably in the crook of Jay's arm when he whispered against her hair.

"Nightcap? My house?"

Warm, erotic sensations surged through Desiree's body as anticipation of another night of lovemaking looked to be a reality. There was nothing contrived; no "owe me's." It seemed like the most natural thing in the whole world.

"I thought you'd never ask." Desiree smiled coyly.

"Why, you vixen!" Jay laughed and squeezed her shoulder. Brushing her hair with his lips, he leaned forward and gave the cab driver the address of his house.

CHAPTER 24

As they pulled up outside the beautiful old brownstone, Desiree was again awed by the varied tastes of this fascinating man. From the Caribbean and an old romantic sailboat to red jeeps and hansom cabs to the refined dignity of this grand old house, Jay was the most eclectic man she had ever met. He could be outrageously witty, slap-stick funny, loving, or romantic. He was sophisticated without being stuffy, rugged without being a jock, sexy without being untouchable.

Inside the house, Jay's varied personality prevailed. His home was as personal as Desiree's. This pleased her. According to him, he had done most of the renovations himself and, from the looks of it, the decorating as well. It was a decorator's nightmare but wonderfully comfortable and homey.

There was a beautiful antique baby grand piano that had belonged to his father and old, worn leather furniture that had come from a long-defunct men's club. The oriental rugs and the lamps he had bought at a flea market were his own investments. All it needs, Desiree found herself thinking, is a woman's touch. She gazed around the room, imagining antique satin drapes and vases of flowers and throw pillows of every size and fabric. But truly, the conversation piece was an enormous oil portrait over an oval side table in the living room.

"*Who* is that?" Desiree pointed to the grande dame with white hair piled heavily on her head, brilliant blue eyes, and a Mona Lisa smile.

"That… is Magda. My great, great grandmother. The absolute and only matriarch of the Bennett clan." Desiree studied the portrait with an artist's eye. The work was quite excellent, but the subject demanded all one's attention. She appeared to be a huge woman, not fat, but large and statuesque. Dressed in an elaborate black ball gown, she bespoke power and respect as obvious as the diamond and sapphire necklace that she wore choker-style around her neck. Her presence in this room was overwhelming; she must have done the same a hundred years ago.

"Awesome! I wouldn't want to tangle with her." "Anyone who did isn't alive to tell about it today!"

Desiree continued to stare at Magda while Jay's words settled in. "Well, I guess not." Desiree laughed at his subtle humor. "So, what's her story?"

"Oh, it's all terribly romantic, the stuff novels are made of. Come, I'll tell you as we walk." They continued the tour of the house, through the downstairs kitchen and dining room and up the back stairs to a grand hallway that led to the bedrooms, while Jay filled in the details of his own family history.

Jay had removed his jacket when they came in and rolled up the sleeves of his white dress shirt. It was an effect that Desiree found incredibly sexy. As she followed him up the stairs, Desiree found her interest centering on the curl of his hair, his broad shoulders, and the long tapered lines of his back, now taught under the shirt. She let her eyes fall to his waist and the sway of his hips. She strained to concentrate on his story.

"Magda was a child bride. She was only sixteen years old when she was swept off her feet by Samuel Bennett, a "mature man" of twenty-five. He took her to Barbados, where they worked together, building up a thriving sugar cane business. Their home was the showplace of the island, a beautiful white anti-bellum style house which they named Villa Blanca."

"The name of your house at Los Palmas!" Desiree had interrupted.

Jay nodded and then continued. "They were terribly in love and lived their lives peacefully in an island paradise. But ten years after they married, Samuel was killed in a hurricane, leaving Magda with a substantial fortune and three spoiled children to manage.

Magda was no fool, and she had learned a lot from Samuel. She sold the sugar cane plantation and invested all the money in Europe and America, leaving it in three huge parcels for each of the children when she died. Unfortunately, the two girls married badly, and their husbands squandered their fortunes. The son, however, had acquired his parent's prowess for business and continued to increase his inheritance. That was my grandfather.

"And the rest, as they say," concluded Jay, "is history." "So, Magda's son had the portrait painted?"

Jay laughed. "Are you kidding? Magda commissioned it herself! She was sixty when it was painted. She told the artist she wanted to "keep an eye on things."

"Well, I certainly see where you get your modesty!" Desiree teased.

"It's a Bennett trait that gets stronger with every generation. Just think what our kids will be like."

Desiree turned scarlet. "I beg your pardon?"

Jay came close to her. She could feel the heat from his body; his desires were too, too obvious.

"I said…"

"Never mind. I heard what you said." Desiree felt flustered. She was just beginning to be able to handle such thoughts on her own. But when Jay verbalized them, it was just too much pressure.

Her heart was beating wildly, and her hands were sweaty. The thrill of his words and the promises of what was yet to come amounted to waves of panic subdued by the yearnings of her flesh.

As if this wasn't enough, Jay had reached the last room on his tour and announced, grinning at her obvious discomfort, "And this is the master bedroom!" "Enough!" Desiree hauled off and punched him in the arm. "You are driving me to distraction."

"Ah ha! Now you know how it feels." Jay suddenly picked her up in his arms and carried her over the threshold, bumping her into the door jam on the way!

Desiree started to giggle. "Jay, put me down! You'll kill yourself."

Wincing dramatically, he nearly dropped her on the floor. "My god, woman, how much do you weigh?"

"Now, that is not a very polite question to ask a lady." Desiree feigned indignity. "You should know better. After all, I'm almost as tall as you are!" Then she added playfully. "Ah, but one of my great desires in life is to be carried *gracefully* across a threshold."

"Dream on, my dear, dream on."

Once again, the intensity of the moment was tempered. Desiree walked around the beautiful room, taking in the floor-to-ceiling windows, pocket doors leading to a dressing room, the black and white tiled bathroom with its huge walk-in shower, and finally, the stunning and surprisingly almost modern golden oak sleigh bed, a stark contrast to the mahogany and burled woodwork. Neither one spoke. They stood facing each other for several minutes. Desiree could hear the chimes of a clock somewhere in the house… she counted…10…11…12…Midnight!

"Oh my God! I've gotta go! My train!"

"It's too late, Cinderella. Stay. Stay with me tonight. Will you stay?" His eyes were sparkling, not with tricks and teases but with the fire of passion and a promise that would ignite Desiree's soul.

***

As they laid down together on the oversized bed, it felt like old friends united after a long absence. Relaxing and allowing her emotions to dictate, Desiree took the initiative. "Roll over," she whispered and began massaging Jay's back, kneading his muscles gently while he groaned seductively. Desiree wasn't the only one who felt the tension of the moment. Jay's back shoulders were tight; the muscles knotted into what felt like lumps of clay. Gradually, she felt him relax and loosen his hold on control.

Desiree worked quietly, humming to herself, smoothing his skin with oils and lotions and kneading the muscles more and more deeply. She spoke only once, asking him to turn over. Very, very slowly, with a smile on her lips, she looked deep into his eyes and ran her hand down his long, lean body as if counting every rib. Her slender fingers trailed gracefully over his chest, parting the curly hairs with her nails, sensuously grazing his skin with the rounded tips, raising goosebumps on his taut abdomen until she had him thoroughly aroused. Jay watched, fascinated at her concentration, an artist at work, a sculptor at play. Unable to lay passively a moment longer, Jay reached for her, but she slapped his hands playfully.

"Relax! Tonight, it's my turn to please you."

Oh, God. Jay moaned inwardly. I've died and gone to heaven. I love her more than is possible. But to Desiree, he kept the tone light.

"I like your style, lady." He grinned and closed his eyes, forcing himself to relax under her delicate touch.

She loved looking at him, every muscle and tendon of his tanned body clearly defined against the soft white sheets. Desiree took her time, massaging, touching, teasing, stroking, slowly leading Jay to absolute ecstasy. Blood simmering, heart racing, every nerve in his body alert and ripe for the taking, he was losing all reason. He could contain himself no longer.

"Come to me, Desiree, for God's sake, let me love you." His voice was barely a whisper.

Desiree eased herself onto Jay sucking in her breath dramatically as he arched upward, pulling her close, down into his arms, filling her soul. Throbbing. Pulsating. She was moist and warm and full and loved. Jay opened his eyes to find Desiree gazing down at him, her golden mane loose around her shoulders, her sapphire eyes brimming with the passion of unselfish love. He took her face between his own hands and gently stroked her cheek, tracing the curve of her chin and the soft lines of her full rose-colored lips.

"I love you, Des. With all of my heart, with all my soul."

Then they began to move in unison, gently rocking to and fro, impassioned by their very touching and joining together. Like the ebb and flow of the ocean, with as much feeling echoing in their ears, they seduced each other over and over again until their bodies could refrain no more. Together, yet separately, unique and as one, they burst forth on each other, consumed in their reverent passion.

Desiree was lost on a plain somewhere short of total ecstasy; she was conscious of feeling more alive than ever before. No one had ever made her feel this way. No man had ever loved her so completely. She knew... that night, she knew... she loved this man with all her heart.

CHAPTER 25

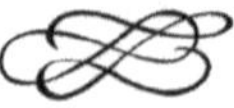

It was late afternoon when Desiree finally took a break from the arduous task of putting out fires and staving off creditors. Sitting back, stretching her back, she reflected on the previous night. Yes, it had been quite an evening, and she was even more positive that everything would work out. Talk about a fairytale romance. A young damsel in distress, rescued by a knight in white armor or a yellow bird! Desiree closed her eyes and relived the dream where her father put the yellow bird into his pocket! Maybe the answer was there all along.

The ringing phone interrupted Desiree's daydream. It was Jay. "Hello, beautiful. How's my favorite heiress."

"Very funny." But Desiree was smiling anyway. Only Jay could get away with such a comment.

"No trouble getting to Brooklyn this morning?"

"Only that I'm wearing the same clothes as yesterday! Haven't had to do *'the walk of shame'* since college! Lil certainly raised an eyebrow." They bantered in their usual style for a few minutes, and then Jay told her the specifics of his call. "I'm afraid I have to cancel lunch tomorrow, Des. I'm sorry, but something's come up, and I have to be at a meeting."

"Oh, boo. And I did want you to meet Janette."

"I'll be glad to accompany you two on your little weekend."

"No chance. This one is all ours. But why don't you come up to my house on Sunday? I'll be back by five."

"That's an offer I can't refuse. I'll see you then." "I'll miss you," Desiree whispered into the phone. "Des?"

"Hmmmm?"

"I love you." click.

Just as Desiree was hanging up the receiver, the other line rang. "Forget something?" Desiree laughed as she answered.

"What? Desiree, is that you?"

"Elliott! Oh, I'm sorry, I was just talking to Janette," she lied, "and I thought she forgot something. Hi. How are you?"

"Fine, thank you. " Elliott was all business. "Listen, I think you better come to my office tomorrow."

"Why? What happened?"

"The guy your father made the deal with has shown up!"

"What? That's wonderful! Who is he? What's his name? Where's he been?" "Hold on, Desiree. I don't know very much. I didn't talk to the guy. He called early this morning and left a message with Eva. He's the president of a company called Morton Enterprises, and he has a letter from your father selling him the invention, and he wants to meet with us."

"How much, Elliott? Did he say what Poppy sold it for?"

"No. I told you I didn't get a chance to talk with him. He'll be here at my office tomorrow at two o'clock if that's ok with you."

"I'll be there. Oh, Elliott, thank you, thank you. It's the answer to everything.

Thank God."

A few seconds later, Lil knocked and opened the door. "Sorry, Desiree, but I just picked up this message at reception. It must have come while you were out at lunch."

Lil handed her the pink message slip. Jay had called. Please call at this number: 555-410-3144.

"Oh, that's all right, Lil, no worries. I just spoke with him."

Lil left, and Desiree smiled, thinking about her conversation with Jay. She stared absent-mindedly at the phone number on the paper. Suddenly, the numbers registered very large to her eyes. 410-3144. It couldn't be! Desiree took her cell and scrolled through her address book. Under B, Jay Bennett, 410-3144. Then she pulled the file that held her father's papers out from under the stack of mail on the desk.

"This can't be." She had a terrible sense of doom. She quickly thumbed through the papers, looking for the scribbled yellow-lined paper that had the numbers with no names. "Damn," she swore under her breath, "where is it?"

She went back and started again. "I know it's here; I just read through the file the other day. Oh, right." Desiree looked to her right near the phone. She rummaged through the stack of files and papers she had piled there. Halfway down, she found it. Thumbing through it, she grabbed the paper. The first number had been Uncle Max. The second number was 410-3144!

"No!" Desiree felt her chest tighten and her breathing quicken. She looked again. There was no mistake. The number on the yellow sheet written in her father's hand was Jay's number. But why? Did her father know Jay? Why didn't Jay say so?

Desiree had another thought. She opened her purse again. Inside, she had the handwritten invitation that Jay had sent to her yesterday. She pulled the two letters from her father's file and compared the handwriting. They matched! What the…. there was no doubt. Jay Bennett knew about Poppy's invention! How did they ever meet? Was HE the secret buyer?

Desiree leaned back in her chair, staring into space. All the mysteries and questions began to form into an answer. She finally verbalized her thoughts. "That means Jay will be at the meeting tomorrow! And he canceled lunch with me, knowing he would see me there. What is going on? What's it all mean?"

Desiree rubbed her temples and laid her head down on her arms. She felt angry, betrayed, nervous, excited, and, least of all, hopeful. She tried to be optimistic. Remember the yellow bird, she told herself. Poppy had the yellow bird in his pocket. Surely, there was an explanation for it all.

The next day, at lunch with Janette, Desiree never stopped talking. She told her friend everything from the moment she met Jay until the call from Elliott late yesterday afternoon. Janette was incredulous.

"Your life never ceases to amaze me. I work in the most exciting industry in the world (Janette had her own PR Firm), and you, little Miss Conservative, with her children's drawings and family heirlooms, managed to put together a scenario that could have jumped off the pages of a Harold Robbins' novel."

Desiree laughed at the comparison and looked fondly at her best friend. She and Janette had known each other since college. Janette was as dark as Desiree was blonde and full of a no-nonsense attitude that comes from growing up too fast. Janette was an army brat. She was born in Germany, lived in England, Hawaii, Greece, Iran, and Texas, went to two grammar schools and three junior high and high schools, won a journalism award at the age of 19 for a story she did on Iran, and graduated suma cum laude.

Janette always told Desiree that they should switch names. "It really doesn't fit you," she had said during their first year at school. "You look like a Janette. I, on the other hand, am definitely the Desiree type!"

True to her statement, Janette was flamboyant, aggressive, assertive and constantly advising Desiree on the matters at hand, whether it be men, sex, business, clothes, or the best restaurant in town.

When it came to feelings, though, Janette was unshakable. She loved Desiree like a sister and would go to the ends of the world for her. The feelings were mutual; Desiree was the rock in Janette's crazy, often-times tumultuous life. Janette could come 'home' to Desiree; she was the port in the storm, the home-cooked meal, the mom waiting at the front door after school. Desiree and Janette were each other's alter egos. Together, they were an awesome duo.

As it was nearing two o'clock, Desiree and Janette finished up quickly and re-confirmed their plans to meet at Penn Station at five. They were taking the train to East Hampton, where Janette had a cottage near town. It wasn't on the beach, but it was hers, and it was private. The two women had shared many tears and much laughter at that little house.

"Well, good luck, Des. I can't wait to hear the next chapter of this story!"

Desiree looked at her watch. "God, I'm already 10 minutes late and a nervous wreck. Do I look all right?"

"Yes, you look gorgeous, as usual. Just remember, Des, don't lose your temper until you hear all the facts!" It was one of Desiree's worst traits, and Janette knew it well. She had been at the other end of Desiree's temper more than once.

"Right. Bye." Then she grabbed her purse and dashed off to hail a cab.

Traffic was horrendous, and by the time Desiree reached Elliott's office at Columbus Circle, she was 40 minutes late and feeling completely on edge. She didn't know how she was going to handle this meeting. She figured if Jay hadn't confided in her, then he certainly hadn't confided in Elliott. At least that was one less problem to worry about for now.

The receptionist at Grayson and Grayson welcomed Desiree with a big smile. "Hello, Miss O'Conner! Have you set the wedding date yet?"

Desiree stopped. Just like Elliott, to not let anyone know that anything was different. She was already testy, but she smiled politely.

"Hello, Helen. No, not yet." Then, she abruptly changed the subject. "I'm rather late for an appointment with Elliott. Are they in his office?"

"No, ma'am. In the conference room. I'll just let Mr. Grayson know you're here." She dialed the number. "Mr. Grayson, Miss O'Conner's here. Yes, sir. Right away."

"Go right in. You know the way?"

"Thank you." Desiree went through the big double glass doors and down the lushly carpeted hall. The conference room was on the left. As she opened the door, she heard a familiar laugh. Her heart skipped a beat. She'd know that laugh anywhere.

She saw Elliott on the far side of the big mahogany table. Then she saw the back of his head. There was his beautiful curly hair. Visions of the day on My DESIRE with the wind blowing his hair away from his face and of almost every minute of their growing, passionate and intimate relationship overwhelmed Desiree. He stood up as Elliott started making introductions.

"Desiree, this is…" the man turned around and held out his hand. His beautiful blue eyes were twinkling; he looked totally at ease and in control. Not only did he not seem embarrassed at facing Desiree like this, but he acted as if he was delighted at the whole situation.

"Morton Bennett of Morton Enterprises," continued Elliott. "He's the gentleman…" But Desiree didn't hear the rest. She just stood there and stared.

Face-to-face with Jay made her feel foolish. Foolish that she had played right into his hands. He must have been laughing behind her back the whole time. She obviously didn't mean a thing to him; he had had an elaborate game of post office, all at her expense. And to think she even asked him for help, "want to buy a bankrupt company," she had asked so innocently. Well, she wasn't going to play the fool any longer. She controlled her urge to turn and walk out of the room and used her anger to give her the courage and composure to play out this charade.

She held out her hand. "Why, Mr. Bennett, what an 'unexpected' surprise." Only Jay caught the double meaning in her words. "We had almost given up hope of finding the man my father sold his invention to."

"My pleasure, Miss O'Conner. And I do apologize for not getting in touch sooner." Was he trying to tell her something? Desiree felt a glimmer of hope. "I've been out of the country for a while, and there was still some paperwork to be completed before I could come forward."

Desiree's hopes were dashed as quickly as they had risen. She clenched her teeth; she wanted to scream. Obviously, Elliott knew nothing of their relationship. She continued to go along with it.

"So, Mr. Bennett. Let's get down to business." Desiree purposefully walked around the table and sat next to Elliott. She spoke slowly and with enormous self-control. "We are in the dark as to the details my father made with you. All we have had to go on are the two letters (which I have here) that Elliott has already discussed with you."

When Desiree went to sit with Elliott, the smile on Jay's face died. He could see the hurt and confusion in Desiree's eyes and sensed her absolute anger. His worst fears had been realized.

She was furious that he hadn't confided in her, and now, she undoubtedly felt betrayed. But for the sake of her father's wishes, he had no choice but to go on. "It's really quite simple. Your father sold me the water purification and filtration system that he invented, along with the full patent and all the rights for future modifications."

"That we know," offered Elliott. "But what Miss O'Conner is waiting for is the purchase price." Elliott had assumed his lawyer mode again and proceeded to protect his client. He had sensed a change in Desiree's mood since their conversation late yesterday afternoon. For some reason, Desiree did not like Morton Bennett. Elliott's protective attitude did not go unnoticed by Jay.

"It's all right here in these papers, signed by Miss O'Conner's father on February 9th," Jay passed copies to both Elliott and Desiree. He waited while they read them over. Suddenly, Desiree gasped.

"But this is for $75,000!"

"That's right. It's a very generous price since the Cranford experiment isn't completed yet. I told your father that I would be willing to pay much more if he waited until the final results were tabulated. But your father wanted to sell immediately."

"This is ludicrous!" Desiree's temper erupted like Mt. St. Helens. "Not three days ago, a company twice the size of yours, Brown and Ferris to be exact, offered me $100,000 for the same rights and admitted that it was worth at least three if not ten times that amount."

"And they're quite right. Your father was a genius, Miss O'Conner. And the closer you get to October and the end of the experiment, the more it will be worth to a buyer. But the bottom line is that your father sold me the rights."

"My father is dead. I'm the owner now."

"No, Des, I mean Miss O'Conner. You are not. This deal was signed, witnessed, and notarized prior to your father's death. It's all very legal."

"But Jay, you can't do this to me. You know what it means!"

Desiree hadn't even realized her faux paux. She had lost all of her composure. She was crushed. Jay had used her. Obviously, he didn't care for her at all. It would be very easy to negate the deal, but he had no intention of doing so. She had fallen hook, line, and sinker for his self-centered lies.

"Jay?" Elliott looked up quickly from studying the papers to see Jay, or rather Morton Bennett, and Desiree glaring at each other, oblivious of Elliott or anything else around them. Elliott saw the desolation in Desiree's face. She knew this man?

Jay reached across the table to touch her. "Desiree, I'm sorry. Who would have ever thought that we would meet."

She yanked her hand away as if burned. "What does that matter? You took advantage of a sick old man. You're a smart businessman! You know what that water system is worth. You used him, and then you used me."

"What's going on here! Who are you?" Elliott glared at Jay.

Desiree shot a sideward glance at Elliott. He could see the angry fire in her eyes. He knew that look; it was not one to be taken lightly. "Mr. Morton Jay Bennett is a very rich, very successful businessman who buys anything that can be of use to him," spit out Desiree. "He merges businesses, restructures them, and then sells them for a profit." Desiree couldn't stop. "Obviously, he got wind of Poppy's experiment and talked him into selling it. He'll use it to build up one of his own businesses and reap all the profits."

"80% of any profit earned from your father's invention, Desiree, goes back to his estate." Jay's voice was calm and maddeningly reassuring.

"Don't you understand, *Mr.* Bennett? There is no "estate," Desiree said sarcastically. P.O.C. and that water system were the only equity my father had.

P.O.C. is bankrupt, and you have the invention."

"Desiree," Elliott interrupted again. "How do you know this guy?"

Desiree broke down sobbing. "Because, Elliott, this is the man I fell in love with while I was away! This is the man I broke up with you for." Desiree gasped and looked in horror at Jay and Elliott.

"Oh, my God! What have I said." Tears streaming down her face, Desiree flew from the room, leaving Elliott and Jay glaring at each other.

If looks could kill, Elliott and Jay would have slaughtered each other on the spot. Hatred and absolute anger, all in Desiree's defense, left Elliott with a stone-cold expression. His blue eyes were the color of the grey carpet in the room, and he sat perfectly still, poised, and in control, eyeing Jay like a mountain lion, ready to pounce on its prey.

Jay stared back, equally cool. But inside, he was devastated. Desiree had run like a frightened deer, confused and broken-hearted. He knew she felt betrayed; if only he could take her in his arms right now and explain everything. But that would have to wait. Right now, he had to deal with Elliott.

Elliott broke the silence. His voice was low, cold, and unemotional. "Who the hell are you?"

"Like the lady said, I'm the man she fell in love with while she was away." Jay hated this tough guy act. But now he had to carry it through.

"You must have presented quite a different picture of yourself for that to have happened. She would never have fallen for a cheat and a liar."

"Look here, Grayson. I really don't care what you think. But here are the facts. I own O'Conner's invention. He sold it to me fair and square. I didn't lie or cheat anyone, least of all O'Conner. He approached me, and he set the price of the deal."

"That may be. But the man was eccentric and emotional. I can't believe you didn't know what you were being offered."

"I'm a good businessman. I know a good deal when I see one."

"So why didn't you just leave well enough alone? Why did you have to involve Desiree in it? Couldn't resist another deal? You want her inheritance, too?"

"Knock it off, Elliott. I don't need Desiree's inheritance. I never set out to involve her in this. Meeting her was an accident."

"Sure, it was. But boy, it really sweetened the pie when you found out who she was, didn't it?" Elliott's voice had risen about three octaves. His pupils were dilated, and poison was dripping from every word. For the first time in his life, he was beginning to lose control. He was clenching and unclenching his fists; sweat broke out on his brow.

"Desiree is my fiancée, Bennett. I love her more than anything in this whole world. And everything was going just fine before you came into the picture. We were planning our wedding when her father died."

He rose from his seat and started around the table, talking the whole time. "She was devastated over his death, and you just sucked up her emotions like a sponge. You played on her grief and seduced her into your plans."

Now, Jay stood up and faced Elliott face to face. His own self-pride couldn't take much more of this. He would protect O' Conner's confidence on the business side, but he refused to let this pompous ass think that he had abused and used Desiree to further his own desires.

"Look, here, Grayson, let's get two things straight. First, there's a lot more to this business deal with Pat O'Conner than either you or Desiree know. But I can't disclose the details."

"Convenient for you, isn't it?" Sneered Elliott.

Jay ignored him and continued. "It's not my decision. But in time, it will all be made clear. And you and Desiree will know the truth of the whole situation." "I can't wait. You know, you're really scum, Bennett." Elliott was beyond reasoning now. He was angry and hurt and felt totally vulnerable. It was bad enough that he had lost Desiree, but to a man like this was the final insult.

Jay continued, raising his voice in his own defense. "And second, whether you believe it or not, and quite frankly, I don't give a damn, I don't use women, period! Desiree was already doubting her feelings for you when I met her. All I did was give her an opportunity. I loved her from the moment I saw her, but I never pushed her into anything she didn't want. Desiree came to me of her own free will."

"Why, you…" suddenly, Elliott lost it all, rolled back his right arm and threw a punch that landed right in the center of Jay's right eye! "You son of a bitch… owww! " Elliott was shaking his hand, watching it swell. Jay fell back against the doors, totally stunned. The pain in his eye was excruciating.

"Are you nuts? You bastard!" Jay coiled his own fist back, instinctively ready to defend himself and then stopped mid-air.

And Desiree had said Elliott had no emotions. Ha! If she could see him now. Jay lowered his fist, muttering under his breath. Elliott was still standing in the same place, staring at Jay, lying against the door frame. He couldn't believe it either. He had never hit anyone in his life. "My God! I'm sorry, man. I really don't know what came over me."

"You have some swing, Grayson." Jay's eye was throbbing.

Elliott went to the phone and called his assistant. "Eva, bring in a towel and a bucket of ice. Now, please!" Then he went to the bar and took out a bottle of bourbon. Eva came in moments later. She gasped when she saw Jay and then again when she noticed Elliott's limp right hand.

"Eva, pour us a couple of drinks, please. And then leave us. And Eva… you won't say a word about this." She nodded as she poured two rather large portions into the crystal glasses. "Thank you."

As she left, Elliott pushed the towel and ice towards Jay. "Here, put some on your eye." Then he stuck his own hand down into the bucket, wincing as the cold numbed his broken skin.

For the next few minutes, there was complete silence in the room. Only the ticking of the grandfather's clock in the corner broke the quiet. Elliott and Jay continued to stare at each other with a newly formed mutual respect.

Finally, with all of his former composure, Elliott raised his glass to Jay. "To Desiree."

"To Desiree." Echoed Jay.

CHAPTER 26

Janette poured Desiree another glass of wine. Desiree's eyes were swollen and red, and her nose was raw from where the Kleenex had scraped at least a hundred times. A pile of the crumbled white fluff lay at Desiree's feet, on the table and by her side. She sat curled in a ball, feet tucked up under her with Janette's favorite blue afghan wrapped around her. She smiled weakly at Janette as she accepted the glass.

Desiree had managed incredible self-control during the train ride out to East Hampton, but once they reached the seclusion of Janette's little cottage, her emotional dam broke all barriers. She ranted and raved, making no sense for well over an hour. Words spewed forth, tumbling over each other in rampant confusion. But, finally having cried herself out, she was trying to put some sense of order into the chain of events of the last month.

"Men are Pigs!" declared Desiree disdainfully. "To hell with them! There isn't a decent one in the bunch. Pompous, self-righteous, egotistical, chauvinistic, obnoxious, stubborn, conceited… did I leave anything out?"

"Only worthless, vain, good-for-nothing, fickle, womanizing scums of the earth!"

Desiree added. "Don't forget underhanded, childish, greedy, manipulative, and genuine creep."

"I'll drink to that." Janette took a sip of her wine, contemplating Desiree. Finally, she said, "So how come we love them so much?"

"I don't love anyone."

"Oh, yes, you do. You're in love with Jay Bennett, hook, line, and sinker. If you weren't, this wouldn't hurt so much."

"Janette, please," Desiree protested. "This isn't the time to discuss this."

"Oh, yes, it is. It's the perfect time. Because right now, you can really be totally objective. Your defenses are down, and you are completely vulnerable."

"That's the worst time."

"Not for affairs of the heart. Trust me, I know."

Well, all I know is that I never want to see the man again."

"That's not true, either. If he walked through that door right now, you'd be putty in his hands."

"Wrong."

"So, you'd rather be with Elliott."

"I didn't say that." Desiree got up from the couch and went over to the big window that had been left open for earlier breezes and eased it shut, shivering. She peered out through the trees, staring towards the old dirt road that led to the beach. Though the sun was gone, dusk hadn't quite settled into night, and she could still see the outlines, though muted, of the tall trees that protected the house from sightseers.

Outside, Desiree could see the still bare branches swaying slightly in the spring breeze. The crisp smell of other people's fireplaces drifted through the ocean air. It was so peaceful here this time of year, so secure. After hours of emotional upheaval, Desiree was beginning to relax. She rolled her head back and forth over her shoulders and kneaded the back of her neck.

Janette watched quietly from her chair across the room, waiting patiently for her friend to continue.

"What was I thinking?" Desiree finally confessed. "I slept with him, Janette. More than once. The man told me he loved me…. on the beach." Janette gasped, "You made love on the beach?"

Desiree turned around. She tried to put all the pieces together. "No, no, no – not there! But that was when he told me he loved me – the first time. We were on the beach. It was beautiful, lonely, so pure. We only kissed, then. God, I wanted more, and so did he. But we didn't. And I was so torn. Why did I want more? Then…after I broke up with Elliott – that's when we made love for the first time. It started the first night we met – the electricity between us. It was crazy. The feelings, the expectations, a mounting tension between us every time we were together. Then two weeks ago…. finally…it was so right." Desiree paused, remembering. "Twice…. the first time in my house, then a few days later in his. Janette, it was magical. So spontaneous. So erotic. So incredibly, absolutely fantastic! He took me to places I've never been before! He was gentle, then aggressive, romantic, then playful; he challenged my own inhibitions…. oh, God Janette…."

"You know, " Desiree continued with a weak smile on her lips, "that's the irony of this whole thing. Jay made me realize that I definitely don't and didn't love Elliott. Probably never did. And now, Jay turns out to be a rotten, low-down liar and cheat."

"You don't know that." "I know what I heard."

"Desiree, now you listen to me. Once again, you've let your damn temper control your emotions, and you stormed out of that meeting before you heard the whole story. There's got to be more to this than what you think you know. Give your father some credit, Girl. He might have been sick and dying, but you know as well as I do that he was perfectly coherent. He was working with a full deck right up to the end, and there's no way in hell he would have denied you your inheritance."

"But, Janette, nothing makes sense. He sold Jay Bennett the invention for only $75,000. Why? Why did Poppy do that? If he was so aware of things, why didn't he know it was already worth more than $200,000?"

"Maybe he did. Maybe there's more to this deal than you've allowed yourself to hear. You've been so caught up with getting enough money to pay off those creditors that maybe you haven't seen the old forest for the trees."

"OK. Fine. Maybe. But that doesn't excuse Jay for using me. He knew all along who I was and never told me a thing. None of this would ever have happened if he had confided in me in the beginning."

Desiree's voice cracked with emotion; her eyes filled with tears. "Oh, God, Janette. What am I going to do? You're right. I love him."

"Oh, Des." Janette took her friend in her arms and hugged her. "You've got to talk to him. Swallow that Irish pride of yours and give him a chance to explain."

"I don't know. He'll have to come to me. He owes me that much." "Desiree. Don't be stubborn."

"He's insulted me and my family. He can come to me."

"I love you, Des. But you're a fool. And if you're not careful, you're going to miss out on what may be the best thing that ever happened to you. You have nothing to lose by going to Jay and asking him for the truth. And you have everything to gain."

Desiree looked at Janette and knew she was speaking the truth. But she hated to admit it. It was, indeed, her pride, and it had been the cause of many misunderstandings throughout her life.

"I'll see." Desiree finally conceded. "I'll think about it. Now, I'm starving.

What shall we eat?"

Janette burst out laughing. "Oh…. Desiree O'Conner…. I DO love you! But you never change! And I love that, too! If I was as depressed as you, I'd die of starvation! Let's go! Down to Luigi's for a plate of pasta."

"My treat." Desiree offered graciously. "You deserve it after listening to me all night."

CHAPTER 27

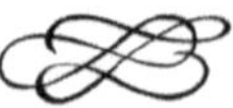

The two days passed uneventfully. Janette and Desiree had a great "girl" weekend, shopping and antiquing and catching up on the news of the last three months, including the scoop on Janette's new beau.

Janette had been very closed-mouthed about Ted Harris but was now ready to admit that 'things were progressing nicely.' But she was treading very carefully in this relationship, having been burned too many times.

On Saturday night, they went down to Willies, the regular "hang out" for the local set. Dark, pubby, with green checkered tablecloths and memorabilia on the walls, a visit to Willies was like going to a class reunion. Janette knew just about everyone and, as usual, had an entire collection of anecdotes that kept her audience in stitches.

Saturday night was bandstand night; the only person missing was Dick Clark (rest his soul). But Rory Ralbutton, the local rock and roll mavin, more than made up for the icon's absence. Rory's band played everything anyone could dance to, and Janette and Desiree didn't want for partners. They danced till their feet hurt and didn't get home until after two.

* * *

Sometime in the early morning, before dawn, Desiree opened her eyes to see a yellow bird sitting at the foot of her bed. The little bird cocked its head to the left, to the right. "What is it?" crooned Desiree. A sweet chirping came from its tiny body as if the bird was telling her something. "Tell me. What are you trying to tell me?" The little bird hopped down onto the covers, making its way up through the mounds of the comforter, disappearing and then reappearing, continually chirping its sweet song. Finally, the bird settled on Desiree's chest. Gently, she stroked its little head and was amazingly comforted by the touch. The feathers were soft. Desire cupped her hands together, picked up the little bird, and held it close to her heart. She felt a calmness wash over her as she fell back into a deep sleep.

* * *

When she woke a few hours later, Desiree's hands were cupped on her chest. Startled, she opened them wide, but of course, they were empty. She closed her eyes again as she tried to revive the dream. It was so real, so vivid, and her feelings were equally intense. She shivered with the memory, but she wasn't afraid or freaked out. She had a distinct sense of resolve. She must call Lil later.

Throughout the weekend, during the quiet hours, Desiree sat lost in thought about Jay and the overwhelming situation she found herself in. Over and over again, she imagined his kisses, her own passions sending pangs of desire through her belly. When she closed her eyes, she saw the little stretch of beach and felt the sun beating on her back; then she would smile as she relived the rollicking melodramatic chase through her house that ended in a totally unexpected, romantic and erotic "slumber party" in front of a roaring fire. No man can be that at ease, that unassuming, that flexible, that open with his feelings, and with just a touch, a look, make a woman feel the way Jay made her feel and not love her in return.

Then why, Jay, why? Desiree asked herself over and over again. Why didn't you trust me? Or are you really using me as part of your own little deal? Desiree kept tormenting herself first by remembering his looks, his touch, and their sincere and open conversations, and then by doubting Jay's motives. I have to stop this, she finally said to herself. Call him. And then Desiree remembered that Jay was supposed to come to her house on Sunday…. OMG, tonight!??? Surely, he won't come after what happened on Friday? He can't possibly think that everything is fine? Now, Desiree had one more thing to worry about.

Desiree didn't arrive home til 8:00. The whole way home, she debated over whether Jay would be there, whether he had come and then left again, or left a message, or whether he would call or whether she should call him. She finally decided not to decide.

But everything at home was just as she left it. There was nothing. No messages, No flowers. She had to admit to herself that she had hoped there might be something, some gesture of an apology.

Turning on the lights, Desiree was only reminded of the last time Jay had been there. In the evening light, like it had been the night of the storm, in every corner of every room, she was reminded of his touches, his whispers, his laughter. The memories sent goosebumps up and down her spine once more. And their "date" in the city, the carriage ride, dinner, the romance, and the unexpected and spontaneous night in his arms. It was like a love song filled with passion and anticipation of a future. Everything had seemed so right. Now, all she felt was a disquieting emptiness. All the fun and all the romance had gone out of her heart. Finally, she ran a bath and sunk down into the bubbles. This was her favorite thinking spot. Whether she was depressed or elated, Desiree found her bubble baths the best place to put things in perspective. Only a few days ago, she had pondered over her dreams of the yellow bird. How fascinating, she had thought. All the clues to our own desires and needs are locked up in our subconscious. She had been unhappy with Elliott, and the yellow bird helped her accept it. She had been falling in love with Jay, and the yellow bird pointed that out, too. Somewhere in their brief relationship, there must have been some hint, some clue that Poppy had known Jay Bennett, for the yellow bird was trying to make her see that as well. She kept trying to fly with the yellow bird, and she kept trying to recognize the truth and accept it. And just the other night, she held the yellow bird to her heart.

According to Lil, the yellow bird was symbolic of everything in her life right now, from her innermost fears and frustrations to her hopes and dreams. The little bird is her spiritual guide, taking on many roles to help her recognize the truth, understand and trust what's around her, and even to help strengthen her confidence and to believe in herself, that she is wise enough and strong enough to prevail. Was Jay the yellow bird? Was it really that simple? Did he hold the answers to her quest for the truth, for her entire destiny?

Here, with the hot water up to her chin, floating in the old tub like a baby in a womb, she realized her desires, her hopes, and her dreams. She needed him, to see him, to touch him. Even if her worst fears were to be confirmed, any kind of confrontation with Jay, even a fight, would be better than nothing.

"Face it, kid," she said to herself. "Janette's right. You're hopelessly in love with the jerk."

Suddenly, her cell phone rang, breaking the silence and Desiree's reverie. "Where's my phone??. Jay! Damn it! What lousy timing. Why do they always call when I'm either on the john or in the tub!" One ring… two rings… three rings…

She grabbed a big terry towel, wrapping it quickly around her. Dripping water and bubbles across the floor, she ran into the bedroom, around the bed, and grabbed her phone from the nightstand. The call disconnected.

"Damn! Damn! Damn!" Desiree flopped down on the bed, feeling tears well up in her beautiful blue eyes. "Now stop this, Desiree. It was probably the wrong number anyway." She checked the call log.

But it wasn't the wrong number. Jay put down the phone, equally disappointed. He had been calling all day. It usually went straight to voice mail. This time, it connected. Maybe he should send a text. Why didn't she answer the phone? Why? He knew the answer. "She's probably putting pins in a voodoo doll right now," he said dejectedly to himself.

All weekend, and even now, as he lay stretched out on his big bed, he kept thinking back to Friday, reliving that horrendous scene in Elliott's office. What a fool he'd been. He thought he knew Desiree so well. He figured she'd be annoyed, but he never expected the full wave of emotions that he witnessed in that brief half hour.

"She loves me," he said aloud with a matter-of-fact tone. He was both elated and saddened at the same time. "She loves me, and she thinks I've betrayed her."

Never had he anticipated Desiree's overwhelming sense of betrayal. The hurt he saw in her eyes as she ran from the room burned him to the quick. He had felt her pain and was so helpless. If only he had grabbed her and held her and soothed her anguish. But he didn't, and now the damage was done.

"God, this whole thing is a mess." He rubbed his head tiredly, suddenly wincing as his hand grazed his right eye. Slowly, he got up and went to the mirror and looked again at Elliott's signature. The eye was three shades of purple, yellow, and green and still swollen shut. It would be weeks before it would be back to normal.

Jay sighed and decided to get to sleep early. Tomorrow, he has to start the second part of his agreement with Pat O'Conner. He had to follow it through, and now, the quicker, the better. His only hope was that, eventually, Desiree would let him explain and that she would understand.

Jay turned out the light and stretched tiredly under the covers. Light from the street lights sifted through the slats in the shutters, throwing long lines across the opposite wall. In these last moments before sleep, Jay thought about Desiree. He could smell her perfume, so soft and flower-like, and feel the silkiness of her hair. He smiled as he remembered her laugh and then shuddered as he relived her temper.

"A sobering thought," he said to himself and concentrated again on his plans for tomorrow. Somehow, he had to get hold of P.O.C.'s accounts, payables, and receivables. Now, with Desiree on the warpath and Lil, no doubt on her side, it was a formidable challenge.

CHAPTER 28

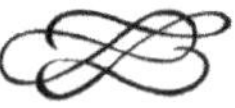

Monday morning was rainy and cold. It felt more like fall than spring, and it contributed nothing to Desiree's mood. She woke up cranky, plagued with her period and an ache in her neck that ran all the way down to the middle of her back. Obviously, she had slept wrong. That's probably what had given her the nightmare. Sometime in the middle of the night, she had awakened with a start. She had felt frightened, and the sheets and her nightgown were soaked. Now, she reached over to the table and looked at what she had written. It was the yellow bird again.

* * *

Desiree was walking in her garden when she found a nest in the rose bushes. At first, she thought the nest was empty. Then she noticed that deep inside were three little baby birds, all a beautiful bright yellow. When they saw her, they started to cry for their mother. Desiree looked up into the sky. There was the mother yellow bird sitting high on the peak of the roof. Then, the bird took flight, leaving the babies in the nest. They cried and screeched for hours, but the mother never came back. Desiree had become hysterical and tried to comfort the baby birds. Then, as quickly as she had found the birds, they all disappeared.

* * *

The dream haunted her all morning. She kept thinking about it as she showered and made coffee. She watered her plants, dusted the furniture, and vacuumed her rugs. Try as she might, she couldn't understand it. Finally, she called Lil.

"Lil, these yellow birds are driving me to the nut house! They're going to come and take me away!" Desiree expounded as soon as Lil picked up the phone.

Lil chuckled. "So, these dreams are getting to you, are they? Is my favorite skeptic becoming a believer?"

"All right, Lil, so you've convinced me, sort of. All I know is that these damn birds are ruining my beauty sleep!"

"So what happened last night." Lil was all ears.

First, Desiree told her about the dream from the other morning when the little bird sat on her chest, and she held it to her heart. Then she read to Lil exactly what she had written down from the night before.

"Ummmm." Lil was taking notes as she listened. Finally, she said, "OK, Desiree. I'll have to check on this. I'll call you when I get home tonight, OK? Are you coming in today?"

"No. I'll be in on Wednesday as usual. I've got to work on the illustrations, or I'm going to lose the contract."

"You haven't mentioned the meeting on Friday. What happened? I've been dying to talk to you all weekend."

"Don't ask!" "That bad?"

"Worse. Lil?" Desiree took a deep breath. "Yes, dear?"

"Jay Bennett is the guy who bought the rights to Poppy's invention." "Jay Bennett? *Your* Jay Bennett?"

"The one and only." "Well, I'll be damned!"

"That's an understatement." "But that's marvelous!"

"Are you crazy?"

"It's a hell of a coincidence, your father choosing to sell his invention to the man you've fallen in love with? Desiree, if that isn't fate, I don't know what is." "Lil! The man's a cheat and a liar. He bought the water system, knowing what it's worth, for $50,000! Then, when he met Me, hey, what a bonus!" "Desiree! What are you saying?"

"Lil, are you dense? He used Poppy, then he used me." "How did he use you?"

"He played on my emotions. He knew all along I was Poppy's daughter, and he never told me. There I was, like a love-sick puppy, sharing my innermost feelings with him. And to make matters worse, I...." Desiree stopped short of telling Lil she had slept with him...twice. Desiree felt another piece of her heart break off as she remembered their last night together. She ached with embarrassment and a feeling of betrayal.

"And then, when I walked into Elliott's office, he played as if he never saw me before in his life!"

"Desiree, there must be more to this. I know you, and I know what you've told me about Jay. I can't believe you would fall in love with a man if he was the creep you describe."

"Haven't you ever heard of con men, Lil?"

"He's not a con man. Not from what you've told me. Con-men aren't that good. Believe me."

"Lil, you weren't there."

"I don't care, Desiree. Call it my sixth sense. I still think you're missing something."

"Well, you do have a point about that…your sixth sense. Anyway, I still want to know about my dreams."

"Of course. I'll call you later." "Bye!"

Desiree went upstairs and stood staring into the drawers of her dresser, trying to decide what to wear. It was an old habit that had started when she was only four years old. Whenever she was cranky or sad, Desiree's mother would find her gazing into her closets. "Are you looking for answers in there?" her mother would ask sympathetically.

Desiree would laugh and eventually come out with some outlandish outfit on, realizing only years later that she had been looking for the proverbial security blanket. For her, when her mood was blue, or she was sick, or tired, or feeling sorry for herself, there was nothing like an old flannel nightgown, a favorite cotton shirt, or a pair of big fuzzy slippers to blanket her emotions.

"Ah," Desiree finally said to herself. From the very bottom of the drawer, she pulled out an old pair of grey sweatpants and a matching grey sweatshirt. They were far too baggy, and the string was long gone, but they fit her mood and the color of the day. Then she wrapped her hair up on top of her head and, with her cup of coffee and her favorite chocolate donut, settled down in her studio to work on the illustrations.

It was as drab and grey in the studio as it was outside, even with all the lights on. The sun was totally lost behind the clouds, and little specks of drizzle had started to beat against the window. Desiree usually liked days like this, finding them cozy and pleasantly melancholy. But today, it was just downright depressing. She kept staring out the window, looking for a glimmer of sunlight, wishing she could just close this chapter of her life.

An hour later, she found herself doodling pictures of birds with broken wings and baby birdies with their little mouths open to the sky. Amid the sketches, she found her own handwriting, "Mrs. Jay Bennett," "Desiree Bennett," "D. O'Conner Bennett," "Mr. and Mrs. Morton Bennett," "Desiree and Jay Bennett."

"Damn him! He permeates my entire life." She took the pencil and scratched everything out. Just then, her phone rang.

"Hello?"

"I was right!"

"What? Lil? Is that you?"

"Yes, I was right! You are definitely missing something in all of this intrigue!" Desiree laughed. "What are you talking about?"

"You're dreams, dearie, your dreams. Are you ready for this?" "Lil, where are you? I thought you went to work today?"

"I did, I did. But I was so intrigued with your dreams, and there really isn't much happening here today. I took a few minutes to do research on Google."

"You're unbelievable." Desiree laughed in spite of her mood. "I'm all ears. Just give me two minutes. OK?" Desiree grabbed her cup and ran down the stairs to the kitchen, pouring herself another cup of coffee. Putting her phone on speaker, she curled up on the couch with her cup.

"OK, I'm back."

"First off, your dreams of yellow birds are escalating, becoming more frequent. It's actually quite common when the dreamer is feeling scared or unsure of herself. Think about it…. with everything happening so fast – your father's illness and death, and the discovery of his secrets and mismanagement at POC. Meeting Jay, acting on your doubts about Elliott. And now, I'm finding out about Jay's involvement in it all. It's a tangled web, and you, my dear friend, are right smack in the middle of it all! You are facing enormous challenges and decisions. You can cave in, or you can rise to the occasion. Most people would just throw up their hands and surrender to the fates. But you and I both know you're not a quitter."

"Thanks for the confidence, Lil. I'm not feeling very encouraged. I'm exhausted and worn out. It's like I was never in St Martin…. where is that girl now?"

"Cheer up, Dearie! I firmly believe that your dreams are all quite positive. The recurring visions in different places and the roller coaster feelings you experience in the dreams are normal. The birds are simply telling you in many different ways that you're stronger than you think. So.... the little bird who visited you in your bed? And how you end up cradling it in your hand, over your heart? I love this one! That little bird brought you some peace and made you calm. Smoothing its feathers on its little head was a gentle, loving gesture. Very, very positive. You showed your inner self to yourself. It was full of reassurance and a reminder – for you - of who you are. You needed that dream, and so it was."

Desiree felt goosebumps rise up and down her arms and shivered slightly in her cozy room.

"Desiree, you there? Are you alright? Shall I go on?"

"Yes, of course. I'm sorry. I'm just thinking about what you said."

"Ok. In the second dream about the baby birds.... I think your yellow birds in this one are only yellow because that's what you expect. In this one, the color really has nothing to do with the message. But the baby birds are very important. By the way, were the roses blooming on the bushes?"

"Ah…" Desiree searched her memory. "yes, they were. They were magnificent.

But I don't remember their color."

"That doesn't matter either. Roses traditionally mean love between a man and a woman. Now, the first time you saw the baby birds when they were just sitting in the nest, that could have to do with successful business dealings – everything is steady, wrapped up, in its place. Perhaps it's about your illustrations and your own career. But, since the nest is in the rose bush, I'm sure it's more about your relationship with Jay."

"What do you mean?" Desiree asked cautiously. "Because of the thorns?" she finished sarcastically.

"No," Desiree could feel Lil smiling through the phone. "Just the opposite.

Successful business dealings between lovers."

"Nonsense. Lil, you're reading too much into this. I've told you too many details. I think your crystal ball is cloudy."

"Hmph…You say nonsense." Lil was not to be discouraged. "I say it's right there in your dream. You have to look harder, Desiree. I really believe the answer is there."

"What about the birds?" Desiree's interest, though skeptical, was still peaked. "Oh, that's the easy part. The fact that the birds start screaming for their mother and are eventually deserted is completely symbolic of your feelings right now. Your father, his invention, and his eccentric business dealings with Jay have caused you great anxiety. Everything that's happening now is the result of your father's actions. Those little birds are deserted in your dream because you feel deserted and alone. Desiree? Are you there?"

''Yes…. yes…I'm here." Desiree had tears in her eyes, and her voice was choked. Poppy *had* deserted her, and she did feel so vulnerable.

"Desiree, honey. It will all work out. I just know it, I wish I was there with you. I'd give you a hug."

"I could use one." Desiree smiled into the phone. "But I'll be ok. Thanks, Lil. I'll see you on Wednesday."

"Call me if you need me."

"Of course."

Desiree went back up to the studio. Suddenly, the thunder roared through the sky, bringing sharp stabs of lightning to brighten the garden. Rain pelted down, beating against the sides of the house from every angle. Soon, Desiree couldn't even see out the windows. A heavy mist seemed to rise from the flower beds where the rain flattened the tiny blossoms trying to push through the dirt. The storm only lasted a few minutes, and when it cleared and the sun pushed its hazy rays out from behind the clouds, the whole world seemed brighter.

This time, when Desiree sat down to work, she managed to complete three entire illustrations. Unconsciously, she included a little yellow bird in the context of each drawing. Later that week, when she submitted them to Poppins, he would be ecstatic with her creativity. "There is something very personal in these drawings, my dear," he would say. But he would never be able to put his finger on exactly what it was.

For the rest of the afternoon, Desiree refined her drawings, glad of no further interruptions. She kept waiting with half an ear for the phone to ring, hoping it would be Jay. But his call never came.

Not that he didn't try. During the day, his schedule was hectic, running all over the city, visiting a few sites and working on his plans for securing the accounts from P.O.C. But every hour or so, he always managed to text or call Desiree's cell. No response, straight to voicemail. In the old days, people could call an operator and have them check the connection. Some things were just better then.

Jay looked grimly at the phone in his hand, this time letting his frustration and guilt turn to annoyance. "Damn her. What kind of game is she playing? Tit for tat?" Then he reigned in his hostility. "Whoa, guy. What right do you have to be annoyed at her?"

Jay felt so alone. His normal response to a crisis would be to man it out, but this was different. He never could have foreseen how this deal and the promise he made would isolate him so much. He needed a sounding board. Picking up his phone again, he punched in the name of his partner and best bud. Dave had met Pat O'Conner several times – they had all gone fishing together in Cranford, and of course, he knew of the deal, though not of the mounting intrigue.

"Hey, guy, how 'ya doin? I'm heading over to The Hole…can I buy you a beer?"

"Hey, Jay, yeh, sure…. what's up? Where you've been these last couple of days?"

"Sorry, I didn't mean to be evasive…. but I'll fill you in. See you in a few." When Dave arrived, Jay was halfway through his beer. "Hope you don't mind I started without you." He turned to face his friend.

"What the hell?" Dave gasped when he saw Jay's eye. "Care to elaborate?" he said as he smothered a grin. "You're a little old for playground fights, aren't you?"

"Very funny." Jay motioned to the bartender, holding up two fingers while downing the rest of his drink.

"So, give…" Dave took a swig of his own as the bartender went to another customer.

"Geez, man, I'm in so over my head. I think I've really fucked up what could be the best thing that ever happened to me. It's turned into a total nightmare."

"So wait…back up. Who and what are we talking about?" "That crazy old man… O'Conner's secret deal."

"The water filtration deal?" "Yeh, it's turned into a circus."

"Who punched you?" Dave stared at Jay's eye, wincing. "His lawyer."

"What? When… and why?"

"Jealousy. He… the lawyer…thinks I slept with O'Conner's daughter and cheated her out of her inheritance."

"What the… hey… you better start at the beginning." Dave held up his hand to the bartender and ordered two more.

Starting with the night Desiree sauntered into the bar at Las Palmas, Jay began an accounting of the events leading up to his black eye. He told his friend everything – what she looked like, her beautiful eyes, her hair, how he felt when he looked at her. He described her style, her passion, her love of food, and her fiery Irish temper! He recounted how they both love old movies, antiques, and heirlooms and her passion, kindness, and unwavering loyalty to friends and family. 'She's wicked smart,' he continued, 'witty, funny, with a quirky sense of humor. And a talented artist to boot, an illustrator with a bright future. Most of all, she's determined to save her father's company, not for herself but for the people who work there. She's convinced, Jay told his friend, that despite her father's "creative funding" of his inventions, he would never have put his daughter and his employees in jeopardy. "She's convinced," Jay confessed, "her father had a plan."Holding back his comments, Dave went from being incredulous to totally impressed with his friend's narrative. "So, this girl, this smart, gorgeous, ingenious woman you met, is O'Conner's daughter? What are the odds!"

"No shit."

"And she broke off her engagement with this guy Elliott, who happens to be O'Conner's lawyer and fell in love with you?" "Exactly, except I'm pretty sure she hates me now."

"Because she now knows you bought her father's company AND the rights to the filtration system?" Dave laughed, shaking his head in disbelief. "Damn, Jay, you can't make this shit up!"

Jay nodded grimly, his lips tightening in resolve. "Like I said, I'm in so over my head here. I love her, Dave, and I want to tell her everything. And

I feel so guilty. I just hate the lies. She deserves the truth. But… I promised O'Conner. I'm sure he never foresaw me meeting his daughter. Talk about fate. This whole crazy, convoluted deal, including her future, depends on me seeing it through." "My friend, you are caught between the proverbial rock and a hard place.

But you know the answer. You gave your word. Your honor's at stake here. Your integrity and the promise you made to her father, and indirectly to her. From what you've said, she has the same values. And if everything you told me is true about her, once she knows the whole story, she'll understand. But ironically, if you break any part of that promise, if you don't see this through exactly the way he wanted, she'll find out….and you, my friend, will definitely lose her because she'll never, ever trust you."

And for the second time in several days, two men raised their glasses and toasted, "To Desiree!"

CHAPTER 29

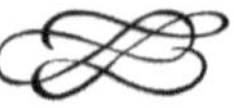

That night, the yellow bird soared high above the earth, diving and climbing again until it landed on the sand. There was Poppy, in his baggy old corduroys, standing on the far shore of a vast river flowing in front of him. He whistled to the bird. The bird took flight, and when it landed on his finger, he put it in his pocket and smiled. Then he said, 'Desiree, the bell is ringing.... the bell is ringing.... the bell is ringing.'

Suddenly, Desiree was awake. She heard a bell ringing loudly in her ear. She shook off the dream and became conscious that the bell wasn't a dream. Her cell was vibrating and ringing beside her bed.

Fumbling in the dark, she finally answered it. "Hello?" Silence.

"Hello?" she repeated. "Desiree. It's me…Jay."

Reacting on reflex, Desiree curled up, fetus-like, under the covers, pulling the pale pink sheet up around her ears. With her eyes closed, she cradled the phone with one hand, unconsciously clenching the other. She had known his voice immediately. She had dreamed it a hundred times, rehearsing what she would say if and when he called. Now, all her words were gone.

"I know." She finally said quietly and waited. Her heart was pounding. She opened her eyes and stared into the dark. The moment was excruciatingly long. Desiree loved him. She knew it without any doubt. But the pain of feeling betrayed and used was more than she could bear. She wanted to blurt it all out, to rant and rave and scream. But instead, she waited, hoping and praying for an explanation.

Jay grimaced at her silence, at her incredible self-control. He felt like a little boy caught stealing money from his mother's purse to buy her a birthday gift. No explanation would make it right without breaking a secret, jeopardizing the pledge he had made.

"Des, I know how you must feel. Believe me, I never wanted you to be hurt. I thought everything could be taken care of before you found out who I was."

"Stop it, Jay. You're making things worse. I don't want your apologies. I want the truth." Desiree squeezed her eyes tight to keep the quiver out of her voice. But despite her attempts at self-control, Jay could sense her struggle. He wanted to be with her, to hold her. Instead, he took a deep breath and tried again.

"Desiree, please, listen to me. You don't have to say anything. Just listen. I love you. I feel absolutely terrible about what happened on Friday (in more ways than one, he thought as he touched his eye). I've been trying to call you since Sunday night!... thought your phone was broken, or worse... you blocked my calls."

"I know." Desiree felt a glimmer of hope. So he *did* try to call. That must have been him last night while I was in the tub and all day today while the phone was on silent. "Thank you for that. It was an accident," she continued. "I turned the phone off while I was working today. But I'm here now. I'm listening."

"I love you," he repeated. "I'll say it a hundred times! I fell in love with you the moment I saw you. And when I found out you were Pat O'Conner's daughter, I loved you even more. It was better than fate that we met."

"So, why didn't you tell me you knew my father. Why didn't you tell me about the water system and about the money?"

"I couldn't, Des. I can't." "Why?"

"Because I couldn't," he said with finality. "And I can't tell you why I couldn't."

"Well, what can you tell me?" Desiree asked sarcastically.

Jay continued calmly. "That I admired your father. That he was a shrewd and brilliant man. That he loved you ...and loves you still...more than you know. And that he trusted me. And so should you."

"Trust you? Why? You've given me absolutely no reason for that. For all I know, you're just a very, very good con man. Why, this whole conversation might be part of your scam!"

"Desiree, it's not. I am the one and only Jay Bennett. I'm the man your father struck a deal with. The man you met at Los Palmas. The man who kissed you on that deserted piece of beach. The very same man *you* kissed, laughed with, and danced with, caressed, touched and..."

"Stop it, Jay." She felt herself weakening.

Jay persisted. "…and fell in love with." He finished. "You are in love with me, aren't you?"

Desiree sat straight up in bed. He was not going to lure her into submission. She deserved the truth, and she was going to get it. She took a deep breath, and with all the fortitude she could muster, she laid down her ultimatum. "This conversation has gone far enough. I have nothing more to say to you. If you can ever come to me and tell me the entire truth, then… we can talk about love. But not now. And certainly not under these circumstances."

"Desiree, I promise you, it will all become very clear very soon. I love you, and I will take care of you forever, one way or another. Remember that. Goodnight, my sweet Desire. Sleep well."

CHAPTER 30

The following morning at his office, somewhat boosted by his conversation with his friend and partner Dave, Jay sat with his head in his hands, staring at the desk and the document before him – Pat O'Conner's directive, including details of their final conversation, written three days before he died, immediately after Jay's last visit with his friend. The deal was simple, at least on the surface:

You buy POC for $1.00 – I'll sign a Quit Claim deed over to you.

In return, you pay back all POC's creditors – <u>anonymously.</u> No one, absolutely no one, is to know where the money is coming from. *'I was going to give you copies of the debts, but now there's no time for me to get them to you,' he had said. 'You're a clever lad. You'll figure out how to get to them.' Jay grimaced at the thought. The requirements continued:*

I sell you the invention & patent at its current value of $75,000. When the full value is established after the final EPA review, all future profits and ongoing proceeds belong to you and to my daughter: 80/20. Desiree gets 80%. You get 20%. No one, not even my daughter, is to know any of the details of this deal until it's complete. *'Promise?' Pat had held out his now thin hand, gripping the young man's in sincerity, and with a humorous twinkle in his voice, 'Ye know this could get a bit prickly? Are Ye in?'*

At the time, Pat's terms were intriguingly challenging and a once-in-a-lifetime chance to help the old man save his reputation and honor. Now, the whole deal, especially the promise, only served to haunt him. And falling in love with the man's daughter? That's just too, too much. How the hell did fate deal with these cards? Couple that with the fact that Desiree and everyone else now know I'm the buyer of the filtration system. And on top of it all, just the icing on the cake, Des and Elliott think I'm a scam artist.

"How on earth do I get to those books? What was I thinking?" he mused aloud. "Aside from the fact I own the rights to Pat's invention, I can't reveal the rest. I gave my word. What does Des know?" he continued aloud to himself. "Nothing…she knows nothing, or she still wouldn't be so pissed at me. Hmmm. Elliott's still managing the deal, the paperwork… he must know who the creditors are…but he's certainly not going to help me. I can't even ask…but what if …. no…that's not good…. and I can't tell him either…. does Des know what Elliott doesn't know? Unlikely. Unless…. hmmm… alright…let me think…. I need a plan." About an hour later, a clever, if not wily, idea lit up Jay's mood as a grin spread over his face.

First thing Wednesday morning, the office phone on Lil's desk lit up.

"Good morning, POC Outfitters, Lil speaking."

"Good morning. May I speak with Desiree O'Conner, please," asks a male voice.

"I'm sorry. She's not in today. What's this in reference to? Can I take a message?"

"Oh, when will she be in? It's important." "Who's asking?"

"Oh…yes…of course…. or maybe you can help me." He had a slight accent – British? Australian? Lil couldn't tell.

"My name's Sparrow from Elliott Grayson's office. Jack Sparrow." He offered in his delightful accent. "I work in the firm's accounting department. I've been asked to get an accounting of POC's payables and receivables for Mr. O'Conner's case. Seems they were missing from the paperwork Ms. O'Conner provided last week, so Mr. Grayson suggested I ring you up to see if we could come by and pick them up."

"Hmmm, did you call Desiree? I mean, Ms. O'Conner?"

"Not me, but I s'pose they did. I was just told to call and make arrangements."

"Well, that seems rather unusual. I'll have to call Ms. O'Conner to confirm. What's the best number to reach you? I'll check and call you back."

"Hold on, please." The caller put his call on hold. A few seconds later, he was back. "H'llo Luv, just checked with my boss, he said I could come there and just take photocopies if that's alright? Shouldn't take long…maybe an hour or so?"

"Well, alright…in that case, why don't you come in at 11? I'll set you up in one of the offices."

"That will do. Thanks so much. Cheers!"

At about 10:30, Lil looked up from her paperwork, startled to find a young man in a three-piece suit standing in front of her. Strange, she thought, I never even heard the doors open and close. I must be going deaf.

"Hello? Can I help you? Who are you? How did you get in here?" demanded Lil.

He smiled charmingly with a slightly lopsided grin. "Sorry, ma'am. There wasn't anyone out in the reception hall. I just came right on in through those doors." He nodded over his shoulder. "Are you Lil?"

"I am. Do I know you?"

"Oh, sorry, ma'am. I'm Jack Sparrow. From Elliott Grayson's office? We spoke this morning? You can call me Jack," he said as he winked at her.

Cheeky. She thought. Still, in her own inimitable fashion, Lil studied the man from head to toe in only a few seconds. Wow…he looked like a GQ ad right off the runway. Obviously, he is well off, has good manners. Maybe one of those entitled rich kids who got a job through his dad. Popular Brooks Brother's banker's grey suit, no doubt, perfectly fitted. His crisp black shirt gave a nod to the roguish modern man. His official-looking briefcase, which he balanced on the corner of her desk, was weathered and had seen better days but was obviously old leather and expensive.

Lil had to admit he was handsome in a spirited sort of way. He looked like the kind of guy who always got away with murder… and could charm his way out of any misunderstanding. He was tall and tanned, his hair was kind of windblown, and he stood there peering down at Lil with a mischievous twinkle in his brilliant blue eyes. Or rather, one eye. A black patch covered the other.

"You're early," she pointed out. "And how did you know I was Lil?"

"Oh, sorry, Luv…another appointment canceled…hope it's no bother." Jack pointed to the nameplate on Lil's desk, grinning …. "Lillian McInnis… isn't that you?"

"Yesssss," Lil said slowly. "I am." The nameplate on her desk was barely visible. But Jack was quickly fumbling in his breast pocket.

"Oh, forgive me." He produced a crisp, official-looking white business card. "My ID."

It all looked normal – picture and all, though the picture was a bit blurry. Jack M. Sparrow, C.P A.

Grayson & Grayson, LLC

Attorneys at Law

450 Columbus Circle

New York, NY

"Your ID is without the eye patch, Mr. Sparrow." Lil had a reputation for letting her tongue speak her thoughts. The man shrugged it off with a smile that bordered on a Cheshire grin. The effect was charming.

"What can I say. I had a slight encounter with a woman a while back. Kind of liked the look, so I kept it." He paused a moment, watching for Lil's reaction. Then he continued, lowering his voice intimately. "Quite frankly, I love those Johnny Depp movies – you know *Pirates of the Caribbean?*" Lil shrugged her shoulders, giving him an *I have no idea what you're talking about* look.

"Though…," he mused, "I do love those old black and white classics. As a kid, I always fantasized myself as a swashbuckling hero…" He raised an imaginary sword – swishing it right and left and then flamboyantly put it back in its sheathe… "you know one of those famous pirates played by Charles Laughton, or Douglas Fairbanks, Laurence Olivier…." Lil nodded, smiling, now knowing exactly who he referred to! "…though my all-time favorite is Errol Flynn in *Sea Hawk*! Now *he* was a pirate!"

Lil was mesmerized. The man was charming, engaging, and, yes… very handsome.

"So…" continued Jack… it gave me a chance to live my fantasy! "Hence…the patch! But I digress…"

Lil swallowed a laugh. "Well, that's quite a story, Mr. Sparrow. Let's hope you're one of the good guys."

"I am indeed…. So, about those books."

"Right. You can come here. Lil led Jack Sparrow down the hall to the small office beside Desiree's. "If you need anything, just let me know."

"I will, indeed. Thank you." Jack removed his jacket and rolled up his sleeves. Opening his briefcase, he removed a ledger, pen, calculator, and a small camera.

Lil looked alarmed. "What's the camera for?"

"Oh… I'm going to write down all the information in this ledger, but then I'll just take a screenshot of each page from your books to make sure nothing was missed. Don't worry. It's fine. Just a formality."

Nevertheless, Lil felt a wave of doubt. "Oh dear, I really do wish Desiree was here," she said half to herself. She hated these unexpected events. This was always her weakness. Tell her what to do and when it's to be completed, and Lil was as efficient as a robot. But throw her a left curve, and she just didn't think well on her feet. Later, she would confess that something about this man, his character, despite his charm, mystified her. She had never seen an accountant, or a law firm employee for that matter, act so flamboyantly and flippant. Just short of arrogant. Again, probably spoiled and entitled. Oh well, we're all human.

"Let's start with the accounts payables and receivables. Then we'll go from there. OK?"

While Jack was working, Lil tried to get in touch with Desiree. But either she was on her way into the office or wasn't answering her phone. Something just didn't seem right about this guy, though all of his identification seemed quite legitimate. She also called Elliott's office, just to be sure. Maybe he would have some advice. But Elliott was in court. Lil left a message and shrugged her shoulders in acceptance.

A little over two hours later, Jack Sparrow glanced at his watch. "Damn," he thought. "This took a lot longer than I thought. He quickly packed up his briefcase and left the little office.

"Well, thank you, Ms. McInnis. Everything seems to be in order. Too bad the company is at such a cross roads. Hope things work out for you. Cheers!" Sparrow tipped his hand in a half salute and left through the glass doors as quietly as he had arrived, leaving Lil staring after him, speechless.

CHAPTER 31

Back out on the street, Jay (a.k.a. Jake Sparrow) turned right, heading back to the subway. Suddenly, he stopped short. Halfway down the block, there was Desiree! As she walked towards him, juggling her portfolio and a handbag, looking down at her phone, his breath caught in his throat while his heart skipped a beat. Dressed in tight jeans, an ivory-shaded silk blouse, leather jacket, and short-heeled leather boots, she looked hot! Her hair was pulled back in a casual loose ponytail that bounced as she walked….or rather as she glided with all the grace he remembered – memories of that first time he saw her in the bar at Las Palmas.

As she walked, Desiree was totally immersed in a text message with Janette.

Hey, girlfriend, what's going on? How are you?

Overwhelmed. Too much to text. More dreams.

Really? About Jay?

He finally called.

That's good.

He's still on my s*** list. (crazy face with scrolling eyes). Won't tell me anything. Says I should trust him. Hey, I'm just picking up lunch – let's talk later, OK?

K…. luv you. Remember…you got this.

You too.

Feeling his blood rise from just the sight of her, he also felt a moment of panic. "Crap…what's she doing here? She can't see me!" With no time to cross the busy street, Jay quickly weighed his options and darted into the deli next door. Moving to the side, he ducked behind tall shelving while still being able to see out the window. Jay watched in horror as Desiree came through the front door.

"Hi Gus," she called cheerily to the man behind the counter as she moved deeper into the store.

"Hey there, pretty lady! What'll it be today?"

Jay's heart was in his throat. "You've got to be kidding me!"

"Let's see…." Desiree was looking at the menu posted on the wall above the deli cases. "I'll have the usual, Gus, grilled chicken parm for me, and…. for Lil… uh…" Desiree was half talking to herself, "How about chicken salad on rye with lettuce and tomato. And I'll grab a couple of ice teas…"

Jay shook his head and hid his laugh. What a woman! How can she eat like that and stay looking like that?

Desiree started to turn towards the cooler. God, he wanted to stay. He wanted to just end this charade and tell her everything. But he couldn't.

Lowering his head and covering the side of his face with his hand, and with the most amazing self-control he could muster, he pulled open the deli door, causing the tinkling of the little bell and himself to cringe! "Shit!" he said to himself for the umpteenth time in the last half hour.

Absentmindedly, Desiree glanced towards the door to see the man in a grey suit exit the store. Subconsciously, she noticed the curl of his hair just brushing the top of the collar of his impeccably tailored jacket, his long back, narrow hips, and the gait of his walk as he made his way out the door.

"Here you go, Desiree…. you're all set." Gus broke her reverie, handed her the bag of sandwiches, and rang up her bill.

Jay was practically hyperventilating. "That was way too close!! And way too risky! It could have ruined everything!" he reminded himself as he headed down the stairs to the subway train.

Meanwhile, Desiree pushed open the glass doors to the office. "Hey, Lil! I brought lunch!" she said cheerily. Even though it was brief, a conversation with Janette always boosted her spirits. Plus, she had just come from Mr. Poppins' studio after delivering the next five illustrations. As agreed, he had advanced her three-quarters of her fees. She was elated. It was the best day she had had in weeks. "So, what's going on here today?"

Lil told her about the strange young man from Elliott's office who had been there not a half hour before. But Desiree wasn't focusing. She was checking her emails on her phone while she ate her sandwich.

"I'm sorry, Lil? Come again. Who was here from Elliott's office?"

"I said an accountant from Elliott's office was here today to review the books."

"Did he say why?"

"He said information was missing from the paperwork you gave Elliott last week. They needed the payables and receivables."

"Who's he?"

"The young man from Elliott's office. And what a strange bird. Had an Australian accent, I think. Told me he loves old pirate movies and always had fantasies of being a Pirate… even had an eye patch!"

"Who?" Desiree still wasn't really listening.

"The accountant, Desiree, from Elliott's office. Name's Jack Sparrow."

Desiree laughed. Pirates. An image of Jay waving the fire poker in his imaginary sword fight flashed through her mind. "It takes all kinds, I guess. But I'm more concerned about why he was here. I wonder why Elliott needs the payables and receivables. What did he do? … this guy?"

"That's strange too. He was here for about two hours. He went over the books, wrote down the info he needed, took some pictures of the documents for verification, and left saying he wished us luck."

"Well, that's nice. But maybe I should call Elliott."

"I already did, but he was in court. But the guy's gone now. You just missed him, actually. He said everything looked fine."

"Hmmm. Well, don't worry about it. I'll speak to Elliott tomorrow." Desiree's phone was ringing.

"Janette! I was going to call you!" Desiree smiled up at Lil. "I'll just be a minute, Lil." And to her friend, "Hey…. how are you?"

"I want to pick up where we left off a few minutes ago…you can't do that to me, you know! How are you feeling?" "Fabulous! Poppins loved the drawings!"

"I don't mean about your artwork. I mean about Jay. How are you?"

Desiree stared off for a moment, remembering his late-night call and her contradictory feelings of love and anger, trust and betrayal that she had wrestled with in the dark. Softly, she said, "He called last night."

"Jay?"

"Said I should trust him." "What did you say?"

"I told him I didn't want to have anything to do with him until he was ready to tell me the whole truth."

"Well, I guess you made a decision." "That I did. And I feel better for it, too."

And after they hung up, Lil was there. "I'm sorry, dearie, I couldn't help but hear." And Lil knew, and Desiree knew that she knew she was lying. She didn't feel better about anything except her drawings. She was miserable, and it was getting worse all the time.

CHAPTER 32

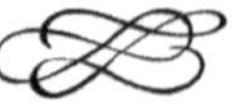

Over the next two weeks, Desiree had to make some unpleasant decisions. According to Elliott, the check for $75,000 from Jay Bennett for her father's invention would not be paid for thirty more days. Again, it had to do with some sort of agreement that had been struck between Bennett and her dad. Jay had produced a legal and valid letter from Pat O'Conner, laying out the requirements for payment.

It was all very upsetting and beginning to get very annoying. Elliott's need for the creditors' list remained a mystery and was quite forgotten in light of Desiree's latest decisions. She simply forgot to ask Elliott about it. And, thought Desiree, if it was necessary and proves otherwise, I'll worry about it then.

In the meantime, Desiree was left with very few options to keep the company going. She laid off all the kids that had been hired for the summer. Then she cut the work week down to four days and split the rest of the week into two shifts, giving those employees who wanted to stay part-time jobs.

At a meeting she held before instituting these changes, Desiree told everyone of the bleak situation. With every ounce of encouragement and positive thinking she could muster, she told these loyal employees that somehow she would put this company back in business and that when she did, they would all be welcome back. In the meantime, anyone who wanted to leave to find better work could go without any remorse.

Only three of the twenty-five full-time employees took the option. The rest were willing to try and wait it out. Relieved when the meeting was finally over, Desiree quickly said her goodbyes and left the room, silently praising her father for building up such loyalty and damning him for his eccentricities.

Lil was helping to keep up everyone's morale, but the faces around the warehouse were long, and even the people who said they would stay were getting restless. Desiree was no exception.

Each day started with calls and letters from their creditors. She had barely scraped together enough money to pay the telephone and electric bills, and now Friday was payday again. Desiree really didn't know where the money would come from.

Her belief that everything would work out was waning. The handwriting was on the wall. Without money, there simply was no future for Poppy's company. As she walked through the halls that she used to run through and among the barren shelves where she once played hide and seek, she could hear the echoes of years gone by, the laughter and camaraderie that grows in a well-run, successful family company. Everyone Poppy and her grandfather had cherished, everything they had worked so hard to achieve, soon it would all be a memory.

On Friday, Desiree sent Lil to the bank with a personal check written out for cash. It was for half the money she had received for her drawings. "Get it in hundreds, fifties, and twenties," Desiree had instructed her. When Lil returned, Desiree divided it into envelopes and paid the salaries of the twenty-two employees that had stayed, Lil included.

Lil stormed into Desiree's office, a deep frown on her face and determination in her voice. "I won't take this." Lil threw the money down on Desiree's desk and stood with her arms folded across her chest.

The effect was dramatic. Desiree looked at the envelope and looked up at Lil. It was like Deja vu. Desiree remembered a time over twenty years ago when Lil had caught her giving away her doll clothes to the children who lived next door to the warehouse. It had been a benevolent gesture on Desiree's part, but the result was futile. The children had no dolls, and Desiree's dolls ended up with no clothes.

Desiree smiled at the memory and at Lil's expression. "Don't be silly," she said stubbornly.

"Your father would roll over in his grave if he knew you were doing this, Desiree." Lil felt her throat tighten with emotion, looking at the young woman who had once been the little girl she had seen grow up, sitting at her father's desk, doling out her own money to pay salaries. "It's not right."

"Yes, it is." Desiree's chin came up, and the Irish fire shot from her eyes.

"Poppy would have done exactly the same thing."

Lil opened her mouth to argue with her young friend and then closed it again. Desiree had grown up these last six months. A rather spoiled little girl had suddenly blossomed into a mature, responsible young woman, and Lil felt very, very proud for any part that she may have played in the metamorphosis. Anyway, Lil had also learned long ago not to meddle when an O'Conner had made up his or her mind.

"Yes," said Lil slowly, appraising Pat O'Conner's daughter. "Yes, I suppose he would have." Lil turned and left but still did not take the envelope.

Moments later, the phone rang. "Hello?"

"Desiree? It's Elliott."

A soft smile spread across Desiree's face. Elliott! Dear sweet Elliott. He was probably the only solid, respectable, secure thing in her life right now. She knew what she was getting with Elliott. With him, there were no surprises.

"Elliott. I was just thinking about you." "Really? Good thoughts, I hope."

"Yes. Good thoughts. How are you?"

"Fine. In fact, I was hoping you might have dinner with me tonight. That is if you're not busy."

Desiree hadn't had a pleasant evening in over two weeks. Jay had never called again, and the last few hours had left her totally exhausted. An evening with Elliott could be just what she needed. It would be like a visit with an old friend. "I'd love to."

Actually, Elliott had been especially communicative these last weeks. He called every other day or so to see how she was and kept her abreast of what was happening with Jay Bennett. Not that she cared, except where her money was concerned. Yes, dinner with Elliott would be a pleasant break, indeed.

CHAPTER 33

Soon after, Desiree left for the day. As she walked past Lil's desk, she bent and gave the woman a kiss and a hug. "Thank you, Lil. I don't know what I would do without you."

Lil looked closely at Desiree's face, noticing a rather sad look around her eyes. She was very concerned about Desiree. No one should go through such stress and unhappiness at such a young age. But she kept her tone light as she asked, "So where are you off to so early?"

"Well, first, I'm going off to buy myself a new dress. There's nothing like a new dress to stave off depression. I guess if we still wore hats, I'd buy a hat!" Desiree laughed, but it sounded fake. "And then, I'm meeting a handsome man for dinner."

"Desiree!" Lil's eyes twinkled. "Was that Jay who called?"

Desiree looked at Lil, amazed. "Don't be silly. I'm having dinner with Elliott." "Desiree!"

"What?" Desiree said defensively.

Lil's maternal instincts came right to the forefront. "Now, Desiree, don't you dare lead that man on. He's still crazy about you, and he deserves some TLC."

"Lil. Please. Give me some credit. Elliott's a good friend, and I need some male attention."

"Your French blood is showing, Desiree. I loved your mother like a sister. But she could be unwittingly coy. You are hurt and lonely. Don't do anything you'll regret."

Desiree caught her own expression in the reflection of the old glass doors. Maybe Lil was right. Reign it in, Desiree, she said to herself. "I'm good, Lil, no worries."

As she left the building, she noticed the old clock that had stopped at four. Funny, she passed that thing a hundred times before, never seeing it.

But now, with the memory of Jay's artful courtship vivid in her mind, not to mention her heart, the old clock was all too obvious. Damn. It seemed everywhere she went, everything she did brought back some reference to Jay Bennett's presence.

"Enough." Desiree chastised herself. "Go and have some fun."

Desiree took the subway to Manhattan and went to Taylor's, browsing through the main floor for a few minutes, enjoying the hustle and bustle of well-heeled shoppers amid the bright, mirrored, almost deco decor. Upstairs, in one of her favorite departments, she found a stunning black cocktail dress.

The rich, soft jersey material was cut on the bias and draped dramatically in the front, crisscrossing over the bodice to show just a hint of her black laced bra. Long raglan sleeves tightened at the wrist, showing off her long, slender hands and manicured nails. The newer, shorter length of the dress just brushed her knees and skimmed her lean body like a second skin. It was both sexy and sophisticated at the same time. Combined with her tan and the gold jewelry she had worn that day, she looked absolutely fabulous.

Desiree informed the sales lady she would wear the dress, and while she was in the dressing room, she reapplied her makeup and tied up her hair in a sophisticated knot. The sales lady was fawning all over her, impressed with Desiree's beauty and panache.

As she looked in the mirror, turning this way and that, complimenting herself on her taste, Desiree realized she had chosen the dress with Jay in mind. She could see his eyes light up and that smile curl the corner of his lips. He would say something sexy like, "Here's looking at you, kid." And she would respond, "If you need me, just whistle."

Desiree's heart skipped a beat, and she felt an aching between her thighs, a desire and hopeless yearning for what could now never be. "Elliott will love it," she heard herself say. Then she turned and went out to pay for her purchase.

* * *

She could feel all eyes on her as the Maître 'D led her down the long front dining room to the banquets at the back. The old, established French restaurant was filled to capacity, a wonderful place to see and be seen.

Desiree was stunning and carried herself with an air of sophistication. Elliott had been ready to take a sip of his drink, but when he saw Desiree, he stopped mid-air to stare at the vision. My God. She was more beautiful than he remembered. Her dress was dramatic, and she wore it with great aplomb. But there was something different about Desiree as she strode so graciously towards him; she had a wild, animal look about her tonight, and he found it terribly arousing.

The Captain pulled the table out to allow Desiree to slip in beside Elliott on the banquet. As she slid in beside him, she kissed him on the cheek. He looked as handsome and sweet as he always did. But there was something new about Elliott, too. An air of acceptance, an aura of excitement. Or was it Desiree's imagination and wishful thinking?

After ordering a cocktail for Desiree and exchanging pleasantries, they took care of the business at hand. Desiree told Elliott that things had just gone too far. The money from Jay was too distant; she had just used her own money to pay salaries. She was paying people to sit around and twiddle their thumbs. It was time, she said despairingly. "I hate to admit it. But I have to close down. I'm tired. I can't play the game anymore."

Elliott squeezed her hand. "This isn't a surprise, you know. I knew you would see it this way," he said in his lawyer voice. "But don't you worry? I'll take care of everything. I'll start drawing up the papers first thing Monday."

Desiree finished her drink and leaned back in the banquet. She felt enormously relieved to have Elliott take over. It would be wonderful for a change not to have to think about what to do next. But a sickening feeling had spread over her belly, a feeling of betrayal to her father and to the people he loved. Elliott became aware of her pain and put his arm around her. "Leave it all to me, Desiree. It'll be all right. You'll see."

Soon after, they ordered dinner and a bottle of wine, and Desiree proceeded to get drunk. She didn't mean to. It just happened. After all of the pressures and intense emotions of the last weeks and hours, the wine just went right to her head. Accidentally, she spilled her glass of wine, becoming a little too loud and a little too amorous, leaning against Elliot and rubbing his leg under the table. And in his own predictable fashion, Elliott became terribly embarrassed.

As soon as dinner was finished and before dessert, Elliott asked for the check and, as quickly and unobtrusively as possible, escorted Desiree out of the restaurant and immediately to his apartment.

The view from Elliott's penthouse was breathtaking. Reflections of lights from all over the city glistened against the huge panoramic windows that wrapped around the apartment. From the front door, it appeared that there was no glass at all in those windows, and if you stepped up to them, you could touch the stars.

Below, as far as the eye could see, flowed the East River, from the north at Hell's Gate, past the promenade at the Mayor's Mansion, and south to the Brooklyn Bridge. It was almost overwhelming and wasted, Desiree thought, on such tasteless decor.

All beige and black and chrome, Elliott's apartment was a decorator's statement of contemporary elegance. Desiree hated it. She always had. It lacked personality and charm. It was cold and uninviting. She thought now that it really didn't do Elliott justice. He wasn't that bad. In fact, she thought, as she watched Elliott move around the room, turning on lights and making his way to the kitchen, Elliott was really quite sexy.

While Desiree contemplated Elliott's apartment, taste and body, not necessarily in that order, he made some coffee. But she had other ideas. "Elliott," Desiree reclined seductively across the couch. "Come here."

Elliott put the cups down on the coffee table and sat down beside her. He was annoyed. "Drink this. I can't believe you could allow yourself to get like this. It's embarrassing, Desiree."

Desiree leaned towards him, smiling into his face and pursing her lips while she rubbed his thigh, this time much farther up his leg. She was driving him crazy. Since he had seen her come through the door at the restaurant, Elliott had been attempting to control every male response he had. Her very touch set fire to his heart. He ached to touch her, to hold her, to stroke her breasts and feel her body under his again. Why had he never realized what he had all along.? How did he lose her?

Elliott pushed her hand away, attempting to be stern with her. But Desiree completely ignored him, draped herself over his lap, and wrapped her arms around his neck. The neckline of her dress fell open, revealing the black lace bra. Try as he might, Elliott couldn't contain himself any longer. He grabbed Desiree around her waist and pushed her down on the couch, kissing her hungrily.

Elliott thrust his tongue into Desiree's mouth, searching for her own tongue. When he found it, he sucked it into his mouth and released it gradually until it was almost gone, then he sucked it back again, hard, causing Desiree to wince with excitement. He continued passionately, caressing, almost kneading Desiree's breasts, down her thighs, and under the hem of her dress, which had risen high above her knees. He pulled her dress until it was up around her waist and began caressing her gently between her legs. Desiree felt him gyrate his hips against her own, in no way mistaking his passion.

Desiree lost her breath. She felt herself wanting him, opening up to him, begging for more with her body until her eyes flew open, focusing on the ceiling, adjusting to the light. Elliott had never, ever kissed her like that before. Not even at the cabin after their dip in the lake. It had an immediate sobering effect.

She struggled to push Elliott up away from her. "Elliott. Stop. This isn't right." "Yes, it is. I love you. I want you. God, I never should have let you go. And you need me. I'll take care of you."

"Elliott, it's all wrong." She pushed her hands against Elliott's shoulders. She pulled her legs together and struggled to pull down her dress. Annoyed, Elliott finally got the picture.

"Are you nuts? You have some nerve, Desiree. Leading me on like that and then turning it off like a water faucet!" Elliott got up and paced the floor, finally turning and staring at Desiree.

"I know. I'm so sorry….really sorry. I don't know what came over me. I drank too much. I was lonely…." She finished straightening herself. Her hair had fallen out of its knot and was tangled around her shoulders. No more the vixen, no more the sophisticated woman who had entered the restaurant; Desiree sat gazing back at Elliott, tired and burned out. Her shoulders sagged, and she finally laid her head back against the sofa, closing her eyes to hold back the tears. Elliott's look softened as he watched her pull herself back together. He still loved her. And he felt her pain. But he knew then he could never be more than a friend, even if she would let him. Somehow, those things never did work out. "Desiree. I'm the one who's sorry. I shouldn't have taken advantage of you.

I could tell when you walked into the restaurant you were wired; it's no wonder you got drunk. You've been living on a tightrope for weeks. I'm sorry I brought you back here."

Desiree opened her eyes and looked at Elliott, appreciative of his apology. "It's not your fault, Elliott. I'm a big girl now. I should know better. Elliott, I think we have to talk."

At long last, and for the next two hours, they discussed the relationship, or rather the lack of one, between them. Desiree told Elliott about meeting Jay at Los Palmas and her feelings of guilt and betrayal. She told him how she had felt, and as delicately as possible, without going into details, she confirmed what Jay had said about her going to him freely as true.

Then Elliott told her his story. He had tried to blame their failed relationship first on Desiree and then on Jay Bennett, , but how he had realized it was really himself that was to blame. And finally, embarrassed, he told Desiree how he had punched Jay Bennett in the eye while defending what he thought was Desiree's honor. In reality, he realized it was his own self-pride.

"You punched Jay in the eye? You? Elliott! I'm impressed?" Desiree burst out laughing and hugged Elliott warmly. "Good for you. He probably deserved it."

"Desiree." Elliott changed the subject. "The man really loves you." "How do you know."

"He told me."

"Why should you believe him?" "I just do. Lawyer's intuition."

"Oh, Elliott. Not you, too. I'm sorry. I just don't buy it."

"Don't let this stuff about your father interfere with your logic. Face it, Desiree. Your father was a flake. Everything he ever did was done clandestinely. He never told me or any lawyer anything. He seldom kept any records, and when he did, they were on little scraps of paper. Luckily, in his brilliance, he chose competent people to run that company for him. I haven't the foggiest idea what your dad had up his sleeve, but it's just possible that everything Bennett is saying is true. Maybe you should give him some time to prove it to you."

Desiree just stared at Elliott. The whole world was crazy.

CHAPTER 34

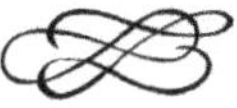

Desiree was in the office bright and early Monday morning. She was still feeling very embarrassed over the way she had acted with Elliott. But, at least she had gotten a lot off her mind and finally knew in her heart that the relationship with Elliott was over…really over. Their conversation had been the beginning of a new friendship. Perhaps in time, it would be a lasting one.

"So, how was your "date" Friday night?" Lil asked as soon as she saw Desiree. "Interesting." Desiree looked down at the coffee she had just poured. When she looked up, Lil was peering at her over her bifocals, waiting for an explanation.

Desiree laughed. "You know, Lil, you're worse than a mother."

"Who, me?" She smiled at the compliment. For that's exactly what it was, coming from Desiree.

"Well, if I didn't look out for you, I don't know who would. I'd say you're in no shape to make very many rational decisions these days, at least where your love life is concerned. So? I'm waiting."

"Lil! Mind your own business." "That bad, eh?"

"All right. So you were right. I behaved rather badly. But it's all been cleared up, and both Elliott and I have a new understanding." Desiree said with finality. Lil knew when she had gotten all she could get and changed the subject.

Over coffee, Desiree told Lil of her decision to close the company, though her words sounded as if she was still trying to convince herself. They sat in Poppy's - now Desiree's- office and, almost at the same time, looked around at the old walls and ancient windows of the Brooklyn warehouse, hundreds of memories reverberating from every corner. The office was cozy, with its chipped paint and 1930's decor. Any minute, one half expected a character from some old black-and-white movie to walk through the door.

"I really don't have any choices left," she said. "I've tried everything I know, and there just isn't any money anywhere. Elliott's putting together all the paperwork. This is the best thing to do."

"You don't sound very convinced, Desiree," Lil observed quietly. She knew Desiree. When the girl had her convictions in order, there was a spark to her voice, even if the decision was negative. She says she'll close the doors, thought Lil, but she's still looking for an out.

Desiree observed Lil. She knew what the older woman was thinking. "I refuse to go to Jay Bennett."

"I never said a thing." Lil smiled innocently. "You didn't have to. I could see it in your eyes."

"Then what you saw in my eyes, my dear, was your own reflection. You have no intention of letting these doors close. And you've probably already thought of talking to Jay Bennett."

"I never…" Desiree stopped short. Actually, she really hadn't thought about it. But why not? Maybe he would give her a personal loan. Why couldn't he advance her the 75,000 until the legal due date?

"Lil, you're a genius!" "What did I say?"

"Never mind. I'll let you know how it works out." Lil took that as her cue to leave and retrieved her cup. At the door, she looked back at Desiree, but she was already holding the phone, ready to try again. Determination was written all over her face. She dialed the now familiar number of Jay's home, sensing the recurring/ache in the pit of her stomach. She remembered only a few weeks ago that these same feelings were butterflies of excitement, of new love, of anticipation. Now, they were pangs of anxiety and uncertainty. She took a deep breath. There was no answer. He wasn't at home. She tried his cell and then Googled Morton Enterprises to get that number. He wasn't there either; he was 'out in the field.' OK. Patience. I'll keep trying."

Despite her anxiety about actually speaking to Jay, just making a positive decision not to give up improved her mood. She felt enormously better. When the phone rang, and it was Uncle Max calling, she felt better yet.

"Uncle Max, when did you get back?" He had been in Canada these last two weeks with Lydia. It seemed like months since Desiree last spoke with him. Obviously, he knew nothing of the latest twist of events, for his deep lilting brogue trilled over the phone; his sing-song voice was as happy as ever.

Talking to Uncle Max was like taking a drink of champagne. The bubbles always made Desiree laugh.

"Just last night, Lassie. And it was wonderful. I caught the biggest muskie ye've ever seen. Why, the Indian guide said he hadn't seen one that long in four lunar years."

"Another fish story, Uncle Max?"

"Fish stories are like women, Desi. Ye never have enough o'them. And they're always better than the last! Speakin' of which, how is that young man of yours?"

Desiree hesitated. "Are you free for lunch? It's a long story." "For you, darlin', I'm always free. Meet me at my club." "Twelve o'clock?"

"Twelve, it is. See you then, Lassie."

Uncle Max's club was his last hold on his life on Wall Street. He had been one of the founding members of this now prestigious club, and whenever he graced its hallowed halls with his presence, he was granted enormous respect, not only from the other younger members but the staff as well. Desiree had been there many times. Gone were the days when women were relegated to certain rooms. Traditions had been updated years ago, but nonetheless, John, the old captain, who was as much revered as Uncle Max, knew her well and took great pleasure in escorting her personally to Uncle Max's table.

Seeing Uncle Max was exactly what Desiree needed. She hadn't realized until this minute how much she had missed him these last two weeks. His phone calls always made her laugh, and just a hug from him made Desiree feel secure and loved. He was such a wonderful old man. She prayed he'd lived to be a hundred.

As usual, Uncle Max came right to the point. "So, me Bonnie Lassie, how's your love life?"

"It's over."

"Nonsense. It's never over." He spoke from great experience. "Maybe not for you," Desiree said wistfully, "but mine is a disaster." "Now, come, Lassie, it canna be as bad as all that."

"Worse." Desiree poured out the details of the past fourteen days, beginning with Jay as the phantom deal maker. She told the story in great detail, leaving no piece of information out, unaware that she was telling as grand a story as Uncle Max himself. He sat there staring at her wide-eyed; he had already eaten two rolls and drank three iced teas. He never interrupted and never offered commentary. For the first time in her life, Desiree witnessed Uncle Max speechless. Desiree took it to mean disbelief. Uncle Max was impressed!

"I canna believe it! You mean Patty made the deal with your beau before he died?"

"He's not my beau!" interrupted Desiree.

Uncle Max didn't even hear her. He was still being impressed by his brother's scheme. "He had it all planned, wrapped up in a ribbon like a gift to ye? I'll be damned." He cackled gleefully, slapping his knee and shaking his head in approval.

"Uncle Max! Whose side are you on?"

"Desi, darlin', your Poppy, my brother, was a wise judge of character. Emotional, aye, to be sure…but not a fool. There was a reason he sold our water system to young Bennett the way he did. You mark my words. Trust him…and trust those Irish feelin's of your own."

Uncle Max paused, poured them each another glass of iced tea, and buttered his third roll. Desiree could see the wheels turning in his grey head. Finally, he looked at her, blue eyes twinkling like stars.

"You're in love with the rogue, aren't ye?"

The tinkle of silver and glassware in the elegant old dining room became muted. The whole room seemed shaded in maroon and grey. Desiree could focus on nothing but the white tablecloth under her glass. And then, like thunder rolling across the sky during a summer storm, like the waves breaking wildly over a jetty, Desiree's feelings crashed and tumbled over one another in crazy disorder. Love, hate, depression, ecstasy, hopelessness, anxiety, passion, guilt, betrayal, confidence, optimism, trust…and they all had one name. Jay Bennett.

Desiree stared at her uncle with glazed eyes. She had admitted it before, to Janette, to Lil, to Elliott, and even to herself, but never with the conviction that she felt now. "Yes, Uncle Max, I love him."

He didn't say "ah ha," and he didn't joke. He grabbed his niece's hand and squeezed. "Then go after him, Lassie, and trust him."

CHAPTER 35

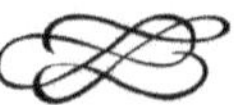

The next morning, Desiree looked at herself in the mirror. Despite all the recent turmoil, she looked the same as she did the night she met Jay Bennett. Her eyes were clear; her hair was shiny; on the surface, she looked like a happy woman.

"Could everybody be right and I be wrong?" Desiree asked herself over and over again as she stared at her reflection. One minute, she believed it, and the next, she didn't.

"What am I afraid of? What's the worst that could happen? Things can't get much bleaker than they are right now, and what if everyone is right? What if Jay really is the good guy? Am I going to pass up the best thing that ever happened to me?"

Her image stared back. Maybe she was blowing everything out of proportion. She knew her father had been eccentric. It was just like him to make a deal like this and not tell anyone. Then, he died without seeing it through. But still, why would Jay not tell her who he was? That really seemed childish. Jay is not an eccentric. Whatever is behind his motive? That's what she had to find out.

The vision of the little yellow bird in her father's pocket came back to her. *'All is not what it seems to be,' the bird had chirped.* Maybe it's simpler than that, Desiree mused to herself. "My brain is telling me to trust Poppy. Poppy put the yellow bird in his pocket; Poppy made a deal with Jay Bennett.

Desiree felt some of the heaviness lift from her heart. But there were still feelings of betrayal to deal with. Jay had no right to lie to her, to mislead her. You don't do that to someone you love. And he had said he loved her.

Her brain was beginning to clear. Her "convictions," as Lil called them, were becoming stronger. Her courage to confront all the issues and to deal with them one at a time surmounted all other fears. She was going to fight this, learn the truth, and get control of her own destiny. Desiree was on a new track.

The morning was uneventful – phone calls and buying time as usual while her new plans were still percolating in her head. When she returned to the office after lunch, she went right to her desk to begin laying some groundwork for her new plans. She called Jay's office again. He was still out. There was no answer on his cell either.

Desiree sat back in Poppy's old chair, still mulling over all the information she had at hand. If she could get the loan from Jay, she could begin to pay off a few of the bills and maybe keep on a skeleton crew. But how much time would $75,000 buy? Maybe she really should just forget it. Let Elliott go ahead with closing the company. No, she had to hear what Jay had to say first.

But wait a minute. Once, he had said maybe he could buy the company. That's an even better idea! Desiree closed her eyes a moment, letting her brain sort through all the options until she could think no more.

When she looked up, the late afternoon sun was streaming through the left windows, sending beams of hazy summer light across the room to the doorway. She blinked. Then she blinked again. Surely, she was seeing things. Jay was leaning in the doorway, looking at her with half-closed eyes, sipping a yellow bird cocktail, subtly stripping her naked with only a look. His free hand was stuck deep into his pockets, and he cocked his head, boyishly grinning at her, inviting her towards him with only his eyes. Desiree felt the pangs of love in her heart and aching passion in her belly. Her legs were numb, and her knees were weak, but she got up from the desk, awkwardly moving across the room. She wanted to leap into his arms and beg for his kisses.

He sensed her hesitation. He watched her, not moving, and then suddenly, he was beside her, holding her in his arms, whispering his apologies for hurting her and deceiving her. "I love you," he said. "Marry me," he said. "Let me make it all up to you?"

Suddenly, Lil came rushing into the office, breaking Desiree's reverie. Her face was flushed, and she was so excited that she didn't even notice Desiree's disorientation.

"Desiree, something very strange just happened! I just got a call from Bob Jenkins.

Desiree was still in a fog, terribly disappointed that it had all been a daydream, but she managed to pull her thoughts back to the present.

"Who called?"

"Bob Jenkins from L.C. Lewis."

L.C. Lewis Company was P.O.C.'s biggest supplier of camping equipment. Practically everything they carried in their catalog came from L.C. Lewis. Unfortunately, it was also their biggest creditor.

"So?" said Desiree. "I've spoken to him at least ten times in the last month." "You don't understand," Lil continued excitedly. "He called to thank us for the check and said he'd send out the last two orders right away!" "What check?" Desiree was dumbfounded.

"That's what I asked him. He told me he received a bank check for everything we owed him."

"But that's over $30,000!" Goosebumps jumped all over Desiree's arms. "Let me call him." She looked up the number and called Bob Jenkins immediately. Lil sat down across from Desiree as she put the call on speaker.

"Bob? Desiree O'Conner." She leaned back in her chair. "Fine, thank you. Yes, well, that's why I called." Desiree couldn't get a word in. Bob just kept going on and on about how pleased he was that they would still be able to do business. Finally, Desiree asked, "Bob, this may seem strange to you, but it seems that we've both benefited from an anonymous donor. Was there a note with the check? I see, yes, of course. You're very welcome. Goodbye."

Desiree hung up and looked at Lil. Despite her disbelief, it was still hard to keep a smile from her lips. "You heard it! It's all true. He received the check this morning in a certified envelope, and the only note was a typewritten one referring the check to P.O.C.'s account; it was for all of it $35,052.56."

Desiree looked at Lil and burst out laughing. "I don't believe it! Who on earth would bail us out like this? Why, this is wonderful! Between that and the $75,000 we'll get from Jay Bennett, we just might be able to keep this old lady going. I'll be damned."

The next day, it happened again. Two different suppliers called Desiree personally to thank P.O.C. for their payments.

"Really glad you people got yourselves back on track," said Fern Davies. "Hate to see a good family go down the tubes."

And "It's wonderful, Miss O'Conner, really wonderful. We've enjoyed doin' business with you for over twenty years, and now I'm sure we'll be doin' it for another twenty. We'll get that order you need out this week," promised Jack Perdy. "By the way, I'll be in town next month, allow me to take you to dinner." And on it went. All week letters arrived--payment received; balance paid; thank you for your payment; paid in full; and one even had a credit statement of $41.00. Amid the letters and statements, it dawned on Desiree that whoever paid these bills had done their homework. It was easy enough to find out what was owed by calling each creditor. But how did this person or persons know who the creditors were?

"Lil," Desiree asked as she walked past Lil's desk. "Where do we keep the records of all of our suppliers?"

"In the shipping room and the email and telephone lists, and of course, they each have a file with our contracts."

"Nowhere else? Is what we owe them in the files?" "No. Only in the account books."

"Where are they?"

"Right here. I always keep them unless Mary's working on them." "Anyone else ever use them?"

"No."

"Are you sure no one else has seen those books since Poppy died?"

"No, just Mary, Elliott, of course. Oh, and Mr. Sparrow, the accountant from Elliott's office."

"Who?"

"I told you last week about the young man from Elliott's office. He was here for about two hours, recorded the accounts and took photos of the documentation."

"Yes, but what did you say his name was?"

"Mr. Sparrow. Jack Sparrow. What's wrong?" Lil was concerned. Desiree had a very queer look on her face.

"What did he look like?" Desiree was starting to put two and two together, and it all kept adding up to one thing.

"Very tall, handsome, kind of cherubic. He had a strange sense of humor. He wore a grey banker's suit." Lil paused and thought back. "Oh, and he had one very blue eye."

"One?"

"A black patch covered the other one. What a character. Definitely not your typical accountant type – kept making references to pirates."

"Tall, handsome, cherubic smile?" Desiree's temper was starting to climb. "Weird sense of humor, one blue eye? Ha! That's because Elliott punched him in the other one! Jack Sparrow, my foot! A pirate? I'll kill him. I swear I'll tar and feather him, tie him to the yardarm, and set him adrift on his own boat to fry in the sun!"

"What are you talking about?"

"Jay Bennett…aka Jack Sparrow! Jack Sparrow's a pirate, Lil! A character from *Pirates of the Caribbean*! I'm surprised at you! How could you not see through that bullshit? He was no accountant from Elliott's firm. He disguised himself, came in here, pried into our accounts, and has been sending them all money in our name." Desiree was livid.

"Why would he do that?' Lil had no idea who or what *Pirates of the Caribbean* was.

"To humiliate me, that's why. I'm going to find that bastard and set him straight once and for all if I have to sit on his doorstep until Tishibuv!" Desiree turned back into her office, grabbed her purse, and stormed out the door, leaving Lil staring after her.

A few minutes later, after the dust had cleared from Desiree's outburst, Lil started to laugh. Desiree was right. She had really been pretty stupid to not have seen through that pirate story. But she had been so distracted by the man's accent and the stories he was weaving that she never caught the symbolism of the name. And now everything seemed to make sense. So that was Jay Bennett. No wonder Desiree was in love with him. He was wonderful. The girl couldn't have done better. Now, it was only a matter of time.

"Humph, I'll be damned." Lil grinned again and started to hum a few bars of YELLOW BIRD. Then she called the employees who had gone on part-time and told them to report as usual on Monday. "We're back in business" she advised them.

CHAPTER 36

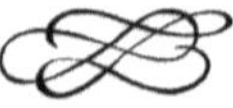

By the time Desiree reached Jay's house, she had had plenty of time to cool off. Instead, she had kept the fires burning by rehashing what seemed like a lifetime of experiences with Jay Bennett. Fueling her mood was a crowded, rush-hour-packed subway train with broken air-conditioners. From Brooklyn to the Upper East Side, she had rubbed elbows and other parts of her body with what seemed like every despicable character in New York City.

Her temper was hot, and she was not going to be pooh-poohed or coddled. She was Desiree Dubois O'Conner, the daughter of Francine and Patrick O'Conner, and no one, not even the great-grandson of some old sugar queen, was going to make a fool out of her.

The front door opened before Desiree even had a chance to take her finger off the bell. She was sure Jay had been peering out the window waiting for her. It would be just like him, she thought indignantly.

He threw open the door, exposing himself to the dusky light dancing through the budding leaves of the trees. In the deepening shadows of the spring sunset, he was as masculine as ever, his animal-like virility simmering just below the surface of his cool and controlled demeanor. Seeing him like this brought memories crashing into Desiree's mood, interfering with her anger. Visions of Las Palmas and the giant whispering palms surged through Desiree's heart, and memories of his hard body and the unyielding passion of every look, every touch, and of the way he made love to her seemed anchored to her very soul.

His face was freshly scrubbed and still tanned. He wore an old, now faded red polo shirt and blue jeans. His feet were bare, cool looking against the old oak floor. She noticed a white mark across his wrist where he had forgotten to remove his watch, and his hair was disheveled, begging for her fingers to comb it. If she stared at him much longer, she would lose all her constraint. She was totally torn between fury and passion, though it was probably a fine line between the two.

Then she saw his eye, and a vivid picture of Elliott's fist punching it dead center flashed through her mind, reminding her of her real mission. Her anger was fueled once more.

Sensing Desiree's mood immediately, Jay made the first move and invited her in before she could say a word. He smiled slyly, lowering his voice to a whisper, and beckoned, "Come into my Parlor, said the spider to the fly."

Desiree ignored the raillery, but as she passed by him, stepping into the foyer, she nodded to his eye, now only two shades of blue and almost normal in shape. "I see you and Elliott got along quite well."

"How observant of you." So, he thought, we're going to be sarcastic, are we? Jay had to admit that she was incredibly sexy when she was angry like this. He could feel her heat emanating from her body and could smell the sweet aroma of her perfume as it mixed exotically with her ire. As he stood so near to her, so close he could feel her breath on his cheek, he was instantly aroused.

"Heard it from the horse's mouth." Desiree brushed past him into the living room. Feeling his eyes boring into her back, it was all she could do to maintain her dignity. Instead, she looked up at Magda's portrait. Was she laughing at her or smiling in agreement?

"Oh, you and Elliott are on speaking terms again?" Jay felt the twinges of jealousy. He was still right behind her.

"Now and then." Desiree pulled her eyes away from Magda's and started to pace the room. As she passed by Jay, on the second time around, he grabbed her shoulders and swung her around to face him.

"Do you think we could have a real conversation, or are you just here to churn up stormy waters?" All Jay wanted to do now was to clear the air. Finally, after all the turmoil of the last weeks, he could tell Desiree the entire story. But Desiree seemed in no mood for a fairy tale and a happy ending; she wanted a fight and probably wouldn't stop until she got it.

Desiree stared into Jay's eyes. For days and weeks, she had waited to face him like this, to confront him in person and hear him account for his actions. She had rehearsed the words and had organized her thoughts. His phone call the other night had taken her by surprise, but now she was here, and he was facing her, so why wouldn't the words come.

Desiree's heart beat wildly. Her eyes were brilliant; little specks of fire shot through the now stormy dark centers, her velvety lashes framing them like a fire screen, keeping the sparks from igniting everything in their path. Her nostrils quivered, her lips trembled. Finally, she spoke.

"I don't want your charity!" Her voice was firm and controlled.

Jay swallowed a smile; he knew what she meant. "What are you talking about?" he asked anyway.

"All those paid-in-full notices I've been getting lately, Jack Sparrow!" Her mouth turned up to one side as she sneered at the name.

"Ah… those."

"Those?" she repeated. "What's with you?" Desiree shrugged loose of Jay's hold and started to pace again. The words were beginning to take shape. "Finally feeling guilty? Maybe there's truth to my suspicions, after all." She was angry. Really angry, and Jay was reminded of the day on the beach.

"Which are…" Jay had no idea where she was going with this conversation. "That you really did use me to get to as much of Pat O'Conner's estate as you could."

"Then why would I give you charity?" Jay was fascinated by Desiree's scenario.

"Well, you keep telling me you're in love with me. What better way to appease the irate heiress than by paying off her debts."

Jay almost laughed. Wait till she hears what he had to tell her next. He prepared himself for Hurricane Desiree to strike again.

"I'm not 'appeasing the irate heiress' as you so colorfully put it. I'm not even paying off your debts. Those bills are owed by my company."

Desiree spun around and glared at Jay in total disbelief. "What? Your company!" She felt sick to her stomach. "What do you mean your company."

"It was part of the deal. Your father sold it to me for one dollar plus the current market price for the invention."

"A dollar! You ripped him off for that, too?" "Desiree! Listen to me."

But she wasn't going to listen to anyone. She was livid. She was so furious she couldn't see straight. She had maneuvered herself across the room again, in front of the table that stood under Magda's portrait. In her fury, she had an uncontrollable urge to throw something, to somehow unleash the turmoil inside her. There on the table, she spied a small carved box that just fit her needs. She grabbed it and, in one fell swoop, threw it across the room. Horror flashed through Jay's eyes.

Instinctively, he reached up and caught the box in midair, bruising his finger in the process.

"Are you crazy? That box is priceless!"

But Desiree heard nothing. She had something to say, and she was going to say it. Her high-pitched voice shook the room as she spewed every emotion that she had out into the air.

"Everyone kept telling me there must be more to the story, that Poppy must have trusted you. So finally, I decided to trust you too, to really go with my gut!" Desiree stood rooted to the spot in front of the table. Her anger had erupted into tears, and now she took a gulping breath, choking back her sobs.

"You opened up a whole new world for me, passion and understanding. You made me laugh, and you made me love you! And I do love you. Oh, God, Jay, I really love you. I wanted to trust you and share everything with you. I've been trying to find you for two days to give you a chance to tell me the whole story. But you told me nothing. And now this, a big game, a great charade. Jack Sparrow? Really? What a fool I've been."

Jay moved close to Desiree, but when he reached for her, she cringed and turned away. "DON'T touch me."

"Desiree!" Jay felt all her pain and anguish. He saw her sagging shoulders and could hear her deep breathing as she fought to control herself. But he had taken about all of her insults and abuse that he could. He had his own frustrations, too. Desiree had been so caught up in her own impressions of things that she allowed her logic to go right out the window. Her own pride and stubbornness had created more difficulties than the situation deserved.

He reached out for her again and firmly turned her around to face him. "Are you blind? Don't you see? Sit down here, now."

Jay led her to the sofa, not exactly gently, and handed her a box of Kleenex. "Now you sit there and don't move. You've been trying to find me for days? To hear an explanation? Well, here I am. And you're going to hear it."

Desiree started to protest but took one look at the determination on Jay's face and changed her mind. She grabbed a handful of Kleenex and blew her nose six or seven times. Finally, she leaned back against the sofa, arms crossed, but still wouldn't look at him. "FINE. Talk."

Now, it was Jay's turn to pace. "For your information, I've had more than my share of problems with this whole God damned chain of events. What started off as a simple, though I admit lucrative, business deal has been blown way out of proportion. Do you know why?"

Desiree stared at him with eyes wide. She had never seen this side of Jay. He paced like a caged animal, back and forth over the same stretch of carpet, turning at the same point, talking quickly and efficiently, using his hand for every point that he made. He was in control. His thoughts were ordered and logical.

"It's all because of two stubborn people. Your father, who died before he wanted to, and you, whom I had the misfortune of meeting before I wanted to."

"So you did plan on using me!" Desiree flared.

Jay shot Desiree a warning glance and continued. "Your father had been taking money out of the company for years to subsidize his inventions."

"I know all that."

"Can you possibly sit quietly and listen?" Desiree nodded. She had calmed down considerably but was still wary. Jay went on.

"It was really no big deal. There was nothing illegal about it; it was his company, and he could do anything he wanted with the money. There were no shareholders nor anyone else he had to account to. But fortunately, or maybe unfortunately, your father was also a very moralistic and emotional character. He loved you, Desiree…so much…more than life itself. He wanted to leave you an inheritance. And he felt terribly obligated to all the people who had worked for him for all those years. Plus, he truly respected his clients, his customers – the hundreds of people and small companies out there he had done business with for all those years."

Desiree felt the tears brimming in her eyes. Jay told the truth, yet it was no more than she had already shared with him. But she kept quiet and sat listening with her arms folded across her chest. Jay stopped pacing now and came across the room and pulled up a chair, sitting opposite Desiree.

He leaned forward, resting his elbows on his knees, locking Desiree's eyes into his.

"Your father had always planned on repaying the money and keeping the company going. But things had gone too far. One day, he realized just how much in debt he really was. And he was desperate to find a way to put things back in order.

"When he learned the invention was a success, he knew he could sell it for a lot of money and save the company for you. But at about the same time, he learned how sick he was. He started to lay the groundwork, but God seemed to have other plans for him, and he started to decline. He had to move fast. He didn't tell you or anyone about his plans because of his damn Irish pride…which, I might add, you seem to have inherited. Pat was sure he could handle it all."

"How long did you know Poppy?" Desiree interrupted, ignoring Jay's sarcasm.

"Almost a year."

"A year? I never had any idea. How did you meet him? How did you know about the water system?"

Jay leaned comfortably back in his chair and crossed his left foot over his right knee. Desiree just sat perfectly still, refusing to relax.

"My partner, Dave, knew your dad from Cranford – and we often went there on weekends. Then one weekend by accident, I met your dad in the tackle shop with your Uncle Max... well, kind of.. your dad and Max were having one of their animated discussions over fishing and women." Jay grinned at the memory. "But we ..your dad and I …ran into each other later in the lodge bar, and by some strange twist of fate, we hit it off; I don't know what it was," Jay smiled rather wistfully. "And then last spring, I started spending most weekends in Cranford. We just became friends…we bonded…a lot of long chats over those fishing poles, you know? I guess it was kind of a father/son relationship or would have been if he had lived longer.

"Anyway, like I said, right about the time he found out how sick he really was, he also learned that the invention was a success and knew he could sell it for a lot of money and save the company for you. So, he called me one day and asked for a meeting, where he laid out his crazy scheme. It was all very dramatic…must run in the family," Jay cocked his head towards Desiree with a lopsided grin. Desiree was not amused.

* * *

Jay continued, quoting Pat O'Conner's terms, vividly remembering every word of the conversation: "*One – I'll sign a Quit Claim Deed, and you buy POC for one dollar. Two – You pay back all POC's creditors – anonymously. You put POC back in the black and set up a pension fund for the key employees. No one, and I mean no one, is to know where the money is coming from. I was going to give you access to the books, but now there's no time for me to get them for you. You'll figure it out…you're a clever boy,*" Pat had winked at Jay. "*Three – I sell you the patent for the purification system and all rights, including any ongoing and future modifications, for its current value of $75,000. Once the full value is established when the EPA review is complete, all profits belong to you, to be shared with my daughter…that would be 80% of the final value and ongoing proceeds to Desiree, 20% to you. Four -- And lastly, NO ONE, not even my daughter, is to know the details until the entire deal has been completed. This could get sticky. Are ye in?*"

* * *

Jay had lowered his voice reverently and become quite emotional. Desiree could hear it in his voice; she could see it in his eyes. He really had cared for Poppy, of that she seemed sure. "I just can't believe he never mentioned you, the deal, or anything to me…or to anyone."

"Your pride is showing again, Desiree." Jay grinned at her.

Desiree glared back. She still wasn't ready to forgive the cad. Nothing yet excused the way he had treated her. And she said so.

"I'm glad you and Poppy met, and I'm sure that the two of you did hit it off.

But that's not really the issue here, is it?"

"Hold on, Desiree, the fat lady hasn't sung yet."

Desiree bit her tongue. He was certainly milking this story for all it was worth; she didn't know how much longer she could sit here. "Get to the point, Jay."

"Didn't you hear what I just said? Your father knew the water filtration system was the key, and the pride he felt about his life's work finally paying off was his personal reward. But the challenge, the overall purpose, the very main objective of his crazy plan was to keep his honor intact by paying back the debt, taking care of his employees, and not leaving you to face an otherwise grim reality."

"You mean, there really are pension funds for everyone?" The impact of Jay's words was beginning to register. "The company will still be able to operate? You're not going to close it down?" Desiree was speechless. This was all too amazing. It was like something out of a book. But she still had questions, and Jay wasn't done with his story.

"Your father was ashamed of where he had allowed his pride to take him, which is why he wanted it all to be done without the benefit of lawyers and in cash. But I insisted on some kind of document for both our protection. Finally, your father agreed, but only if my lawyer did the paperwork."

"So, when exactly did you buy the company?"

"That was written up in the original document between us. It was only a formality that made the rest of the arrangements easier. At that point, I was to own the company on paper only. Your father was still planning on putting everything completely back to normal before he died. But he didn't make it."

Desiree sat silently, thinking about everything Jay had said. Finally, she added, "So that's why you came to Las Palmas? To meet me? To finish the deal, you started with my father?" Desiree was close to tears again. She still felt used. Now, Jay seriously lost his patience.

"Woman, you're impossible! I met you completely by accident. Why can't you believe that? I fell in love with you long before I knew who you were!"

Desiree still felt leery, but dawn was beginning to break in her muddled head. Things were beginning to take a clearer shape. He loved her. He had loved her from the moment he saw her. He had loved her before he knew who she was. "That must have complicated things," she said out loud to Jay and smiled shyly.

"An understatement, my dear."

"But you could have told me, Jay." She refused to give in on that point. "No. I couldn't. And I wouldn't." Jay was totally frustrated with the woman's stubbornness. "Desiree, of course! I wanted to tell you everything from the very beginning, but I had to fulfill my commitment to your father. Don't you understand? I'm as much an emotional slob as your father. I made him a promise. But he's dead, and I could never explain to him why I broke it. I could not and would not. But you *are* here. And I knew, at least I hoped, that eventually, I could explain it all to you and that you'd understand! But I've certainly had my doubts lately; you're so damn stubborn!"

Desiree felt totally embarrassed. "I guess Poppy really did know you. He had a sixth sense about people…. like me." she smiled impishly.

"You!" Jay jumped up and came over to Desiree. Desiree blushed. "Well, I did love you even when I thought you had betrayed me."

"And if I remember right, you said you loved me now? Do you, Des?

Do you love me?"

"Oh, Jay." Desiree took a huge breath and let it out slowly. "Can you forgive me for being so pigheaded?"

"I can forgive you for anything. I love you." Jay grabbed her hands and pulled her to her feet, took her in his arms, and hugged her with all his strength. And when he placed his lips on hers, the fire that had almost died was reignited between them. Frantically, they searched for each other, holding and caressing each other like starved lovers. Jay kissed her deeply, passionately, thirsting for all that he had missed these last weeks. Desiree was far from passive. She drank down every ounce of love that Jay gave her, grabbing onto the moment with all of her strength. It was wonderful to be back in his arms, to feel his strong iron-like body against her own, and to know that they would love again.

Then suddenly, a sobering thought interrupted Desiree's reunion. She broke her embrace with Jay, pushing him back so she could look at his face.

"What's wrong, Des?"

"I just realized. You own me. You own the invention, the company, and everything I thought was mine."

"Not for long."

Desiree looked at him hopefully.

"I'm about to put it all in the name of my wife."

"Your wife!" Desiree's heart sunk to her belly, churning up bile she had long ago swallowed. She looked in horror at Jay, completely missing the twinkle in his eye.

"That is if you'll marry me!" Desiree hauled off and hit him, laughing at her own horror. Jay kept on teasing. "I'd hate to see all this property and money go to some stranger."

Desiree grabbed him and pulled his head towards her, planting a huge kiss right on his lips. It was the only way to shut him up. It wasn't long before their comical kiss became one of passion, one of deep mutual love. They held each other tightly, hearts pounding as one. Soon, however, Jay broke the embrace and whispered in Desiree's ear. "Sit down…. don't go away."

CHAPTER 37

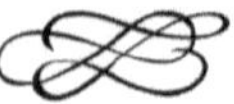

Jay left the room, heading through the large double doors to his office. Desiree sat in stunned silence, trying to wrap her head around everything she had learned in just the last couple of weeks and hours. It was really overwhelming. Her father was indeed a genius. His life's work had been recognized. But too late, he was dealt a lousy hand of cards, and his fate was sealed. Through some mystifying coincidences, he had befriended and engaged a brilliant young entrepreneur to help him save his reputation while protecting his daughter and beloved employees from humiliation and financial ruin. Fates intervened, and the young man met and fell in love with the man's daughter, and she with him.

And through it all, a simple little yellow bird invaded her dreams, spiritually guiding her to the truth and her destiny. Amazing.

Desiree watched him move with the grace of a tiger and felt the stirrings of love between her thighs. She couldn't wait to be with him, to hold him and love him. She was focusing on Jay's back, the curl of his hair on his neck, his long back, broad shoulders, and narrow hips…the same way he looked sneaking out of Gus's Deli a week ago…. WHAT? She nearly choked on the thought!

Desiree shook her head to clear the cobwebs. The foggy image of the man in the tailored grey suit appeared with crystal clarity. Desiree jumped up and rushed after Jay as he went into the office, and not very quietly. "YOU… you were there! YOU…you were in the Deli! YOU were standing not 6 feet from me, and you didn't speak with me? You were hiding there? And just sneaked out the door without saying anything?" Desiree's voice had gone up two octaves.

Jay spun around. The deli? Really? Oh, boy, here we go again. He grimaced with dread, rubbing the side of his head. "Des," he spoke quietly, "Seriously?

Again? I couldn't…for all the reasons we just discussed…please calm down." Jay started to reach for her.

"DON'T! TOUCH ME! PLEASE." Desiree grabbed the arm of the club chair in front of the desk and slumped down into it…. exhausted. All of the events and all of the pressure and all of the feelings, the good, the bad, and the ugly …came rushing back again. Just when she thought it was at last behind her. "Really?" she all but shouted. "You are so clever," she spit out. "Such a talented liar and a con artist… pure and simple… you were obviously hiding that day, clandestinely avoiding me after duping Lil in that ridiculous charade! Jack Sparrow!" she practically spit out the words. "Who does that?"

Ignoring her tirade, Jay went around the desk, opened the center drawer,and removed an envelope.

"Des…. look at me," he moved to stand in front of her. His heart ached. She looked so fragile and sad. "Des," he whispered almost reverently, "This is for you."

Desiree gasped. On the front of the envelope, she saw her own name, scrawled in her father's nearly unreadable handwriting. She looked quizzical, searching Jay's face for some clue.

"Open it." Jay leaned down and kissed the top of her head, caressing her cheek as he did so, noticing she didn't flinch. "He left this with me for you." And then Jay quietly retraced his steps to the other room.

With shaking hands, Desiree slipped her finger under the seal and pulled out the paper inside.

* * *

Lassie, me darlin' Desiree, May God, your mother, and you forgive me.

* * *

A sob stuck in her throat. As she began to read, tears rolled gently down her cheeks, and she could hear his wonderful, deep, lilting voice like he was in the room.

* * *

May God, your mother, and you forgive me, she read again. My ego, self-pride and my obsession with inventing things, always lookin' for the next big thing, got the better of me. Fool that I was, I kept tellin' meself, Paddy, ye're a smart man… you'll find a way to pay back the money. In me heart, I always knew, believed, it would be OK. And then it wasn't. But damn, the luck o' the

181

Irish dinna let me down. If ye're readin' this letter, then I know my greatest dream, the plan I made, and my deepest wishes for you came true. You've heard the whole truth, Lassie. It's up to you what you do with it. With all a me heart, I trust the young man in front of ye. At the very least, I hope you are friends or will be.

Twas your mother, ye know, the letter continued, who helped me. She came to me one night in a dream…tellin' me how it was time, how I needed to put an end to me foolishness. Aye, there she was in her blue weddin' dress, holding a little yellow bird on her finger. Strange dream, it was…but it was right about the time the doctor told me 'twas over, it was time to put my affairs in order. And so, Lassie, I made a plan….

* * *

The rest of the letter told her what she knew…how much he loved her, how full his life had been with her and her mother in it. And he had a few words to say about Jay Bennett as well. Yes, they had developed quite the friendship, and he trusted Jay with everything that was dear to him.

When Jay returned to the room, Desiree was sitting quietly with the letter in her lap. He handed her some water and the Kleenex, then pulled the other club chair to sit next to her. She remained silent, staring at her hands. She could feel her heartbeat slowing and hear the soothing melodies of Kenny G filling the beautiful rooms in the background. Every moment of the last couple of months and hours tumbled through her brain like scenes from an epic novel.

At last, Desiree looked up at Jay, her beautiful blue eyes filled with emotion and forgiveness. "He trusted you," she spoke softly, "He asked me to forgive him for making you promise to help him and his request to follow his rules. He loved you like a son." She shook her head, taking another deep breath. "He was crazy…my father…."

"Sshh," Jay touched his finger on her lips. "You don't have to say anything. I love you, Desiree Dubois O'Conner, with all my heart and forever. Do you love me?"

"Oh yes…yes…yes…can you forgive me? I love you more than life itself." "Come here," Jay took her arm and pulled her to sit on his lap. Wrapping his arms around her, he held her close, feeling her heart quicken as he gently kissed her and stroked her hair. The tension went out of her body, and she relaxed into him.

They sat like this for quite a while, not speaking, listening to the music. "So…" Jay said at last, reaching around her to retrieve a small carved box sitting on the desk…the same box that, only an hour ago, had narrowly missed his head.

Desiree recognized it immediately. His blue eyes twinkled with mischief, and a smile curled slyly at the tips of his lips. "Let's try this one more time. Desiree, my sweet desire," he held the box towards her, "will you marry me?"

"What's in the box?" Desiree's own eyes glittered in anticipation, feeling her mood lighten.

"Say yes, and you'll find out."

"Weeeeel," she hesitated. "I don't know…" but then she burst out laughing. All the pain, worry, and anger dissipated. She felt truly happy, so elated, and all she could do was giggle. "Oh, forget the box. I'll marry you anyway!"

Jay grinned like a little boy at Christmas and winked as he placed the box in Desiree's hands. "For you, darling. You earned it."

Desiree looked quizzically at Jay. "Open it."

Desiree slowly lifted the old lid and peeked inside the velvet-lined box. Suddenly, she gasped. "Oh, Jay, it's magnificent, it's oh, my…. this is…" As she stared at the diamond and blue sapphire necklace, the same one that adorned Magda's neck in the portrait, Desiree was totally speechless.

"For my heiress, the next Bennett Matriarch!" Jay laughed gleefully as he gazed lovingly at Desiree's beautiful, astounded, thrilled expression. "For my beautiful wife."

EPILOGUE

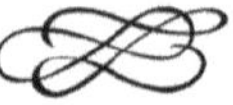

High above the ocean, on a stony bluff sheltered by the same giant palms that graced the walks of Las Palmas, sat a little stone church, rich in history and still alive with memories of ghosts past and the dreams of those present. A full moon was just beginning to rise in the Eastern sky, its bright light casting long shadows against the night. Millions of stars twinkled like distant candles and seemed to sway in the Caribbean breezes.

Desiree stood in the vestibule behind the huge oak doors that led to the altar. She kept checking and rechecking her reflection in the mirror. But no matter how hard she looked, all she saw was a beautiful, happy woman about to be married. Her exotic blue eyes were clear and bright, her lips full and rosy pink. Her golden hair, brushed a hundred times till it was sleek and shining, was pulled dramatically back from her face and cascaded down her back. White mini orchids, shaped in a half-moon crown, held three layered tiers of ivory tulle, framing her face like a misty cloud.

Desiree let her eyes drift downward and turned again to catch the full effect of her gown in the long mirror. Yards and yards of silk satin enshrouded Desiree in exquisite splendor. The shimmery fabric gathered dramatically to one side and, like the headpiece, was inset with hundreds of tiny pearls and crystals, each one glittering and sparkling with her every move. The deep, sweetheart neckline draped off her shoulders and down her back, cascading majestically to the floor, spreading out behind her like a giant silk fan.

"You are absolutely magnificent," whispered Janette in her ear as she caught her friend gazing at herself once more. "Quit being so nervous. You have nothing to be nervous about. I've never seen anyone so sure of anything in her entire life."

"Oh, Janette, I'm so happy! I almost can't stand myself! I feel like a princess in a fairy tale." Desiree hugged her friend tightly as they shared a few tears.

"Don't you dare!" Janette quickly dabbed Desiree's eye gently with her own handkerchief. "Princesses don't cry. Now, ready?"

Desiree nodded. Everyone was here. Henry and Raoul, Georgia and her husband, Lil and her daughter, Uncle Max and Lydia, Janette and Tom, Jay's whole family from the West Coast, Jay's partner Dave and the Mayor of Cranford Lake and his wife, and a hundred other friends and guests from New York and natives of the island. It was a wedding that no one would soon forget.

Desiree heard the first strains of the quartet as Uncle Max moved in silently beside her. "Ye are a sight, me lassie," he crooned softly. "You are as beautiful as your mother and as sound and strong as yer father. God bless ye, Desiree." Uncle Max kissed his niece on the cheek and wiped a tear from his own eye just as someone opened the big doors, and Desiree saw the church for the first time. A hundred candles lined the aisle to the altar and cast romantic shadows along the old stone walls and high up to the cathedral ceiling. The soft amber light flickered and danced against the stained-glass windows, mixing a hundred colors together like an artist's palette. And when the gentle island breezes briefly disturbed the shadows, Desiree was sure she saw her mother's and Poppy's ghosts drifting among the guests.

Slowly and softly, like the love song it's meant to be, the familiar strains of Yellow Bird echoed through the little church as Desiree moved gracefully down the aisle, never taking her eyes from Jay as he waited so still, so statuesque, mesmerized by the sight of his island princess. He had eyes only for her. She was a dream come true, a vision beyond words. She walked in a cloud of white, her dress and veil catching the flicker of candlelight and tossing it back into the night like diamonds and ice. Magda's diamond and sapphire necklace, now worn in its full length, lay proudly across her bare skin, a symbol of their incredible love.

As they stood together, hand in hand at the altar, repeating their vows to each other, and again many times throughout the evening during the reception at Las Palmas, Desiree thought of the little yellow bird and knew that at last, she was soaring through the sky, unafraid and with no chance of falling.

Later, when they returned to Villa Blanca, finally to be alone, Jay effortlessly lifted her off her feet and successfully (this time) carried her across the threshold. With her still in his arms, Jay moved into the bedroom before gently lowering her to her feet. The room was bathed in moonlight, and the lightest of breezes drifted through the wide open doors as they kissed again for the hundredth time that evening. And then, as yet another sign of their love, they noticed an oddly- shaped cloth-covered object sitting on the table across the room.

"What on earth….?" Desiree went to the table and opened the gift card. "It's from Lil…but she didn't write any message."

"Pull off that cloth."

Together, they lifted the cloth. There perched in a huge, gilded antique bird cage, side by side, wingtip to wingtip, were two beautiful yellow love birds. A little brass plaque above the door read, *"Life Is But A Dream."*

THE END